PARADISE

PARADISE

Abdulrazak Gurnah

*

THE NEW PRESS · NEW YORK

Requests for permission to reproduce selections from this book should be
made through our website: https://thenewpress.com/contact.

Published in the United States by The New Press, New York
Distributed by Two Rivers Distribution

Originally published in the United Kingdom by Hamish Hamilton in 1994

ISBN 978-1-56584-163-5 (pb.)

Library of Congress Cataloging-in-Publication Data
Gurnah, Abdulrazak, 1948–
Paradise / Abdulrazak Gurnah.
p. cm.
ISBN 978-1-56584-162-8 (hc.)
1. Boys–Africa–Fiction. 2. Europe–Colonies–Africa–Fiction.
I. Title.
PR9399.9.G87P37 1994
823–dc20   93-46678
                                                  CIP

The New Press publishes books that promote and enrich public discussion
and understanding of the issues vital to our democracy and to a more
equitable world. These books are made possible by the enthusiasm of our
readers; the support of a committed group of donors, large and small; the
collaboration of our many partners in the independent media and the
not-for-profit sector; booksellers, who often hand-sell New Press books;
librarians; and above all by our authors.

www.thenewpress.com

Printed in the United States of America

HC: 10 9 8 7 6 5 4 3 2
PB: 10 9 8 7 6 5

For Salma Abdalla Basalama

THE WALLED GARDEN

The boy first. His name was Yusuf, and he left his home suddenly during his twelfth year. He remembered it was the season of drought, when every day was the same as the last. Unexpected flowers bloomed and died. Strange insects scuttled from under rocks and writhed to their deaths in the burning light. The sun made distant trees tremble in the air and made the houses shudder and heave for breath. Clouds of dust puffed up at every tramping footfall and a hard-edged stillness lay over the daylight hours. Precise moments like that came back of the season.

He saw two Europeans on the railway platform at that time, the first he had ever seen. He was not frightened, not at first. He went to the station often, to watch the trains come noisily and gracefully in, and then to wait for them to haul themselves out again, marshalled by the scowling Indian signalman with his pennants and whistle. Often Yusuf waited hours for a train to arrive. The two Europeans were also waiting, standing under a canvas awning with their luggage and important-looking goods neatly piled a few feet away. The man was large, so tall that he had to lower his head to avoid touching the canvas under which he sheltered from the sun. The woman stood further back in the shade, her glistening face partly obscured by two hats. Her frilled white blouse was buttoned up at the neck and wrists, and her long skirt brushed her shoes. She was tall and large too, but differently. Where she looked lumpy and malleable, as if capable of taking another shape, he appeared carved out of a single piece of wood. They stared in different directions, as if they did not know each other. As he watched, Yusuf saw the woman run her handkerchief over her lips, casually rubbing off flakes of dry skin. The man's face was mottled with red, and as his eyes moved slowly over the cramped landscape of the station, taking in the locked wooden storehouses and the huge yellow flag with its picture of a glaring black bird, Yusuf was able to take a long look at him. Then he turned and saw Yusuf staring. The man glanced away at first and then looked back at Yusuf for a long moment. Yusuf could not tear his eyes away. Suddenly the man bared his teeth in an involuntary snarl, curling his fingers in an inexplicable way. Yusuf heeded the warning and fled, muttering the words he had been taught to say when he required sudden and unexpected help from God.

That year he left his home was also the year the woodworm infested the posts in the back porch. His father smacked the posts angrily whenever he passed them, letting them know he knew what game they were up to. The woodworm left trails on the beams that were like the turned-up earth which marked the animal tunnels in the bed of the dry stream. The posts sounded soft and hollow whenever Yusuf hit them, and emitted tiny grainy spores of rot. When he grumbled for food his mother told him to eat the worms.

'I'm hungry,' he wailed at her, in an untutored litany he had been reciting with increasing gruffness with each passing year.

'Eat the woodworm,' his mother suggested, and then laughed at his exaggerated look of disgusted anguish. 'Go on, stuff yourself with it any time you want. Don't let me stop you.'

He sighed in a world-weary way he was experimenting with to show her how pathetic her joke was. Sometimes they ate bones, which his mother boiled up to make a thin soup whose surface glistened with colour and grease, and in whose depths lurked lumps of black spongy marrow. At worst, there was only okra stew, but however hungry he was Yusuf could not swallow the slimy sauce.

His Uncle Aziz also came to visit them at that time. His visits were brief and far between, usually accompanied by a crowd of travellers and porters and musicians. He stopped with them on the long journeys he made from the ocean to the mountains, to the lakes and forests, and across the dry plains and the bare rocky hills of the interior. His expeditions were often accompanied by drums and tamburis and horns and siwa, and when his train marched into town animals stampeded and evacuated themselves, and children ran out of control. Uncle Aziz gave off a strange and unusual odour, a mixture of hide and perfume, and gums and spices, and another less definable smell which made Yusuf think of danger. His habitual dress was a thin, flowing kanzu of fine cotton and a small crocheted cap pushed back on his head. With his refined airs and his polite, impassive manner, he looked more like a man on a late afternoon stroll or a worshipper on the way to evening prayers than a merchant who had picked his way past bushes of thorn and nests of vipers spitting poison. Even in the heat of arrival, amid the chaos and disorder of tumbled packs, surrounded by tired and noisy porters, and watchful, sharp-clawed traders, Uncle Aziz managed to look calm and at ease. On this visit he had come alone.

Yusuf always enjoyed his visits. His father said they brought honour on them because he was such a rich and renowned merchant – *tajiri mkubwa* – but that was not all, welcome though honour always was. Uncle Aziz gave him, without fail, a ten anna piece every time he stopped with them. Nothing was required of him but that he should present himself at the appropriate time. Uncle Aziz looked out for

3

him, smiled and gave him the coin. Yusuf felt he wanted to smile too every time the moment arrived, but he stopped himself because he guessed that it would be wrong for him to do so. Yusuf marvelled at Uncle Aziz's luminous skin and his mysterious smell. Even after his departure, his perfume lingered for days.

By the third day of his visit, it was obvious that Uncle Aziz's departure was at hand. There was unusual activity in the kitchen, and the unmistakable, mingled aromas of a feast. Sweet frying spices, simmering coconut sauce, yeasty buns and flat bread, baking biscuits and boiling meat. Yusuf made sure not to be too far away from the house all day, in case his mother needed help preparing the dishes or wanted an opinion on one of them. He knew she valued his opinion on such matters. Or she might forget to stir a sauce, or miss the moment when the hot oil is trembling just enough for the vegetables to be added. It was a tricky business, for while he wanted to be able to keep an eye on the kitchen, he did not want his mother to see him loafing on the lookout. She would then be sure to send him on endless errands, which is bad enough in itself, but it might also cause him to miss saying goodbye to Uncle Aziz. It was always at the moment of departure that the ten anna piece changed hands, when Uncle Aziz would offer his hand to be kissed and stroke the back of Yusuf's head as he bent over it. Then with practised ease he would slip the coin into Yusuf's hand.

His father was usually at work until soon after noon. Yusuf guessed that he would be bringing Uncle Aziz with him when he came, so there was plenty of time to kill. His father's business was running a hotel. This was the latest in a line of businesses with which he had attempted to make his fortune and his name. When he was in the mood he told them stories at home of other schemes which he had thought would pros-

4

per, making them sound ridiculous and hilarious. Or Yusuf heard him complain of how his life had gone wrong, and everything he had tried had failed. The hotel, which was an eating house with four clean beds in an upstairs room, was in the small town of Kawa, where they had been living for over four years. Before that they had lived in the south, in another small town in a farming district where his father had kept a store. Yusuf remembered a green hill and distant shadows of mountains, and an old man who sat on a stool on the pavement at the storefront, embroidering caps with silk thread. They came to Kawa because it had become a boom town when the Germans had used it as a depot for the railway line they were building to the highlands of the interior. But the boom passed quickly, and the trains now only stopped to take on wood and water. On his last journey, Uncle Aziz had used the line to Kawa before cutting to the west on foot. On his next expedition, he said, he would go as far as he could up the line before taking a north-western or north-eastern route. There was still good trade to be done in either of those places, he said. Sometimes Yusuf heard his father say that the whole town was going to Hell.

The train to the coast left in the early evening, and Yusuf thought Uncle Aziz would be on it. He guessed from something in his manner that Uncle Aziz was on his way home. But you could never be sure with people, and it might turn out that he would take the up-train to the mountains, which left in mid-afternoon. Yusuf was ready for either outcome. His father expected him to make an appearance at the hotel every afternoon after his midday prayers – to learn about the business, his father told him, and to learn to stand on his own feet, but really to relieve the two young men who helped and cleaned up in the kitchen, and who served the food to the customers. The hotel cook drank and cursed, and abused everyone in sight except Yusuf. He would break off in the middle of a foul-mouthed harangue with smiles when he caught sight of him, but Yusuf still feared and trembled in front of him. On that day he did not go to the hotel, nor did he say his midday prayers, and in the terrible heat of that time of day he did not think anyone would bother to hunt him out. Instead he skulked in shady corners and behind the chicken-houses in the backyard, until he was driven from there by the suffocating smells which rose with the early afternoon dust. He hid in the dark timber-yard next door to their house, a place of dark purple shadows and a vaulting thatch roof, where he listened for the cautious scurrying of stalking lizards and kept a sharp lookout for the ten anna.

He did not find the silence and gloom of the timber-yard disconcerting, for he was accustomed to playing alone. His father did not like him to play far from home. 'We are surrounded by savages,' he said. 'Washenzi, who have no faith in God and who worship spirits and demons which live in trees and rocks. They like nothing better than to kidnap little children and make use of them as they wish. Or you'll go with those other ones who have no care, those loafers and children of loafers, and they'll neglect you and let the wild dogs eat you. Stay here nearby where it's safe, so someone can keep an eye on you.' Yusuf's father preferred him to play with the children of the Indian storekeeper who lived in the neighbourhood, except that the Indian children threw sand and jeered at him when he tried to get near them. 'Golo, golo,' they chanted at him, spitting in his direction. Sometimes he sat with the groups of older boys who lounged under shades of trees or the lees of houses. He liked being with the boys because they were always telling jokes and laughing. Their parents worked as vibarua, labouring for the Germans on the line-construction gangs, doing piece-work at the railhead, or

6

portering for travellers and traders. They were only ever paid for the work they did, and at times there was no work. Yusuf had heard the boys say that the Germans hanged people if they did not work hard enough. If they were too young to hang, they cut their stones off. The Germans were afraid of nothing. They did whatever they wanted and no one could stop them. One of the boys said that his father had seen a German put his hand in the heart of a blazing fire without being burnt, as if he were a phantom.

The vibarua who were their parents came from all over, from the Usambara highlands north of Kawa, from the fabulous lakes to the west of the highlands, from the war-torn savannahs to the south and many from the coast. They laughed about their parents, mocking their work-songs and comparing stories of the disgusting and sour smells they brought home. They made up names for the places their parents came from, funny and unpleasant names which they used to abuse and mock each other. Sometimes they fought, tumbling and kicking and causing each other pain. If they could, the older boys found work as servants or errand runners, but mostly they lounged and scavenged, waiting to grow strong enough for the work of men. Yusuf sat with them when they let him, listening to their conversation and running errands for them.

To pass the time they gossiped or played cards. It was with them that Yusuf first heard that babies lived in penises. When a man wanted a child, he put the baby inside a woman's stomach where there is more room for it to grow. He was not the only one to find the story incredible, and penises were pulled out and measured as the debate heated up. Soon enough the babies were forgotten and the penises became interesting in their own right. The older boys were proud to display themselves and forced the younger ones to expose their little abdallas for a laugh.

7

Sometimes they played kipande. Yusuf was too small ever to get the chance to bat, since age and strength determined the batting order, but whenever he was allowed he joined the crowd of fielders who frantically chased across dusty open spaces after a flying slug of wood. Once his father saw him running in the streets with a hysterical mob of children chasing after a kipande. He gave him a hard look of disapproval and slapped him before sending him home.

Yusuf made himself a kipande, and adapted the game so he could play it on his own. His adaptation consisted of pretending he was also all the other players, with the advantage that this way he could bat for as long as he felt like it. He chased up and down the road in front of their house, shouting with excitement and trying to catch a kipande he had just hit as high in the air as he could, to give himself time to get under it.

2

So on the day of Uncle Aziz's departure, Yusuf had no qualms about wasting a few hours while he stalked the ten anna piece. His father and Uncle Aziz came home together at one in the afternoon. He could see their bodies shimmering in the liquid light as they approached slowly on the stony path which led to the house. They walked without talking, their heads lowered and their shoulders hunched against the heat. The lunch was already laid out for them on the best rug in the guest room. Yusuf himself had lent a hand in the final preparations, adjusting the positions of some of the dishes for best effect and earning a wide grateful smile from his tired mother. While he was there, Yusuf took the opportunity to reconnoitre the feast. Two different kinds of curries, chicken and minced mutton. The best Peshawar rice, glistening with ghee and dotted with sultanas and almonds. Aromatic and plump buns, maandazi and mahamri, overflowing the cloth-covered basket. Spinach in a coconut sauce. A plate of water-beans. Strips of dried fish charred in the dying embers which had cooked the rest of the food. Yusuf almost wept with longing as he surveyed this plenty, so different from the meagre meals of that time. His mother frowned at the perform-ance, but his face turned so tragic that she laughed in the end.

Once the men were seated, Yusuf went in with a brass pitcher and bowl, and a clean linen cloth draped over his left arm. He poured the water slowly while Uncle Aziz and then his father rinsed their hands. He liked guests like Uncle Aziz, liked them very much. He thought this as he crouched outside the door of the guest room, in case his services were required. He would have been happy enough to stay in the room and watch, but his father had glared at him irritably and chased him out. There was always something happening when Uncle Aziz was around. He ate all his meals at their house even though he slept at the hotel. That meant that there were often interesting morsels left over after they had finished – unless his mother got a clear look at them first, when they usually ended up in a neighbour's house or in the stomach of one of the ragged mendicants who sometimes came to the door, mum-bling and whining their praises of God. His mother said it was kinder to give food away to neighbours and to the needy than to indulge in gluttony. Yusuf could not see the sense of that, but his mother told him that virtue was its own reward. He understood from the sharpness in her voice that if he said any more he would have to listen to another lengthy sermon, and he had plenty enough of that from the Koran-school teacher.

There was one mendicant Yusuf did not mind sharing *his* leftovers with. His name was Mohammed, a shrunken man with a reedy voice who stank of bad meat. Yusuf had found him sitting by the side of the house one afternoon eating handfuls of red earth which he scooped out of the broken outside wall. His shirt was grimy and stained and he wore a pair of the most ragged shorts Yusuf had ever seen. The rim of his cap was dark brown with sweat and dirt. Yusuf watched him for a few minutes, debating whether he remembered seeing anyone who looked dirtier, and then went to get him a bowl of leftover cassava. After a few mouthfuls, which Mohammed ate between whines of gratitude, he told him that the tragedy of his life was the weed. He had once been well off, he said, with watered land and some animals, and a mother who loved him. During the day he worked his sweet land to the utmost of his strength and endurance, and in the evening he sat with his mother while she sang God's praises and told him fabulous stories of the great world.

But then the evil came upon him, and it came with such force that he abandoned mother and land in search of the weed, and now he roamed the world taking kicks and eating earth. Nowhere in his wanderings had he eaten food which had the perfection of his mother's cooking, until perhaps now, this piece of cassava. He told Yusuf stories of his travels while they sat against the side wall of the house, his high-pitched voice animated and his wizened young face cracking into smiles and broken-toothed grins. 'Learn from my terrible example, my little friend. Shun the weed, I beg you!' His visits never lasted long, but Yusuf was always glad to see him and hear about his latest adventures. He loved best to hear descriptions of Mohammed's watered land south of Witu and the life he led during those years of happiness. Next best he loved to hear the story of the first time Mohammed was taken to the house of the mad in Mombasa. 'Wallahi, I tell you no lies, young one. They took me for mad! Can you believe that?' There they had filled his mouth with salt and slapped him in the face if he tried to spit it out. They had only given him peace if he sat quietly while the rocks of salt melted in his mouth and corroded his guts. Mohammed talked of the torture with a shudder but also with amusement. He had other stories which Yusuf did not like, about a blind dog he had seen stoned to death and about children abandoned to cruelty. He mentioned a young woman he had once known in Witu. His mother had wanted him to marry, he said, and then he smiled stupidly.

Yusuf tried to hide him at first, afraid that his mother would chase him away, but Mohammed cringed and whined with such gratitude whenever she appeared that he became one of her favourite mendicants. 'Honour your mother, I beg you!' he would whimper in her hearing. 'Learn from my terrible example.' It was not unheard of, his mother told Yusuf later, for wise people or prophets or sultans to disguise themselves as mendicants and mix with the ordinary and the unfortunate. It is always best to treat them with respect. Whenever Yusuf's father appeared, Mohammed rose and left, making cringing noises of deference.

Once Yusuf stole a coin from the pocket of his father's jacket. He did not know why he did it. While his father was having a wash after returning from work, Yusuf had plunged a hand into the smelly jacket which was hanging on a nail in his parents' room and taken a coin. It was not something he planned. When he looked at the coin later it turned out to be a silver rupee and he was frightened to spend it. He was surprised not to be discovered and was tempted to put it back. Several times he thought of giving it to Mohammed but was afraid of what the mendicant would say or accuse him of. A silver rupee was the most money Yusuf had ever held in his hand. So he hid it in a crevice at the base of a wall, and sometimes teased a corner of it out with a stick.

Uncle Aziz spent the afternoon in the guest room, having a siesta. To Yusuf it seemed an aggravating delay. His father too had retreated into his room, as he did every day after his meal. Yusuf could not understand why people wanted to sleep in the afternoon, as if it was a law they had to obey. They called it resting, and sometimes even his mother did it, disappearing into their room and drawing the curtain. When he tried it once or twice, he became so bored that he feared he would never be able to get up again. On the second occasion he thought this was what death would be like, lying awake in bed but unable to move, like punishment.

While Uncle Aziz slept, Yusuf was required to clear up in the kitchen and yard. This was unavoidable if he was to have any say in the disposal of the leftovers. Surprisingly, his mother left him on his own while she went to speak with his father. Usually she supervised strictly, separating real leftovers from what would serve another meal. He inflicted as much damage as he could on the food, cleared and saved what was possible, scrubbed and washed the pots, swept the yard, then went to sit on guard in the shade by the back door, sighing about the burdens he had to carry.

When his mother asked him what he was doing, he replied that he was resting. He tried not to say it pompously, but it came out like that, making his mother smile. She reached suddenly for him, hugging him and lifting him up while he kicked furiously to be released. He hated to be treated like a baby, she knew that. His feet sought the dignity of the bare earth yard as he wriggled with restrained fury. It was because he was small for his age that she was always doing it − picking him up, pinching his cheeks, giving him hugs and slobbery kisses − and then laughing at him as if he was a child. He was already twelve. To his amazement she did not let him go this time. Usually she released him as soon as his struggles became furious, smacking his fleeing bottom as he ran. Now she held him, squeezing him to her steeping softness, saying nothing and not laughing. The back of her bodice was still wet with sweat, and her body reeked of smoke and exhaustion. He stopped struggling after a moment and let his mother hold him to her.

That was his first foreboding. When he saw the tears in his mother's eyes his heart leapt with terror. He had never seen his mother do that before. He had seen her wailing at a neighbour's bereavement as if everything was spinning out of control, and had heard her imploring the mercy of the Almighty on the living, her face sodden with entreaty, but he had never seen these silent tears. He thought something had happened with his father, that he had spoken harshly to her. Perhaps the food was not good enough for Uncle Aziz.

'Ma,' he said pleadingly, but she hushed him.

Perhaps his father had said how fine his other family had been. Yusuf had heard him say that when he was angry. Once he heard him say to her that she was the daughter of a hill tribesman from the back of Taita who lived in a smoky hut and wore stinking goatskin, and thought five goats and two sacks of beans a good price for any woman. 'If anything happens to you, they'll sell me another one like you from their pens,' he said. She was not to give herself airs just because she had grown up on the coast among civilized people. Yusuf was terrified when they argued, feeling their sharp words cut into him and remembering stories from other boys of violence and abandonment.

It was his mother who had told him of the first wife, recounting the story with smiles and the voice she kept for fables. She had been an Arab woman from an old Kilwa

13

family, not quite a princess but of honourable descent. Yusuf's father had married her against the wishes of her proud parents, who had not thought him grand enough for them. For although he carried a good name, anyone with eyes could see that his mother must have been a savage and that he himself was not blessed with prosperity. And although a name could not be dishonoured by the blood of a mother, the world they lived in imposed some practical necessities. They had greater aspirations for their daughter than to let her become the mother of poor children with savage faces. They told him: 'We thank God, sir, for your kind attentions, but our daughter is too young now to think of marriage. The town abounds in daughters more worthy than ours.'

But Yusuf's father had caught sight of the young woman, and he could not forget her. He had fallen in love with her! Affection made him reckless and foolhardy, and he sought ways to reach her. He was a stranger in Kilwa, only there as an agent to deliver a consignment of clay water-jars for his employer, but he had made a good friend who was a boat-master of a dhow, a nahodha. The nahodha gleefully sustained him in his passion for the young woman and helped him in his stratagems to win her. Apart from anything else it would cause some grief to her self-besotted family, the nahodha said. Yusuf's father made secret assignations with the young woman and eventually stole her away. The nahodha, who knew all the landfalls on the coast from Faza in the far north to Mtwara in the south, spirited them away to Bagamoyo on the mainland. Yusuf's father found work in an ivory ware-house belonging to an Indian merchant, first as a watchman, then as a clerk and a jobbing trader. After eight years the woman he had married made plans to return to Kilwa, having had a letter written to her parents first, begging their forgiveness. Her two young sons were to accompany her to sweep away any vestiges of parental reproach. The dhow they travelled in was called *Jicho*, the Eye. It was never seen again after it left Bagamoyo. Yusuf had heard his father too talk about this family, often when he was angry about something or after a disappointment. He knew that the memories caused his father pain and stirred him into great rages.

During one of their terrible arguments, when they seemed to forget about him sitting outside the open door as they clawed at each other, he heard his father groan, 'My love for her was not blessed. You know the pain of that.'

'Who doesn't?' his mother asked. 'Who doesn't know the pain of that? Or do you think I don't know the pain of love that goes wrong? Do you think I feel nothing?'

'No, no, don't accuse me, not you. You're the light on my face,' he shouted, his voice rising and breaking. 'Don't accuse me. Don't start on all that again.'

'I won't,' she said to him, dropping her voice to a hissing whisper.

He wondered if they had been arguing again. He waited for her to speak, wanting to be told what the matter was, irritated by his powerlessness to force the issue and make her tell him what made her cry.

'Your father will tell you,' she said in the end. She let him go and went back inside the house. In a twinkling, the gloom of the hallway had swallowed her.

4

His father came out to look for him. He had only just woken from his siesta and his eyes were still red with sleep. His left cheek was inflamed, perhaps where he had lain on it. He lifted a corner of his undershirt and scratched his belly, while his other hand stroked the shadowy stubble on his chin. His beard grew quickly and he usually shaved every afternoon after his sleep. He smiled at Yusuf and his smile grew to a broad grin. Yusuf was still sitting by the back door where his mother had left him. Now his father came to squat down beside him. Yusuf guessed that his father was trying to look unconcerned, and he was made nervous.

'Would you like to go on a little trip, little octopus?' his father asked him, pulling him nearer his masculine sweat. Yusuf felt the weight of the arm on his shoulder, and resisted the pressure to bury his face in his father's torso. He was too old for that kind of thing. His eyes darted to his father's face, to read the meaning of what he was saying. His father chuckled, crushing him against his body for a moment. 'Don't look so happy about it,' he said.

'When?' Yusuf asked, gently wriggling himself free.

'Today,' his father said, raising his voice cheerfully and then grinning through a small yawn, trying to look untroubled 'Right now.'

Yusuf stood up on tiptoe and flexed his knees. He felt a momentary urge to go to the toilet, and stared anxiously at his father, waiting for the rest of it. 'Where am I going? What about Uncle Aziz?' Yusuf asked. The sudden damp fear he had felt was quelled by the thought of the ten anna. He couldn't go anywhere until he had collected his ten anna piece.

'You'll be going with Uncle Aziz,' his father said, and then gave him a small, bitter smile. He did that when Yusuf said something foolish to him. Yusuf waited, but his father said no more. After a moment his father laughed and made a lunge for him. Yusuf rushed out of the way and laughed too. 'You'll go on the train,' his father said. 'All the way to the coast. You love trains, don't you? You'll enjoy yourself all the way to the sea.' Yusuf waited for his father to say more, and could not think why he did not like the prospect of this journey. In the end, his father slapped him on the thigh and told him to go and see his mother about packing a few things.

When the time came to leave it hardly seemed real. He said goodbye to his mother at the front door of the house and followed his father and Uncle Aziz to the station. His mother did not hug and kiss him, or shed tears over him. He had been afraid she would. Later, Yusuf could not remember what his mother did or said, but he remembered that she looked ill or dazed, leaning exhaustedly against the doorpost. When he thought of the moment of his departure, the picture that came to mind was the shimmering road on which they walked and the men ahead of him. In front of all of them staggered the porter carrying Uncle Aziz's luggage on his shoulders. Yusuf was allowed to carry his own little bundle: two pairs of shorts, a kanzu which was still new from last Idd, a shirt, a copy of the Koran, and his mother's old rosary. She had wrapped all but the rosary in an old shawl, then pulled the ends into a thick knot. Smilingly, she had pushed a cane through the knot so that Yusuf could carry his bundle over his shoulder, the way the porters did. The brownstone rosary she had pressed on him last, secretively.

It never occurred to him, not even for one brief moment, that he might be gone from his parents for a long time, or that he might never see them again. It never occurred to him to ask when he would be returning. He never thought to ask why he was accompanying Uncle Aziz on his journey, or why the business had to be arranged so suddenly. At the station Yusuf saw that in addition to the yellow flag with the angry black bird, there was another flag with a silver-edged black cross on it. They flew that one when the chief German officers were travelling on the train. His father bent down to him and shook his hand. He spoke to him at some length, his eyes watering in the end. Afterwards Yusuf could not remember what was said to him, but God came into it.

The train had been moving for a while before the novelty of it began to wear off for Yusuf, and then the thought that he had left home became irresistible. He thought of his mother's easy laughter, and began to cry. Uncle Aziz was on the bench beside him, and Yusuf looked guiltily at him, but he had dozed off, wedging himself between the bench and the luggage. After a few moments, Yusuf knew that the tears were no longer coming, but he was reluctant to lose the feeling of sadness. He wiped his tears away and began to study his uncle. He was to have many opportunities for doing so, but this was the first time since he had known his uncle that he could look him full in the face. Uncle Aziz had taken his cap off once they boarded the train, and Yusuf was surprised by how harsh he looked. Without the cap, his face looked more squat and out of proportion. As he lay back dozing silently, the gracious manners which caught the eye were absent. He still smelt very fine. Yusuf had always liked that about him. That and his thin, flowing kanzus and silk-embroidered caps. When he entered a room, his presence wafted in like something separate from the person, announcing excess and prosperity and daring. Now as he leaned back against the luggage, a small rounded pot-belly protruded under his chest. Yusuf had not noticed that before. As he watched he saw the belly rise and fall with his breathing, and once he saw a ripple of movement across it.

His leather money pouches were belted round his groin as usual, looping over his hip-bones and meeting in a thonged buckle over the join of his thighs like a kind of armour. Yusuf had never seen the money belt unattached to him, even while he slept in the afternoon. He remembered the silver rupee he had hidden in the crevice at the base of a wall, and trembled at the thought that it would be discovered and his guilt would be proclaimed.

The train was noisy. Dust and smoke blew in through the open windows, and with them came the smell of fire and charred meat. On their right, the land they travelled across was flat plain with long shadows in the gathering dusk. Scattered farms and homesteads hugged the surface, clinging to the hurtling earth. On the other side were lumpy silhouettes of mountains whose crowns flared with haloes as they caught the setting sun. The train made no haste, lurching and grumbling as it struggled to the coast. At times it slowed nearly to a halt, moving almost imperceptibly and then suddenly lurching forward with high-pitched protests coming from the wheels. Yusuf did not remember the train stopping at any stations on the way, but he knew later it must have done. He shared the food which his mother had prepared for Uncle Aziz: maandazi, boiled meat and beans. His uncle unwrapped the food with practised care, muttering bismillah and smiling slightly, then with his palm half open in a gesture of welcome he invited Yusuf to the food. His uncle looked kindly on him as he ate, and smiled at him to see his long looks.

He could not sleep. The ribs of the bench dug deep into his body and kept him awake. At best he dozed, or lay half awake, nagged by the need to relieve himself. When he opened his eyes in the middle of the night, the sight of the half-full, dimmed carriage made him want to cry out. The darkness outside was a measureless void, and he feared that the train was too deep in it to be able to return safely. He tried to concentrate on the noise of the wheels, but their rhythm was eccentric and only served to distract him and keep him awake. He dreamt that his mother was a one-eyed dog he had once seen crushed under the wheels of a train. Later he dreamt that he saw his cowardice glimmering in moonlight, covered in the slime of its afterbirth. He knew it was his cowardice because someone standing in the shadows told him so, and he himself saw it breathing.

They arrived at their destination the following morning, and Uncle Aziz shepherded Yusuf calmly and firmly through the shouting crowds of traders inside and outside the station. He did not speak to Yusuf as they walked through the streets, which were littered with the remains of recent celebrations. There were palm-fronds still tied to doorposts and shaped into arches. Crushed garlands of marigolds and jasmine lay broken on the paths, and darkening fruit-peelings littered the road. A porter was carrying their luggage ahead of them, sweating and grunting in the mid-morning heat. Yusuf had been forced to give up his little bundle. 'Let the porter carry it,' Uncle Aziz had said, pointing to the grinning man who was standing lopsidedly over the rest of the luggage. The porter hopped and jumped as he walked, taking the weight off a bad hip. The surface of the road was very hot, and Yusuf, whose feet were unprotected, wished that he too could hop, but he knew without being told that Uncle Aziz would not wish this. From the way he was greeted in the streets, Yusuf understood that his uncle was an eminent man. The porter shouted for people to make way – 'Let the seyyid pass, waungwana' – and even though he was such a ragged and ill-looking man, no one contested with him. Now and then he glanced round with his lopsided grin, and Yusuf began to think that the porter knew something dangerous which he had no idea of.

Uncle Aziz's house was a long, low building towards the edge of town. It stood some yards from the road and in front of it was a large clearing ringed with trees. There were small neems, coconut palms, a sufi and a huge mango tree at a corner of the yard. There were also other trees which Yusuf did not recognize. In the shade of the mango tree a handful of people were already sitting, so early in the day. Beside the house ran a long crenellated white wall, above which Yusuf glimpsed crowns of trees and palms. The men under the mango tree stood up as they approached, raising their arms and calling out greetings.

They were met by a young man called Khalil who came rushing out of the shop at the front of the bungalow with garrulous cries of welcome. He kissed Uncle Aziz's hand reverently, and would have kissed it again and again if Uncle Aziz had not pulled his hand away in the end. He said something irritably, and Khalil stood silently in front of him, his hands clasped together as he struggled to restrain himself from reaching for Uncle Aziz's hand. They exchanged greetings and news in Arabic while Yusuf looked on. Khalil was about seventeen or eighteen, thin and nervous looking, with the beginnings of hair on his lip. Yusuf knew he was mentioned in the conversation, for Khalil turned to look at him and nodded excitedly. Uncle Aziz walked away towards the side of the house where Yusuf saw an open doorway in the long whitewashed wall. He caught a glimpse of the garden through the doorway, and thought he saw fruit trees and flowering bushes and a glint of water. When he started to follow, his uncle, without turning round, extended the palm of his hand from his body and held it stiffly out as he walked away. Yusuf had never seen the gesture before, but he felt its rebuke and knew it meant he was not to follow. He looked at Khalil and found him appraising him with a large smile. He beckoned Yusuf and turned to walk back to the shop. Yusuf picked up the bundle with the stick, which the porter had left behind when he took Uncle Aziz's luggage inside, and followed Khalil. He had already lost the brownstone rosary, had left it on the train. Three old men were sitting on a bench on the terrace in front of the shop, and their gaze calmly followed Yusuf as he ducked under the counter flap and into the shop.

5

'This is my little brother, who has come to work for us,' Khalil told the customers. 'He looks so small and feeble because he's just come from the wild lands, back there behind the hills. They only have cassava and weeds to eat there. That's why he looks like living death. Hey, kifa urongo! Look at the poor boy. Look at his feeble arms and his long looks. But we'll fill him up with fish and sweetmeats and honey, and in no time he'll be plump enough for one of your daughters. Greet the customers, little boy. Give them a big smile.'

In the first few days everyone smiled at him, except Uncle Aziz, whom Yusuf saw only once or twice in a day. People hurried towards Uncle Aziz as he walked past, to kiss his hand if he would let them or bow their greetings a deferential yard or two away if he appeared unapproachable. He was impassive in the face of the grovelling salutes and prayers, and when he had listened long enough not to seem discourteous, he continued on his way, slipping a handful of coins to the most abject of his courtiers.

Yusuf spent all his time with Khalil, who instructed him about his new life and questioned him about his old one. Khalil looked after the shop, lived in the shop, and seemed to care about nothing else. All the energy and force in his being seemed given over to it as he strode from one task to another with a look of anxiety, talking rapidly and cheerfully of catastrophes that would befall the shop if he paused for breath. *You'll make yourself vomit with all that talking*, the customers warned him. *Don't rush about so much, young man, you'll dry up before your time.* But Khalil grinned at them and rattled on. He spoke with the pronounced accent of the Arabic-speaker although his Kiswahili was fluent. He managed to make the liberties he took with the syntax seem inspired as well as eccentric. In exasperation and anxiety he burst into a powerful torrent of Arabic which forced the customers into silent but tolerant retreat. The first time he did it in front of him, Yusuf laughed at his vehemence, and Khalil stepped forward and slapped him precisely on the meat of his left cheek. The old men on the terrace laughed at that, chortling and rocking and giving each other knowing looks, as if they had known all along that this was bound to happen. They came every day and sat on the bench, talking among themselves and smiling at Khalil's antics. When there were no customers Khalil turned his attention fully on them, transforming them into a chorus to his antic ranting, interrupting their low-voiced exchange of news and rumours of war with unavoidable questions and fertile insights.

Yusuf's new teacher wasted no time in putting him right on a number of matters. The day began at dawn and did not finish until Khalil said so. Nightmares and crying in the night were stupid so they were to have no more of that. Someone might think he was bewitched and have him sent to the masseur to have red-hot irons put on his back. Snoozing against the sacks of sugar in the store was the worst kind of treachery. Suppose he wet himself and tainted the sugar. When a customer makes a joke, smile until you break wind if necessary, but smile and don't dare to look bored. 'As for Uncle Aziz, for a start he ain't your uncle,' he told him. 'This is most important for you. Listen to me, hey, kifa urongo. He ain't your uncle.' That was the name Khalil had for him in those days. Kifa urongo, living death. They slept on the earth terrace in front of the shop, shopkeepers by day and watchmen by night, and covered themselves with rough calico sheets. Their heads were close together and their bodies far apart, so they could talk softly without getting too near each other.

23

Whenever Yusuf rolled too close, Khalil kicked him away savagely. Mosquitoes wheeled around them, shrieking for blood with high-pitched wails. If the sheets slipped from their bodies the mosquitoes instantly gathered to their sinful feast. Yusuf dreamt he could see their jagged-edged sabres sawing through his flesh.

Khalil told him, 'You're here because your Ba owes the seyyid money. I'm here because my Ba owes him money – only he's dead now, God's mercy on his soul.'

'God's mercy on his soul,' Yusuf said.

'Your Ba must be a bad businessman . . .'

'He isn't,' Yusuf cried, knowing nothing about it but not prepared to put up with such liberties.

'But he can't be as bad as marehemu my father, God's mercy on his soul,' Khalil continued, unperturbed by Yusuf's outcry. 'Nobody can be.'

'How much did your father owe him?' Yusuf asked.

'It's not honourable to ask,' Khalil said good-humouredly and then reached over and slapped him hard for his stupidity. 'And don't say *him*, say seyyid.' Yusuf did not understand all the details, but he could not see that it was wrong to work for Uncle Aziz in order to pay off his father's debt. When he had paid it all off he could then go home. Although perhaps they could have warned him before he left. He could not remember any mention of debts, and they seemed to live well enough compared with their neighbours. He said this to Khalil, who was silent for a long time.

'One thing I'll tell you,' he said at last, speaking softly. 'You're a stupid boy and you don't understand anything. You weep at night and cry out in your dreams. Where did you keep your eyes and ears while they were fixing you up? Your father owes him a lot, otherwise you wouldn't be here. Your

Ba would've paid him, so you could stay at home and eat malai and mofa every morning, heh? And run errands for your mother and things like that. He doesn't even need you here, the seyyid. There's not enough work . . .'

After a moment he continued in a voice so low that Yusuf knew he was not meant to hear or understand. 'You don't have a sister, maybe, or he'd have taken her.'

Yusuf kept silent, long enough to show that he had no indecent interest in Khalil's last remark, although he did. But his mother had often told him off for prying, for asking questions about neighbours. He wondered what his mother was doing. 'How long do you have to work for Uncle Aziz?'

'He ain't your uncle,' Khalil said sharply, and Yusuf winced in expectation of another blow. After a moment Khalil laughed softly, then reached out a hand from under the sheet to clout Yusuf round the ear. 'You'd better learn that quickly, zuma. It's important for you. He doesn't like little beggars like you calling him Uncle, Uncle, Uncle. He likes you to kiss his hand and call him seyyid. And in case you don't know what that means, it means master. Do you hear me, kipumbu we, you little testicle? Seyyid, you call him that. Seyyid!'

'Yes,' Yusuf said promptly, his ear still humming from the last blow. 'But how long do you have to work for him before you can go? How long will I have to stay?'

'Until your Ba is no longer in debt, or he is dead maybe,' Khalil said cheerfully. 'What's the matter? Don't you like it here? He's a good man, the seyyid. He doesn't beat you or anything like that. If you show him respect he'll look after you and make sure that you don't go wrong. All your life. But if you cry at night and have those frightening dreams . . . You must learn Arabic, then he'll like you more.'

6

Some nights they were plagued by dogs which roamed the dark streets. The dogs roamed in packs, loping and alert as they scuffled in shadows and thickets. Yusuf was woken by their scuttling paws on the road, and then saw the merciless shapes their bodies took as they ran past. One night he opened his eyes from deep sleep to find four dogs standing immobile across the road from them. Yusuf sat up in terror. It was the eyes which frightened him most and shocked him out of sleep. Their glare in the pale light of a half moon was lifeless, expressing only one kind of knowledge. Focused in them, he saw hardened calculating patience whose object was the emptying out of his life. His sudden movement in sitting up made the dogs yelp and turn away. But they returned the following night, standing silently for a while and then turning away as if to a plan. Night after night they came, their eagerness growing clearer with the swelling moon. Each night they edged nearer, circling the clearing and howling in the cover of bushes. They filled Yusuf's mind with nightmares. His terror was mixed with shame, for he could see that Khalil took no notice of the dogs. If he caught sight of them lurking, he hurled a stone at them and they ran. If he was near enough, he threw handfuls of dust in their eyes. It seemed that when they came at night, they came for Yusuf. In his dreams they stood two-legged over him, their long mouths half open and slavering, their pitiless eyes passing over his soft prone body.

One night they loped in, as he had known they would, keeping far apart from each other and forcing Yusuf's eyes from one to the other. The light was as bright as day. The biggest of the dogs came nearest, standing in the clearing in front of the shop. A long, low growl came from its tensed body, and was answered by soft-footed scuffling as the other dogs moved in to make an arc across the yard. Yusuf could hear their panting, and saw their mouths widen in soundless snarls. Without premeditation or warning his bowels opened. He cried out in surprise and saw the leading dog suddenly start. His cry woke up Khalil, who sat up in panic and saw how close the dogs were. They were growling with fury, working themselves up into an attacking frenzy. Khalil rushed out into the yard, shouting and waving his arms at the maddened dogs, throwing stones and fistfuls of dust at them and whatever else came to hand. The dogs turned and ran, whimpering and snapping at each other like frightened animals. For one long minute, Khalil stood in the moonlit yard shouting curses in Arabic at the fleeing dogs and waving a fist at them. He came running back, and Yusuf saw that his hands were shaking. He stood in front of Yusuf and shook two enraged fists at him, speaking rapidly in Arabic and making his meaning clearer with a variety of angry gestures. Then he turned and pointed an accusing finger in the direction of the dogs.

'You want them to bite you? Do you think they have come here to play with you? You are worse than a kifa urongo, you're a feeble-minded child without any spirit. What were you waiting for? Speak, you maluun.'

Khalil eventually stopped, sniffed and helped Yusuf grope towards the tap on the outside wall of the forbidden garden. There was a shed by the side of the house which they used as a toilet, but Yusuf refused to use it in the dark in case he missed his footing and fell into the evil bottomless latrine pit. Khalil hushed him with a finger across his lips and gentle pats on the head, and when Yusuf still could not stop, he stroked his hair and wiped the tears from his face. He helped him undress and stood nearby while Yusuf did what he could to clean himself at the standpipe.

27

The dogs came back for several nights after that, stopping some distance away from the yard, yowling and yapping in the shadows. Even on nights when they could not see them, they could feel the dogs prowling around the house, and could hear them in the bushes. Khalil told Yusuf stories of wolves and jackals who stole human babies and raised them as beasts, feeding them dog-breast and regurgitated meat. They taught them how to speak their language and how to hunt. When they were grown, they made them couple with them, to produce the wolf-people who lived in the deepest forest and ate nothing but putrid flesh. Ghouls also eat dead meat, human meat preferably, but only of those over whom prayers have not been said after death. In any case, they are jinns created from fire and not to be confused with the wolf-people, who are made from earth like all animals. Angels, if you happen to be interested, were created from light, which is one reason why they are invisible. Anyway, the wolf-people sometimes came among real people.

'Have you ever seen one?' Yusuf asked.

Khalil looked thoughtful. 'I'm not sure,' he said. 'But I think maybe I have. They come in disguise, you know that. One night I saw a very tall man leaning against the sufi tree there, as tall as a house and all white. Glowing like light . . . but like fire not light.'

'Perhaps it was an angel,' Yusuf suggested, hoping it was.

'May God forgive you. You can't see an angel. He was laughing, leaning against the tree and laughing hungrily.'

'Hungrily?' Yusuf asked.

'I shut my eyes and said a prayer. You must not look into the eyes of a wolf-man, otherwise it's goodbye, chomp chomp. When I opened my eyes again he'd gone. Another time an empty basket followed me for an hour. If I stopped it stopped, if I turned a corner it did too. When I walked on I heard a dog howling. When I looked around I saw the empty basket following me.'

'Why didn't you run?' Yusuf asked, his voice hushed with awe.

'It wouldn't have done any good. Wolf-men run faster than zebras, faster than thought. The only thing faster than a wolf-man is a prayer. If you run, they turn you into an animal or a slave. After kiyama, after the day the world ends and God calls everyone to Him . . . after kiyama the wolf-men will live in the first layer of Hell, thousands and thousands of them, and they'll eat the sinful people who don't obey Allah.'

'Will the ghouls live there too?'

'Maybe,' Khalil said after much thought.

'Who else?'

'I don't know,' Khalil said. 'But it is certainly a place to avoid. On the other hand, the other layers are even worse, so maybe it's best to keep away from the place altogether. Sleep now, otherwise you'll nod off when you should be working.'

Khalil tutored him in the ways of the shop. He showed him how to lift the sacks without hurting himself and how to pour the grain into the tubs without spilling it. He showed him how to count money quickly and how to work out the change, how to name the coins, to differentiate the bigger from the lesser. Yusuf learned how to accept money from a customer, and how to hold a note so that it was secure between his fingers. Khalil held his hand so it would not shake while he taught him to measure out the coconut oil with a ladle and how to cut pieces off the long bar of soap with a length of wire. He grinned his approval when Yusuf learned well, and hit him sharp painful blows when he failed, sometimes in front of the customers.

The customers laughed at everything Khalil did, but the laughter appeared not to trouble him. They teased him endlessly about his accent, imitating him and then heaving with laughter. His little brother was teaching him to speak better, he told them. And when he could speak well enough, he would get himself a plump Mswahili wife and live a God-fearing life. The old men on the terrace loved talk of plump young wives, and Khalil was happy to oblige them. The customers made him repeat words and phrases that they expected him to have trouble with, and Khalil repeated them as carelessly as he could, and then joined in the laughter, his eyes blazing with joy.

The customers were people who lived nearby, or country people on their way out of town. They grumbled about their poverty and the cost of everything, and kept silent about their lies and their cruelties, like everyone else. If the old men were sitting at their bench, the customers stopped to chat with them or call the coffee-seller to serve their fathers a cup. The women customers took a liking to Yusuf, mothering him at every opportunity and laughing delightedly at his little courtesies and his good looks. One of the women, her skin glossily black and her face mobile with subtle movement, was besotted with him. Her name was Ma Ajuza, a large, strong-looking woman with a voice which cut through crowds. She seemed very old to Yusuf, cumbersome, bulky, and with a look of suffering when her face was unguarded. Her body shivered and straightened with an involuntary charge when she caught sight of him, and a small cry escaped her. If Yusuf had not seen her, she stalked him until she was near enough to squeeze him into her arms. Then, while he struggled and kicked she ululated with triumph and joy. On occasions when she could not sneak up on him, she approached with ecstatic cries, calling him *my husband, my master*. Then she cajoled him with compliments and promises, tempted him with sweetmeats and offered him pleasures beyond his wildest imaginings if he

30

came home with her. *Take pity on me, my husband,* she cried. Other men who happened to be nearby offered themselves instead because they could not bear her misery, but she spurned them with a look of scorn. Yusuf fled as soon as he caught sight of her, hiding in the deepest darkness of the shop while she wailed for his appearance. Khalil did all he could to assist the woman. Sometimes he accidentally left the counter flap unlocked so that she could come into the shop itself and pursue Yusuf among the sacks and tins. Or Khalil sent him on errands to one of the stores at the side of the shop where the woman would be lurking in wait for him. Whenever she trapped him, she swooped on him with wild cries while her body shook in paroxysms of trembling and sneezing. She smelt of the tobacco she chewed and her embraces and shouts were embarrassing. Everyone seemed to find the business funny − although Yusuf could not see the joke − so they always told Ma Ajuza where he was hiding.

'She's so old,' he complained to Khalil.

'Old!' Khalil said. 'What has love to do with age? And that woman loves you, yet you cause her constant misery. Can't you see how her heart is breaking? Have you no eyes? Have you no feelings? You stupid kifa urongo, you feeble young coward. What do you mean old? Look at that body, look at those hips . . . Plenty good news there. She's perfect for you.'

'She's got grey hair.'

'A handful of henna . . . and no more grey hair. What do you care about hair? Beauty lies deep in the person, in the soul,' Khalil said. 'Not just on the surface.'

'Her teeth are red with tobacco, like those old men. Why doesn't she want one of them?'

'Buy her a toothbrush,' Khalil suggested.

'Her stomach is so big,' Yusuf said plaintively, wanting to be released from the teasing.

'Wah wah,' Khalil mocked. 'Perhaps one day a slim and beautiful princess from Persia will come to the shop and invite you to her palace. My little brother, that fine big woman is in love with you.'

'Is she rich?' Yusuf asked.

Khalil laughed and gave Yusuf a sudden and delighted embrace. 'Not rich enough to get you out of this hole,' he said.

7

They saw Uncle Aziz at least once every day when he came to collect the day's takings late in the evening. He glanced into the canvas bag of money which Khalil gave him, and looked over the notebook into which Khalil entered the day's figures, before taking both away for detailed examination. Sometimes they saw him more often, but only in passing. He was always busy, walking past the shop in the morning on his way to town with a thoughtful look, returning with a thoughtful look, and most of the time looking as if he had weighty matters on his mind. The old men on the terrace looked on calmly as Uncle Aziz fretted with his thoughts. Yusuf knew their names now: Ba Tembo, Mzee Tamim, Ali Mafuta, but he still thought of them as one phenomenon. He imagined that if he shut his eyes while they were talking he would not be able to tell them apart from each other.

He could not bring himself to call Uncle Aziz *seyyid*, even though Khalil hit him every time he called him Uncle. 'He ain't your uncle, you stupid Mswahili boy. Sooner or later you got to learn to kiss the man's arse. Seyyid, seyyid, not Uncle, Uncle. Come on, you say it after me, seyyid.' But he didn't. If forced to speak of Uncle Aziz he said Him, or allowed a gap to develop which Khalil irritably filled.

Several months after Yusuf's arrival – he had taught himself to lose count, and his perverse success made him understand that days could be as long as weeks if there was no desire for them – preparations were being made for a journey to the interior. Uncle Aziz spoke to Khalil for long periods in the evening, sitting on the bench in front of the shop which the old men occupied during the day. A lamp burned brightly between them, flattening their faces into masks of frankness. Yusuf thought he understood some of the Arabic, but he did not care. They went over the little book into which Khalil wrote the day's business, turned the pages backwards and forwards and added up the figures. Yusuf squatted nearby, listening to the two of them talking in anxious voices as if they feared for their safety. Khalil was restless during these conversations, speaking with an intensity he could not check while his eyes glowed feverishly. Sometimes Uncle Aziz laughed unexpectedly, making Khalil jump with consternation. Otherwise he listened in his casual way, unmoved and vaguely preoccupied. If he spoke it was in a calm voice which hardened effortlessly when required.

Then the preparations became more intense, and gave rise to disorder. Packages and cargoes were delivered at surprising times and were taken to the stores which ran down the side of the house. Sacks and woven packs were piled in the shop. Loads of various shapes and smells began to appear in corners of the terrace, covered with sacking and canvas to keep out the dust. With the loads came untalkative retainers who sat in watch, displacing the old men from their bench and chasing away children and customers who found the covered merchandise irresistible. The retainers were Wasomali and Wanyamwezi, armed with thin canes and whips. They were not truly silent, but spoke words understood only among themselves. To Yusuf they looked fierce and vicious, men who were

33

well prepared for war. He dared not look at them openly, and they did not even seem to see him. The mnyapara wa safari, the foreman of the journey, would be waiting for the expedition somewhere in the interior, Khalil told him. The seyyid was too rich a merchant to organize and run the expedition himself. Normally the mnyapara would have been at the journey's beginning, hiring porters and gathering supplies, but he had some business to finish. Khalil rolled his eyes as he said this. The business was not easy or he would have been here. More likely it was something disreputable. Fixing something, organizing contraband or settling an old score – some kind of slime or another. There's always something crooked when that man is around. The mnyapara's name was Mohammed Abdalla, Khalil said, shuddering melodramatically as he spoke his name. 'A demon!' he said. 'A hard-hearted twister of souls, without wisdom or mercy. But the seyyid thinks highly of him despite all his vices.'

'Where are they going?' Yusuf asked.

'To trade with the savages,' Khalil said. 'This is the seyyid's life. This is what he's here to do. He goes to the wild people and sells them all this merchandise and then he buys from them. He buys anything ... except slaves, even before the government said it must stop. Trading in slaves is dangerous work, and not honourable.'

'How long do they go away for?'

'Months, sometimes years,' Khalil said, grinning with a kind of pride and admiration. 'This is trade. They don't say how long will the journey take? They just go over the hills in all directions and don't come back until they've made trade. The seyyid is a champion, so he always does good business and comes back quickly. I don't think this is a long trip, just for a little spending money.'

During the day men came to look for work, to bargain for

terms with Uncle Aziz. Some came with letters of their previous service, among them old men who pleaded with glaring and desperate eyes when they were turned away.

Then one morning, when the chaos around them had become almost unendurable, they set off. A drum, a horn and a tamburi, all played with joyful and irresistible zest, led the men off. Behind the musicians a line of porters carried the packs and sacks, shouting cheerful abuse at each other and at bystanders who had come to see them off. Alongside the porters strolled the Wasomali and Wanyamwezi, flicking canes and thongs threateningly to keep the curious at bay. Uncle Aziz stood and watched the men pass before him, an amused and bitter smile on his face. When the procession was almost out of sight, he turned to Khalil and Yusuf. For a brief moment, more a gesture than an act, he glanced over his shoulder towards the far door in the depths of the garden, as if he had heard someone call. Then he smiled at Yusuf and gave him his hand to kiss. As Yusuf bent over the hand, ducking into a gust of perfume and incense, Uncle Aziz's other hand came over and stroked his neck. Yusuf thought of the ten anna piece and was overpowered by the odours of the chicken-house and the timber-yard. At the last minute, as if it did not matter to him, Uncle Aziz acknowledged Khalil's raucous farewells. He gave him his hand to kiss and then turned to go.

They watched the departing master until he was out of sight. Khalil then looked round and smiled at Yusuf. 'Perhaps he'll bring another little boy when he comes back. Or a little girl,' he said.

In Uncle Aziz's absence, Khalil's frenzy visibly subsided. The old men returned to the terrace, muttering small snatches of wisdom to each other and teasing Khalil about becoming the master again. He took charge of the dealings of the house and went inside every morning, although he was uncommunicative about this when Yusuf showed interest. He paid the old vegetable man who came every day and went through the garden door, his shoulders sloping with the weight of his baskets. Sometime during the morning he gave money to one of the boys in the neighbourhood with instructions for the market. The boy's name was Kisimamajongoo and he whistled tunes through his nose as he strolled from one task to another, running errands for people. His hard-bitten air was a grotesque parody, making everyone laugh, for he was shrunken and unwell, dressed in rags, and was often beaten in the streets by other boys. No one knew where he slept for he had no home. Khalil called him *kifa urongo* too. 'Another one. The original,' he said.

Every morning, the old gardener Hamdani came to attend to the secret trees and bushes, and clean the pool and water channels. He never spoke to anyone and went unsmilingly about his work, humming verses and qasidas. At noon, he performed his ablutions and said his prayers in the garden, and a little later he silently departed. The customers spoke of him as a saint who had secret knowledge of medicine and cures.

At mealtimes Khalil went into the house and came out with two plates of food for them, and afterwards took the empty plates back. In the evening he took the canvas sack of money and the notebook into the house. Sometimes, late at night, Yusuf heard sharp voices talking. He knew there were women hidden in the house. There always were. He had never been beyond the tap against the garden wall, but from there he had seen washing on the line, brightly coloured tunics and sheets, and had wondered when it was that the voices in the house came to hang it out. Women visitors came, draped from head to toe in black buibui. They greeted Khalil in Arabic as they passed, and asked questions about Yusuf. Khalil replied without looking directly at them. Sometimes a hand decorated with henna reached out from under the black folds and stroked Yusuf's cheek. The women smelt of a heavy perfume which reminded Yusuf of his mother's clothes-trunk. She had called the perfume *udi*, and told him that it was incense made of aloe, amber and musk, names which had made Yusuf's heart stir in an unexpected way.

'Who lives inside?' Yusuf asked Khalil in the end. He had been reluctant to ask questions while Uncle Aziz was there. He had not thought of having desires other than those demanded by the way they lived, and that had seemed accidental and capable of unexpected change. It was Uncle Aziz who was the centre and meaning of that life, it was around him that everything turned. Yusuf did not yet have a way of describing Uncle Aziz out of that embrace, and only now in his absence could he begin to feel him apart again.

'Who lives inside?' he asked. They had locked up for the night but were still in the shop, measuring and packing cones of sugar. Yusuf ladled the sugar on the scales while Khalil rolled the paper cones and filled them. For a moment it seemed as if Khalil had not heard Yusuf's repeated question, then he stopped and looked at Yusuf with mild suspicion. It was a question he should not have asked, he realized, and he began to tense for the blow which still followed from many of his mistakes, but Khalil smiled and looked away from Yusuf's apprehensive eyes. 'The Mistress,' Khalil said, then put his finger across his lips to prevent Yusuf from asking any more questions. He glanced at the back wall of the shop in warning. They made sugar cones in silence after that.

Later, they sat under the sufi tree across the clearing, in the cavern of light that their lantern made. Insects dashed their bodies at the glass, driven mad by their inability to throw themselves into the flames. 'The Mistress is crazy,' Khalil said suddenly, and then laughed to hear Yusuf's small exclamation. 'Your auntie. Why don't you call her Auntie? She's very rich, but she's a sick old lady. If you greet her nicely perhaps she'll leave you all her money. When the seyyid married her, many years ago, he became suddenly a rich man. But she's very ugly. She has a sickness. For many years doctors have come, learned hakim with long grey beards have read prayers for her, and mganga from over the hills have brought medicine, but it's no good. Even cow-doctors and camel-doctors have come. Her illness is like a wound in the heart. Not a wound from a human hand. Do you understand? Something bad has touched her. She hides from people.'

Khalil stopped and would not continue after that. Yusuf had felt Khalil's mockery turn to misery as he spoke, and tried to think of something to say which would make him more cheerful. The crazy old woman in the house did not surprise him at all. It was exactly as it would have been in the stories his mother used to tell him. In those stories the craziness would have been because of love gone wrong, or bewitchment in order to steal an inheritance, or unfulfilled revenge. Nothing could be done about the craziness until matters had been put right, until the curse had been lifted. He wanted to say that to Khalil. Don't worry about it so much, it will all be put right before the story ends. He had already resolved that if he ever ran into the crazy Mistress, he would look away and say a prayer. He did not want to think about his mother, or the way she used to tell him stories. Khalil's sadness made him miserable, and he said the first thing which came into his head, just to get him to talk again. 'Did your mother use to tell you stories?' he asked.

38

'My mother!' Khalil said, taken by surprise.

After a short while, when Khalil still had not said any more, Yusuf asked, 'Did she?'

'Don't talk to me about her. She's gone. Like everybody else. Everybody's gone,' Khalil said. Then he spoke rapidly in Arabic and looked as if he would hit Yusuf. 'Gone, you stupid boy, you kifa urongo. Everybody's gone to Arabia. They left me here. My brothers, my mother . . . everybody.'

Yusuf's eyes watered. He felt homesick and abandoned, but struggled to keep himself from crying. After a moment Khalil sighed and then reached out and clouted Yusuf on the back of the head. 'Except for my little brother,' he said, and then laughed as Yusuf burst into a self-pitying wail.

They usually shut the shop for an hour or two on Friday afternoons, but in Uncle Aziz's absence Yusuf asked Khalil if they could spend the whole afternoon in the town. He had caught glimpses of the sea in the heat of the day, and had heard the customers talk about the wonders brought in with the day's catch. Khalil said he knew no one in the town, and had only ever seen the harbour once after the first time, when he was landed off a boat in the depths of night into the arms of the seyyid.

Even after all this time he did not know anybody he could visit, he said. He had not been inside anyone's house. Every Idd he went with the seyyid to the Juma'a mosque for prayers, and once he had been taken to a funeral, but he did not know whose it was.

'Then we should go and look around,' Yusuf said. 'We can go to the harbour.'

'We'll get lost,' Khalil said, laughing nervously.

'We won't,' Yusuf said firmly.

'Shabab! What a brave little brother you are,' Khalil said, slapping Yusuf on the back. 'You'll look after me, eh.'

Soon after they left the shop they ran into some of their customers, whom they greeted. They joined the tide of bodies in the streets and were swept to the mosque for Juma'a prayers. Yusuf could not help noticing that Khalil was uncertain of the proper words and actions. Afterwards they walked to the waterside to watch the dhows and the boats. Yusuf had never been that close to the sea before, and he was made speechless by its hugeness. He had expected the air to be fresh and tangy by the waterside, but the smells were of dung and tobacco and raw wood. There was also a pungent and corrosive smell which he later found out to be seaweed. Drawn up on the beach were lines of outriggers, and further up, the fishermen to whom they belonged lounged under awnings and around cooking fires. They were waiting for the tide to turn, they said. It would happen at about two hours before sunset. They made space for them and Khalil sat among them without any strain, pulling Yusuf down beside him. The meal being prepared in the two blackened pots turned out to be rice and spinach. It was served in a battered round platter from which they all ate.

'I used to live in a fishing village along the coast south of here,' Khalil said after they left.

They spent the afternoon strolling, laughing at everything they dared. In their wanderings they bought a stick of sugar cane and a cone of nuts, then stopped to watch boys playing kipande. Yusuf asked Khalil if they should join, and Khalil nodded self-importantly. He had no detailed idea how to play, but he had seen enough in the few minutes to get the general drift. He rolled up his saruni into a loincloth and chased after the kipande like a madman. The boys laughed, crying out names for him. He energetically acquired the bat at the earliest opportunity and gave it to Yusuf, who scored hit after hit with the casual assurance of a virtuoso. Khalil applauded every score, and when Yusuf was eventually caught, he carried him off from the game on his shoulders while Yusuf struggled to climb down.

On the way home they saw dogs beginning to stir in the early evening streets. In the light, their bodies looked ulcerated and scrawny, and their fur was mangy. Their eyes, so cruel in the moonlight, were runny and clotted with white matter in the daylight. Clouds of flies buzzed around the red sores on their bodies.

After the game of kipande, Yusuf's heroic performance was sung to the customers. Khalil exaggerated Yusuf's exploits with every telling and made his own part sound more and more clownish. In his usual way with the customers, he played everything for laughs, especially if there were any girls or young women around. So that by the time Ma Ajuza came to hear the story, the game had turned into a carnage and slaughter out of which Yusuf had stepped triumphant, while his clown pranced beside him singing his praise-songs. Yusuf the Magnificent, blessed of God, the new Dhul Qurnain, slayer of Gog and Magog! Ma Ajuza exclaimed and applauded at all the appropriate places as one imaginary foe after another was laid low by Yusuf's flashing blade. Then at the end of the recital, as Yusuf could have predicted, Ma Ajuza emitted joyous ululations and came after him. The customers and the old men on the terrace cheered and laughed, egging Ma Ajuza on. There was no escape. She captured him and dragged him as far as the sufi tree, shuddering with passion, before he managed to wrench himself free.

'Who are all those Majogs you named to Ma Ajuza? What's the story?' Yusuf asked later.

Khalil waved him away at first, preoccupied after having been in the house that evening. Later he said, 'Dhul Qurnain is a small horse which flies. If you can catch it and roast it over a fire of clove-wood, and eat a piece from each limb, including the wings, it gives you power over witches and demons and ghouls. Then you can order them, if you wish, to fetch a beautiful slim princess for you from China, Persia or India. But the price you pay is you have to become a prisoner of Gog and Magog – for life.'

Yusuf waited quietly, unconvinced.

'All right, I'll tell you the truth,' Khalil said, grinning. 'No fooling around. Dhul Qurnain means the one with two horns . . . Iskander the Conqueror, who defeated the whole world in battle. Have you heard of Iskander the Conqueror? During his conquest of the world, he was once travelling on the edges of it when he came to some people who told him that to the north of them lived Gog and Magog, brutes who had no language and who ravaged the lands of their neighbours all the time. So Dhul Qurnain built a wall which Gog and Magog could neither climb nor dig through. That is the wall which marks the edge of the world. Beyond that live barbarians and demons.'

'What was the wall made of? Are Gog and Magog still there?' Yusuf asked.

'How do you expect me to know?' Khalil said irritably. 'Can't I get any rest from you? All you want is stories. Just let me get some sleep now.'

In Uncle Aziz's absence Khalil was less interested in the shop. He went into the house more and more often, and was not as angry with Yusuf if he strayed into the garden. The garden was completely enclosed, apart from the wide doorway near the front terrace of the house. The silence and coolness of the garden, which had been evident even from a distance, had entranced Yusuf from his first arrival. In the absence of his uncle he stepped beyond the wall and found that the garden was divided into quarters, with a pool in the centre and water channels running off it in the four directions. The quadrants were planted with trees and bushes, some of them in flower: lavender, henna, rosemary and aloe. In the open ground between the bushes were clovers and grasses, and scattered clumps of lilies and irises. Beyond the pool, towards the top end of the garden, the ground rose into a terrace planted with poppies, yellow roses and jasmine, scattered to resemble natural growth. Yusuf dreamt that at night the fragrance rose into the air and turned him dizzy. In his rapture he thought he heard music.

Orange and pomegranate trees were scattered in parts of the garden, and as Yusuf walked under their shade he felt like an intruder, and smelt their blossoms with a feeling of guilt. Mirrors hung from the trunks of trees, but were positioned too high for Yusuf to see himself in them. As they lay on their earth terrace in front of the shop, they talked about the garden and its beauty. Although he did not say so, when they talked in that way Yusuf desired nothing more than to be banished for a long time in the silent grove. The pomegranate, Khalil told him, was the fulfilment of all fruits. Neither orange, nor peach, nor apricot but something of all of them. It was the tree of fertility itself, its trunk and fruit as sturdy and plump as the quickness of life. The hard, juiceless seeds that Yusuf was offered as confirmation of this doctrine, from a fruit daringly filched from the garden, tasted nothing like oranges, which Yusuf did not like anyway. He had never heard of peaches. 'What are apricots?' he asked.

'Not as nice as pomegranates,' Khalil said, looking irritated.

'In that case I don't like apricots,' Yusuf said firmly. Khalil ignored him.

But there was no mistaking that he spent a lot of time in the house. Whenever he could, Yusuf went into the garden, although he knew when his departure was indicated. He heard the complaining voice inside the house-courtyard rise and knew that it was pitched over the wall at him. The Mistress.

'She has seen you,' Khalil told him. 'She says you are a beautiful boy. She watches you in her mirrors in the trees when you walk in the garden. Have you seen the mirrors?'

Yusuf expected Khalil to laugh at him, as he did with Ma Ajuza, but he was grim and miserable, preoccupied.

'Is she very old?' he asked Khalil, trying to provoke him into teasing. 'The Mistress. Is she very old?'

'Yes.'

'And ugly?'

'Yes.'

'And fat?'

'No.'

'Is she crazy?' Yusuf asked, watching Khalil's growing distraction with a kind of fascination. 'Has she got a servant? Who does the cooking?'

Khalil slapped him several times, and then punched him hard on the head. He forced Yusuf's head down between his knees and held it there for a moment before pushing him suddenly away. 'You are her servant. I am her servant. Her slaves. Don't you use your head? You stupid Mswahili, you feeble idiot . . . She is sick. Don't you use your eyes? You're better off dead than alive. Are you going to let everything happen to you all the time? Get away from me!' Khalil shouted, the corners of his mouth frothing and his thin body shaking with the rage he was keeping in check.

THE MOUNTAIN TOWN

I

His first journey to the interior occurred unexpectedly. He was becoming used to accidents of that kind. Preparations were well under way before Yusuf discovered that he was going on the trip as well. Provisions for the journey had accumulated in the back of the shop and on the terrace. Fragrant sacks of dates and bags of dried fruit were stacked in one of the side stores. Bees and wasps found their way in through the barred windows, attracted by the perfume and the sweet moisture that oozed out of the woven straw sacks. Some other loads, smelling of hoof and hide, were conveyed hurriedly into the house itself. They were awkwardly shaped and covered with hessian. *Magendo*, Khalil whispered. *Contraband for the border. Big money.* Customers witnessed the arrival of the hessian-covered loads with raised eyebrows, and exchanged pleased conspiratorial looks with the old men, who though displaced from their bench on the terrace still watched calmly from under the trees, and nodded and grinned as if they were party to everything which was going on. Whenever Yusuf was cornered by one of the old men, he had to listen to lavish and careful talk about piles and bowel movement and constipation, depending on his captor. But if he could bear with their talk of the tortures of declining bodies, he would hear stories of other journeys, and watch as the old men forgot themselves in the excitement of these new preparations.

The air was filled with the travel-stained scent of other places, and rang with the sound of commands. As the day of

45

departure approached the chaos reluctantly subsided. Uncle Aziz's calm and bemused smile, and his hard, impassive face, insisted that everyone should conduct themselves with dignity. In the end the expedition left in an atmosphere of serenity, led out by the horn player blowing a garrulous melody and the drummer pounding an approving rhythm. People in the streets stood quietly to watch them pass, smiling and waving with a subdued air. None of them would have thought to deny that this procession to the interior was what they were there for, and they knew the form of words which could make such journeys seem necessary.

Yusuf had watched many such departures before, and had come to enjoy the urgency and frenzy of preparation. He and Khalil were required to help the porters and guards, fetching and carrying, keeping watch, taking counts. Uncle Aziz himself took little part in the arrangements. The details were left in the hands of his mnyapara, Mohammed Abdalla. The demon! Whenever Uncle Aziz was ready for one of his long journeys, he sent for the mnyapara from somewhere in the interior. He always came, for Uncle Aziz was a merchant of means who could provision his expeditions himself without having to ask for credit from an Indian Mukki. There was honour in working for such a man. It was Mohammed Abdalla who hired the porters and the guards, and agreed with them their share of the profit. It was also he who kept them to the mark. Most of them were people of the coast, from as far as Kilifi and Lindi and Mrima. The mnyapara struck fear in all of them. His scowling, snarling looks, and the pitiless light in his eyes promised nothing but pain to any who crossed him. His simplest and most ordinary gestures were performed with the knowledge and relish of this power. He was a tall, strong-looking man, who strode around with shoulders thrown back, anticipating a challenge. His face was high cheek-boned and lumpy, bubbling with unquiet urges. He carried a thin bamboo cane which he used for emphasis, swishing it through the air when he was exasperated, landing it on a slothful buttock when his ire was up. He had a reputation as a merciless sodomizer and could often be seen absent-mindedly stroking his loins. It was said, often by those Mohammed Abdalla had refused to employ, that he picked porters who would be willing to get down on all fours for him during the journey.

Sometimes he looked at Yusuf with a frightening smile, shaking his head in small delight. *Mashaallah*, he would say. A wonder of God. His eyes softened with pleasure at these times, and his mouth opened in an unaccustomed grin to reveal teeth that were stained with the tobacco he chewed. When this anguish was on him he released heavy sighs of lust and smilingly muttered lines of a song about the nature of beauty. It was he who told Yusuf that he was to come on the journey with them, making even such a simple instruction sound menacing.

For Yusuf it was an unwelcome interruption to the equanimity his life of captivity had acquired over the years. Despite everything, he had not been unhappy in Uncle Aziz's shop. He had come to understand fully that he was there as rehani, pawned to Uncle Aziz to secure his father's debts to the merchant. It was not difficult to guess that his father had borrowed too much over the years, even more than the sale of his hotel could repay. Or he had been unlucky. Or had spent stupidly with money he did not possess. Khalil told him that it was the seyyid's way, so that when he needed anything there were people who could be asked to do what was required. If the seyyid was desperate for money, he sacrificed a handful of his creditors to raise it.

Perhaps one day, when his father had made something for

47

himself, he would come to redeem him. He wept for his mother and father when he could. At times he panicked at the thought that their images were turning faint in his recollection. The sound of their voices or a particular quality they possessed – his mother's laughter, his father's reluctant grin – came back to reassure him. It was not that he pined for them, and in any case he did so less and less with each accumulating moment, rather that his separation from them was the most memorable event of his existence. So he dwelt on it, and was saddened by his loss. He thought of things he should have known about them or could have asked them. The bitter fights which had frightened him. The names of the two boys who had drowned after leaving Bagamoyo. Names of trees. If only he had thought to ask them about such things perhaps he might not have felt so ignorant and so dangerously adrift from everything. He did the work he was given, carried out whatever instructions Khalil gave him and came to depend on his 'brother'. When he was allowed to, he worked in the garden.

His love of the garden had impressed itself on the old man who came to tend it in the mornings and early afternoons, Mzee Hamdani. The old man rarely spoke, and became irritated if he was forced to stop singing the verses in praise of God, some of which he composed himself, and was required to listen to someone speaking to him. Every morning he began work without greeting anyone, filled his buckets and scooped the water out with his hand as he walked along the paths, as if nothing else existed apart from this garden and this work. When the sun was too hot, he sat in the shade of one of the trees and read through a little book, muttering and gently rocking, lost in his ecstatic worship. In the afternoon, after prayers, he washed his feet and departed. Mzee Hamdani allowed Yusuf to help him whenever he chose, not so much by directing him to any task but by not chasing him away. In the late afternoons, as the sun went down, Yusuf had the garden to himself. He pruned and watered and strolled under the trees and between the bushes. The querulous voice over the wall still rose to chase him away as it got dark, although at other times he also heard sighs and snatches of song in the gathering gloom. The voice filled him with sadness. Once he heard a drawn-out cry of longing which made him think of his mother, and made him stop under the wall and listen with a tremble of fear.

Yusuf had given up asking about the Mistress. It made Khalil angry. *This is not your business and you must not ask useless questions. You'll bring ... kisirani ... bad luck. You want to bring evil on us.* He knew that Khalil's anger required him to keep silent about her, though he could not help intercepting the looks which passed between the customers as they inquired after the household, as was polite. In their afternoon wanderings in the town Khalil and Yusuf had seen the huge silent houses with blank front walls where the rich Omani families lived. 'They only marry their daughters to their brothers' sons,' one of the customers told them. 'In some of those sprawling fortresses are feeble offspring locked away and never spoken about. Sometimes you can see the faces of the poor creatures pressed against the bars of the windows at the top of the houses. God only knows with what confusion they look on our miserable world. Or perhaps they understand that it is God's punishment for their fathers' sins.'

They visited the town every Friday to say prayers at the Juma'a mosque, and play kipande and football in the streets. Passers-by shouted remarks at Khalil, telling him he was almost a father and should not be playing with children. People will talk about you and give you dirty names, they shouted. One day an old woman stopped to watch the game for a few minutes, until Khalil came near and then she spat on the ground and walked away. At dusk they strolled to the waterfront and spoke to the fishermen if any had not gone to sea. They offered them a smoke, which Khalil accepted but forbade to Yusuf. *He's too beautiful to smoke*, the fishermen said. *It will only spoil him. Smoking is devil's business, a sin. But how is a poor man to live otherwise?* Yusuf remembered the tragic stories Mohammed the mendicant used to tell him, of how he had lost the love of his mother and his watered farm south of Witu, and he felt no deprivation at their prohibition. The fishermen told stories of their adventures, and of the visitations and tribulations which befell them at sea. With quiet ceremony they spoke of the demons which descended on them from clear skies disguised as freak storms, or which rose out of dark night-seas in the shape of giant glowing stingrays. Indulgent to each other, they exchanged tales of memorable battles they had fought against powerful and brave foes.

Later they watched a card-game outside a café, or bought food and ate it in the open. Sometimes there were open-air dances and concerts which went on into the early hours, to mark a seasonal occasion or celebrate some good fortune. Yusuf felt comfortable in the town, and he would have liked to go there more often, but he sensed that Khalil was not at ease. Khalil was happiest behind his shop counter, bantering with the customers in his heavy accent. His happiness with them was unfeigned. He laughed at their teasing and mockery of him with as much pleasure as they did, and listened to their tales of hardship and their relentless aches and pains with attention and sympathy. Ma Ajuza told him that if she had not already been spoken for by Yusuf, she would have considered him, despite his nervous airs and his scrawny frame.

One evening they went to the celebration of an Indian wedding in the heart of the old town, not as guests but as part of the unwashed throng which gathered to watch the prosperous display and observance of affection. They were stunned by the eloquence of the brocade robes and the gold ornaments of the guests, and applauded the gay turbans the men wore. Heavy scents of ancient provenance filled the air, and thick fumes of incense rose out of brass pots placed in the road in front of the house. They held in check the smells of the covered gutters which ran through the centre of the road. The procession which accompanied the bride was led by two men carrying a large green lantern in the shape of a many-domed onion-shaped palace. Flanking the bride were two rows of young men, chanting and spraying rose-water on the multitudes lining the streets. Some of the young men were a little embarrassed. The crowd sensed this and shouted words of mockery and abuse to increase their discomfort. The bride looked very young, a slip of a girl. She was covered from head to foot in veils of silk that were shot through with gold, glittering and sparkling with her every movement. Heavy bangles on her wrists and ankles shone dully, and her large ear-rings flitted like luminous shadows behind her veil. The outline of her lowered face was silhouetted by the bright glow of the lantern as she turned into the narrow gate of the groom's house.

Afterwards, platters of food were brought out into the street to feed the onlookers: samosa and ladhoo and halwa badam. Music played far into the night, strings and percussion accompanying voices that rose with beautiful clarity and precision. None of the crowd outside the house understood the words but they stayed to listen anyway. The songs became more melancholy as the night wore on, until in the end the people outside began to disperse silently, driven away by the sadness the songs promised.

2

'Kijana mzuri.' Beautiful boy, Mohammed Abdalla had said, stopping beside Yusuf and taking his chin in a hand that felt as if it was mottled and scaled. Yusuf shook his head free and felt his chin throbbing. 'You're coming. The seyyid wants you ready in the morning. You'll come and trade with us, and learn the difference between the ways of civilization and the ways of the savage. It's time you grew up and saw what the world is like . . . instead of playing in dirty shops.' A smile grew on his face as he spoke, a predatory grimace which made Yusuf think of the dogs that prowled the lanes of his nightmares.

Khalil, to whom Yusuf went for sympathy, refused to commiserate or mourn his fate with him. He laughed and punched him in the arm in a manner that seemed playful but which hurt Yusuf. 'You want to sit and play in the garden here? And sing qasidas like that crazy Mzee Hamdani? There's plenty of garden up there. You can borrow a hoe from the seyyid. He'll be carrying dozens of them for trading with the savages. They love hoes, those savage people. Who knows why? I hear they love a fight too. But you know all about that, you don't need me to tell you. You're part of that savage country up there. What are you afraid of? You'll enjoy yourself. Just tell them you're one of their princes coming home to find a wife.' That night Khalil avoided him, busying himself with the shop and getting into frantic conversations with the porters. When he could not avoid him any more, because they were lying on their mats to sleep, he made a joke of any question Yusuf tried to ask. 'Perhaps you'll meet one of your grandfathers on the journey. That will be exciting . . . and all the strange sights and the wild animals. Or are you afraid someone will steal Ma Ajuza when you travel? Don't worry, my Mswahili brother, she's yours for life. I'll tell her that you cried for her before you left because you were afraid there would be no one to squeeze your zub among the savages. She'll wait for you, and when you return she'll come to sing for you. You'll be a rich merchant soon, and you'll wear silk and perfume like the seyyid, and carry moneybags across your belly and a rosary round your wrist,' he said.

'What is the matter with you?' Yusuf asked in exasperation, his voice quavering with hurt and self-pity.

'What do you want me to do? Cry?' Khalil asked, laughing.

'I'm going away tomorrow, travelling with that man and his robbers –'

Khalil clapped a hand over Yusuf's mouth. They were in the back of the shop, sleeping there because the terrace in the front had long been taken by Mohammed Abdalla and his men, who had also turned the bushes on the edge of the clearing into open-air latrines. Khalil put a finger across his lips, and made a soft hiss of warning. When Yusuf made to say more, Khalil punched him hard in the stomach, making him groan with agony. He felt as if he was being banished, and felt accused of a betrayal he did not comprehend. Khalil pulled him near and held him in a long embrace and then let him go. 'It's better for you,' he said.

In the morning, the hessian-covered packages were all loaded into an old lorry to make part of the journey into the interior on their own. The column would join up with them later. The truck driver was a half-Greek and half-Indian man called Bachus. He had long black hair and a neatly trimmed moustache. His father owned a small bottling and ice-making plant in the town, and sometimes hired his truck and his son out to traders. Bachus sat in the driver's cab with the door open, his soft round body slumped comfortably in the seat. Out of his mouth issued an unstoppable stream of obscenities,

53

delivered with a mild voice and an unsmiling face. In between he sang snatches of love songs and puffed at a biri. 'Please be kind to me for once, you goatfuckers. I'd love nothing better than to sit here and stroke your anuses all day, but I've got other loads to pick up, bob. So can you put a bit of shoulder into it and stop sniffing each other's shit.

> When I think of truth I see your face,
> And every other face is nothing but a lie.
> When I dream of happiness I feel your caress
> And I see envy burning in everyone's eye.

Wah, wah, janab! If a maharaja heard me sing he'd offer his favourite piece of meat to me for a night. There's a funny smell in this place. I am sure I can pick up the perfume of rotting cocks, but maybe that's the food they give you. Hey, baba! What do they give you here? There's a lot of grease in that sweat running down your backs. They love fatty meat up there where you're going, bob, so watch where you put your fannies. Come on, my brother, stop scratching yourself there. Let someone else do it for you. It won't do any good, anyway. There's only one medicine for that kind of wound. Come behind the wall here and give me a massage. I'll give you five anna.' The porters roared and cackled with laughter at the driver's foul mouth. Using such language in front of the merchant! When he faltered, they taunted him with insults about his mother and father, and crude insinuations about his own children. 'Come and suck my cock,' he would say, clutching his crotch. Then he would start off again.

The rest of the goods to be taken on the journey were to be hauled to the railway station in a rikwama, a long handcart drawn by the porters. Until the last moment, Uncle Aziz was talking quietly to Khalil, who was bobbing deferentially beside him, acknowledging his instructions. The porters stood in

54

languid groups, talking and arguing, and exploding into sudden flurries of laughter and hand-slapping.

'Haya, take us to the country,' Uncle Aziz said at last, giving the signal to move. The drummer and horn player struck up at once and set off eagerly ahead of the column. Mohammed Abdalla walked a few paces behind them, head held high while his cane swished a grandiose parabola through the air. Yusuf gave a hand pushing the cart, keeping his eyes on the wooden wheels which could crush unwary feet, and joined in the rhythmic grunting of the porters. It had shamed him to see Khalil slavering over Uncle Aziz's hand at the last moment, looking as though he would swallow it whole if he were given the opportunity. He always did that, but Yusuf hated it more this morning. Yusuf heard Khalil shout something about *Mswahili*, but he did not look back.

Uncle Aziz brought up the rear, now and then stopping to exchange words of farewell with his more notable acquaintances among the bystanders in the streets.

3

The porters and the guards travelled in the third-class carriage, and spread themselves out on the slatted wooden benches as if they owned the place. Yusuf was with them. The other passengers moved to different carriages or retreated into corners, intimidated by their noise and uncouthness. Mohammed Abdalla came to visit them from another part of the train, sneering as he listened to their frenzied grumbling and their ignorant talk. It was cramped and gloomy in the carriage, and smelt of sticky earth and wood-smoke. When he shut his eyes, Yusuf felt a memory of his first train journey. They travelled for two days and a night, stopping often and rarely making much speed. At first the land was choked with palms and fruit trees, and through the verge-side vegetation they could see small farms and plantations. Whenever the train stopped, the porters and guards streamed on to the platform to see what was up. Some of them had been on this route before and knew station employees or platform traders, and wasted no time in renewing acquaintances. They were given messages and gifts to pass on down the line. At one of the stops, in the stillness of the early afternoon heat, Yusuf thought he heard the sound of tumbling water. In mid-afternoon the train stopped in Kawa, and he sat in tense silence on the floor of the carriage, in case someone should see him and embarrass his parents. Later, as the lie of the land rose and their journey turned eastwards, the trees and the farms became more rare. Grasslands intermittently thickened into copses of lush woods.

The porters and guards growled and snapped at each other. They talked a lot about food, arguing about all the wonderful dishes which were unavailable to them at that time, and contesting the excellence of the cuisines of their different regions. When they had made each other hungry and ill-tempered, they argued about other things: about the true meanings of words, about the size of the dowry received by the daughter of a legendary merchant, about the courage of a famous sea-captain, about the explanation for the raw skins of Europeans. For an animated half-hour they could not agree on the weight of the testicles of different animals: bulls, lions, gorillas, all had their supporters. They bickered over their sleeping space, which they saw being encroached on. With oaths and grunts, they pushed at each other for room. As they became more passionate, their bodies gave off a pungent musk of urine-scented sweat and stale tobacco. Before long, fights had started. Yusuf covered his head with his arms, wedging his back against the side of the carriage and kicking out with all his might when anyone came near him. In the depths of the night he heard mutterings, and then small movements. After a while he recognized the sound of furtive caresses, and later heard soft laughter and muted whispers of pleasure.

In the daylight he looked out of the window, searching the countryside and noting its changes. On their right distant hills were rising again, looking lush and dark. The air above the hills was thick and opaque, secreting a promise. On the parched plain through which the train was labouring, the light was clear. As the sun rose the air became gritty with dust. The scorched and dry plain was still covered with patches of dead grass which the rains would transform into lush savannahs. Clumps of gnarled thorn trees dotted the plain, which was darkened by scattered outcrops of black rock. Waves of heat and vapour rose from the burning earth, filling Yusuf's mouth and making him heave for breath. At one station, where they stopped for a long time, a solitary jacaranda tree was in bloom. Mauve and purple petals lay on the ground like an iridescent rug. Beside the tree was a two-roomed railway store. On its doors hung enormous rusty padlocks and its whitewashed walls were spattered with laterite mud.

Several times he thought of Khalil, and was made sad by the memory of their friendship and of his own abrupt and sulky departure. But Khalil had seemed nearly pleased to see him go. He thought of Kawa and of his parents there, and wondered if he could have acted differently.

They alighted from the train late in the afternoon, at a small town under a huge snowcapped mountain. The air was cool and pleasant, and the light had the softness of early twilight reflected in boundless water. On arrival Uncle Aziz greeted the Indian stationmaster like an old friend.

'Mohun Sidhwa, hujambo bwana wangu. I hope your health is good, and your children and the mother of your

57

children are all well. Alhamdulillahi rabi-l alamin, what more can we ask for?'

'Karibu, Bwana Aziz. Welcome, welcome. I hope everyone in your house is well. What news? How's business?' the stocky stationmaster said, pumping Uncle Aziz's hand with barely controlled excitement and pleasure.

'We thank God for whatever he has chosen to bless us with, my old friend,' said Uncle Aziz. 'But never mind about me, tell me how everything has been here. I pray that all your affairs prosper.'

The two of them disappeared into the low, shed-like building which was the stationmaster's office, smiling and chattering as they vied to extend formal courtesies to each other before they began to talk business. A huge yellow flag flew over the building, rippling and snapping in the breeze, making the angry black bird on it seem hysterical with rage. The porters smiled among themselves, knowing that their seyyid had gone to arrange an appropriate bribe with the railwayman so that their freight charges would be reduced. In a moment the stationmaster's clerk appeared, and leaned against the wall with the unconcerned appearance of a stroller pausing to take in the scene. He too was an Indian, a short and slim young man who made sure not to catch anyone's eye. The porters winked at each other over his display and made knowing remarks at him. In the meantime they unloaded the goods, under the gaze of Mohammed Abdalla and the guards, and piled them on the platform.

'Look sharp, you shameful loud-mouths,' Mohammed Abdalla said, shouting for the pleasure of doing so and wobbling his cane in the air threateningly. He smiled his scorn for everyone around him while he absent-mindedly massaged himself through his kikoi cloth, his legs wide apart. 'I'm warning you, no pilfering. If I catch anyone, I'll cut his backside to pieces. Later on I'll sing you a lullaby, but now stay awake. We're in the country of the savages. They're not made of the same cowardly mud as you. They'll steal anything, including your manhood if you don't keep your cloths well tied around you. Haya, haya! They're waiting for us.'

When all was ready, they marched off in procession, carrying whatever had been assigned to them. At the head of the caravan marched their haughty captain, swinging his cane and glaring at the astonished people whom they passed. It was a small, empty-looking town, but the huge mountain under which it cowered gave it an air of mystery and gloom, as if it were the scene of tragedies. Two beaded warriors strode past them, their bodies ochred and sleek. Leather sandals slapped the road in time with their swinging spears, their bodies leaning forward, straining and urgent. They glanced neither right nor left, and in their eyes was a look of assurance and purpose, almost of a kind of dedication. Their hair was groomed into tight plaits and dyed red like the earth, as were the soft-leather shukas which covered them diagonally from shoulder to hip and down to their knees. Mohammed Abdalla turned round to look at his procession with contempt, then pointed his cane at the striding warriors. 'Savages,' he said. 'Worth ten of any of you.'

'Imagine that God should create creatures like that! They look like something made out of sin,' one of the porters said, a young man who was always first to speak. 'Don't they look vicious?'

'How do they get themselves to look so red?' another porter asked. 'It must be the blood they drink. It's true, isn't it? That they drink blood.'

'Look at the blades of their spears!'

'And they know how to use them,' a guard said in a lowered voice, mindful of his captain's glowering looks. 'They may look like clumsy knives on sticks, but they can do a lot of damage. Especially with all the practice they get. It's what they do all the time, attacking other people and hunting. In order to become full warriors they have to hunt a lion and kill it, and then eat its penis. Each time they eat a penis they can marry another wife, and the more penises they eat, the greater they become among their own people.'

'Yallah! You're teasing us!' his listeners cried, mocking him, refusing to believe such tall stories.

'It's true,' the guard protested. 'I've seen them myself. Ask anyone who's travelled these parts. Wallahi, I'm telling the truth. And every time they kill a man they cut off a part of him and keep it in a special bag.'

'What for?' the talkative young porter asked.

'Do you ask a savage what for?' Mohammed Abdalla said sharply, turning round to glance at the young man. 'Because he's a savage, that's what for. He is what he is. You don't ask a shark or a snake why it attacks. It's the same with the savage. That's what he is. And you had better learn to walk faster with that load and talk a little less. You're nothing but a bunch of whimpering women.'

'It's to do with their religion,' the guard said after a while.

'It's not honourable, this way of life,' the young porter said, earning a long, frightening look from Mohammed Abdalla.

'A civilized man can always defeat a savage, even if the savage eats a thousand lion penises,' another guard said, a man from Comoro. 'He can outwit him with knowledge and guile.'

It did not take the caravan long to arrive at its destination. This was a shop at the end of a drive near the main road going out of the small town. In front of the shop was a circular clearing, well swept and ringed by breadfruit trees. The shopkeeper was a short, plump man dressed in a large white shirt and baggy trousers. He had a thin, trimmed moustache which, like his hair, was flecked with grey. Both his appearance and his language marked him out as a man of the coast. He moved busily among them, giving his instructions with firmness and authority, taking no notice of Mohammed Abdalla, who tried to intercede and relay his commands.

4

The air was sharp under the mountain, and the light had a purple tint which Yusuf had never seen before. In the early morning the top of the mountain was hidden by clouds, but as the sun strengthened the clouds disappeared and the peak congealed into ice. On one side, the level plain stretched away. Behind the mountain, he was told by the others who had been here before, lived the dusty warrior people who herded cattle and drank the blood of their animals. They thought war honourable and were proud of their history of violence. The greatness of their leaders was measured by the animals they had acquired from raiding their neighbours, and by the number of women they had abducted from their homes. When they were not fighting, they adorned their bodies and hair with the dedication of brothel queens. Among their traditional victims were the cultivators who lived on the mountain slopes where the rain drenched the ground. These cultivators came to the town several times a week to sell their produce, and looked hardy and flat-footed, not the look of people who would travel far from their land.

A Lutheran pastor had shown them the use of the iron plough, and taught them how to construct the wheel. These were gifts from his God, he told them, who had sent him to this mountain to offer the people salvation for their souls. He announced to them that work was God's divine edict, to allow

61

humans to atone for their evil. His church was also a school outside the hours of worship, and there he taught his flock to read and write. And because he insisted, the whole people had converted their allegiance to the God who had such practical priests. The pastor forbade them more than one wife and persuaded them that their oath to the new God he had brought to them was more binding than anything they owed to the ways of their fathers and mothers. He taught them hymns, and told them stories of green valleys that were lush with fruit and cream, and forests that were teeming with goblins and wild beasts, and mountainsides covered with snow and whole villages skating on frozen lakes. The cattle herders now had another reason to despise the farming people whom they had preyed on for generations. Not only did they grub the earth like animals or women, but they also sang the mournful choruses of the vanquished which filled and defiled the mountain air.

In the dusty shadowlands of the snowcapped mountain, where the warrior people lived and where little rain fell, lived a legendary European. He was said to be rich beyond counting. He had learned the language of the animals and could converse with them and command them. His kingdom covered large tracts of land, and he lived in an iron palace on a cliff. The palace was also a powerful magnet, so that whenever enemies approached its fortifications, their weapons were snatched from their scabbards and their clutching hands, and they were thus disarmed and captured. The European had power over the chiefs of the savage tribes, whom he none the less admired for their cruelty and implacability. To him they were noble people, hardy and graceful, even beautiful. It was said that the European possessed a ring with which he could summon the spirits of the land to his service. North of his domain prowled prides of lions which had an unquenchable craving for human flesh, yet they never approached the European unless they were called.

The coast man who owned the shop where the caravan was gathered, and where Yusuf sat under the breadfruit trees with the men to listen to these stories, was called Hamid Suleiman. He came from a small town north of Mombasa called Kilifi. Yusuf knew that it was not far south of Witu because Mohammed the mendicant had told him of how he had once nearly drowned while crossing the deep channel at Kilifi. It would have been better, he said, if he had perished, and been released from his shameful bondage to the weed. But he had grinned as he said this, baring his broken teeth apologetically.

Hamid Suleiman was genial and good-natured and treated Yusuf like a relative. Uncle Aziz had said something to him before he left. Yusuf had seen him speak, and had seen him look in his direction. There had been no explanations, simply a pat on the head and the instruction to stay behind with Hamid. He watched them leave with mixed feelings. It was a relief to escape the menace of Mohammed Abdalla, but a journey to the lakes in the deep interior, which was where the expedition was headed, had begun to excite him. And he had felt surprisingly at ease in the outcast company of the porters, and had thrilled to their endless stories and uncouth jokes.

Hamid's wife Maimuna was also from the coast, from a lot farther north of Mombasa, from the island of Lamu. She spoke differently, and claimed that the Kiswahili spoken in Lamu was purer than anywhere else on the coast – *Kiswahili asli*, ask anyone – and Lamu itself was little short of perfection in her eyes. Like her husband, she was plump and genial, and seemed unable to sit in silence if someone was within earshot. She had many questions for Yusuf. Where was he born? Where were his father and mother born? Where did his other relatives live? Did they know where he was? When was the last time he had visited them? Or visited his other relatives? Had no one ever taught him how much such things mattered? Did he have a betrothed? Why not? When did he plan to marry? Didn't he know that if he waited too long people would think there was something wrong with him? He looked old enough to her, although looks could be deceptive. How old was he? Yusuf did what he could to avoid the questions. In many cases the best he could do was shrug with defeat at questions he had never faced before, or drop his eyes with shame. He thought he managed well enough. Maimuna grunted incredulously at his evasions, and the look in her eye promised that sooner or later he was going to have to come clean.

His duties were the same as in the other shop, except here there was less to do for the business was less prosperous. In addition to his shop duties he had to sweep the clearing in the morning and late afternoon. He gathered the breadfruit which had fallen under the trees and piled it in a basket which a man from the market came to collect every day. The broken fruit he threw away in the backyard. They never ate the breadfruit themselves.

'Thank God we're not that poor yet,' Maimuna said.

The place had been a stopping-station for the caravans from the interior, Hamid explained. That was in the days before they came to live and work here themselves, when it was a prosperous station. The breadfruit was to feed the porters and the slaves, who would eat anything after their long walk in the wilderness. Not that he thought there was anything wrong with breadfruit. They used to eat it at home cooked in coconut sauce and accompanied with fried sardines. God knows what they ate now instead of breadfruit was humble enough food, although Yusuf was not to think that was reason to despise it. It was simply that breadfruit made people think of bondage, especially in these parts.

Yusuf was given a small room in the house, and was invited to eat with the family. Lamps were kept burning in the house throughout the night, doors were barred and window shutters were bolted as soon as it was dark. It was to keep the animals and burglars away, they told him. Hamid bred pigeons which lived in boxes under the eaves of the house. On some nights the uneasy silence was broken by a flurry of flapping which left feathers and blood on the yard in the morning. The pigeons were all white, with wide trailing tail feathers. Hamid destroyed any young birds which looked different. He talked happily about the birds, and about the habits of birds in captivity. He called his pigeons the Birds of Paradise. They strutted on the roof and the yard with reckless pomp and arrogance, as if the display of their beauty was more important to them than safety. But at other times Yusuf thought he saw a glint of self-mockery in their eyes.

Sometimes husband and wife exchanged looks over what Yusuf said, which made him think they knew more about him than he did himself. He wondered how much Uncle Aziz had told them. They thought something in his behaviour was odd at first, although they did not tell him what it was. They often treated what he said with suspicion, as if they were doubtful about his motives. When he described the parched land over which they had travelled to get to the town, they became irritated, and he felt he had done something ill-mannered or difficult, had drawn attention to an unavoidable constraint under which they lived.

'Why did that surprise you? It's dry everywhere in these parts. Perhaps you expected lush terraces and little streams. Well, it isn't like that,' Hamid said. 'Here so close to the mountain it's cool, at least, and we get some rain, though not so much as on the slopes. But that's how it is.'

'Yes,' Yusuf said.

'I don't know what you expected,' Hamid continued, frowning at Yusuf. 'Except for a few weeks in the year after the rains, and on high ground like here, it's like that everywhere. But you should see those parched plains after the rains. You should see them!'

'Yes,' Yusuf said.

'Yes what?' Maimuna said irritably. 'Yes hyena? Yes animal? Call him Uncle.'

'But it was lush by the sea,' Yusuf said after a moment. 'The house we lived in had a beautiful garden, with a wall running all round it. With palms and orange trees, and even pomegranates, and water channels with a pool, and scented shrubs.'

'Ah-ah, we can't compete with these merchants, these lords,' Maimuna said, her voice rising steeply. 'We're only poor shopkeepers. You're the lucky one, but this is the life God has chosen for us. We live here like beasts at His command. To you He has given a garden of paradise while to us He has given scrub and thickets full of snakes and wild animals. So now what do you want us to do? Blaspheme? Complain that we have been treated unjustly?'

'Perhaps he's just homesick,' Hamid said, smilingly making peace. Maimuna was not placated and muttered under her breath, glaring angrily and looking as if she could have said more.

'Well, there's a price for everything. I hope he learns that before long,' she said.

Yusuf had not meant a comparison with their garden, but he kept silent. Instead of the shade and flowers which Mzee Hamdani had created, and the pools and fruit-laden shrubs, here there was only the bush beyond their backyard which was used for rubbish. It shuddered with secret life, and out of it rose fumes of putrefaction and pestilence. On his first day he

66

had been warned to approach it with care because of the snakes, and had felt the warning to be a kind of prophecy. They waited for him now to say something, to explain, but he could not think of anything to say and sat tongue-tied in front of them, causing offence.

'I used to work in the garden in the afternoons,' he said at last.

They laughed, and Maimuna reached for his face and stroked it. 'Who can be annoyed with a beautiful boy like you? I'm thinking of getting rid of my fat husband and marrying you. But until then, perhaps you can build us a garden,' she said, exchanging a swift look with Hamid. 'We can get him to do some real work while he's here.'

'Do orange trees grow here?' Yusuf asked. They took his remark to be satirical and laughed again.

'You can build fountains for us and summer palaces. The garden will be filled with captive birds of all kinds,' Maimuna said, continuing in her bantering tone. 'Songbirds, not these grumbling pigeons that Hamid loves so much. I hope you'll also hang mirrors on trees as in ancient gardens, to catch the light and see the birds faint as they catch sight of their beautiful reflections. Make us a garden like that.'

'She's a poet,' Hamid said, applauding his wife. 'All the women in her family are. And the men are all layabouts and sharp traders.'

'May God forgive you for your lies. As you can see, he's the one with the stories. Oh, but he's the one,' she said, smiling and pointing to Hamid. 'You wait until he starts. You'll forget about eating or sleeping until he's finished. Just wait until Ramadhan, he'll keep you up all night. He's the joker, without a doubt.'

The next day Hamid went at the edges of the bush with a machete, hacking viciously at the branches within reach. He

67

shouted for Yusuf to come and collect the lopped branches and pile them for firing. 'You're the one who wants a garden,' he said good-humouredly. 'Well, I'll clear the bush for you and you can plant a garden for us. Put your shoulder into it, boy. We're going to clear all this bush as far as that thorn tree.' At first Hamid's wild swipes were delivered with blood-thirsty cries and raucous songs. It was to frighten the snakes away, he said. But soon his exhilaration ebbed, and Maimuna's cheerful cries of encouragement and mockery made him pause irritably between blows. *If we left everything to women where do you think we'd be?* he said. *Still living in caves, I should think.* Sweat bubbled and streamed from his face. After an hour or so, his war cries turned into grunts as he struck feebly at the shuddering bushes. He stopped often, heaving for breath, and taking time to instruct Yusuf on how to arrange the fallen branches. He snapped at Yusuf's clumsiness, and glared at him when he winced at a sharp twig that stabbed his palm. Finally, with a despairing wail he threw the machete on the ground and stormed back to the house. 'I'm not going to kill myself over that forest,' he declared as he brushed past his wife. 'You could at least have brought us a jug of water.'

'It's not a forest, just a few bushes, you feeble old man,' she mocked, grinning and clapping him out of sight. 'You're finished, Hamid Suleiman. Just as well I've found myself a new husband.'

'You'll know me later,' Hamid called out.

Maimuna ululated with mockery. 'Don't frighten the children, shabab. You, leave that terrible weapon alone,' she called out as Yusuf picked up the machete. 'I don't want your blood on our heads. We've got enough trouble without your relatives descending on us. You'll have to get used to the bushes and snakes, and just keep dreaming about your garden of paradise, until your uncle comes back for you. Take a drink of water to your uncle.'

He was required to be at the service of both of them. They yelled
for him when he was needed, and if he was slow in coming they
greeted him with irritable words and sharp looks. Fetch water
from the well. Chop some firewood. Sweep the yard. When he
could be spared from the shop, he went to the market for
vegetables and meat. He took his time if he was sent to the town,
lingering in the open spaces and watching the herdsmen and the
farmers passing through. The cows dropped enormous pats of
dung as they lurched grumblingly by. Every now and then they
flicked their wet tails and sent a spray of dung flying through the
air. Herdsmen hissed and gurgled at them, and occasionally
lunged to prod the animals into line with the points of their sticks.
Yusuf often saw the red-painted warriors striding by, drawing
looks wherever they went. Sometimes he made deliveries to the
homes of Indian and Greek merchants, carrying baskets on a
long yoke across his shoulders and trying not to remember the
decrepit vegetable man who used to come to Uncle Aziz's house.
European farmers came into the town in their trucks and ox-
carts, for supplies and to conduct their mysterious business. They
had no eyes for anyone, and strode about with a look of loathing.
When he got back to the house he was as likely to be sent to fetch
something from the stores as to take one of the children to the
toilet. They had three children. The eldest was a daughter in her
early youth and she was expected to care for the others. She was
too preoccupied to do this properly, too busy with her own inner
life, and she ran about the house and the yard, banging doors and
smiling to herself. Yusuf was at times required to look after the
younger boys and take them places. They were energetic and
noisy, used to being shouted at. When he was with them he
thought of how Khalil had been with him, and tried and often
failed to remain patient.

He told Hamid about Khalil and the work they used to do together – they practically ran the shop by themselves – in the hope that he would be given work other than errands and running between the shop and the stores, but Hamid only smiled. There wasn't the trade in the shop to keep them all occupied, he said. Without the travellers and the interior business there would not be enough to keep them, let alone make anything. 'Don't you do enough? What do you want more work for? Tell me about the merchant, your Uncle Aziz. Has he been a good master?' he asked. 'He's a very rich and very good man, isn't he? His name suits him perfectly. I could tell you stories about him, such astonishing stories. One day I must visit his house. I should think it's like a palace . . . from everything you've said about the garden I'd say it is sure to be. Does he have banquets and celebrations? You and Khalil must have been like young princes, spoiled like anything.'

There were three stores in the house, but to one of these he was never sent and it was kept locked. Yusuf lingered outside the door at times, and thought he could detect an animal smell of hide and hoof. Magendo, he remembered. Big money. Hamid had mentioned the foul-mouthed truck driver delivering a cargo – *he was like a creature who had crawled out of a latrine*, he had said – and Yusuf guessed that the room contained the secret loads which could not travel on the train with them. The stores were at the back of the house, within the enclosed backyard. Across the yard but within the walls were the outhouses, the kitchen and the toilet. His room was also at this end of the house, and one night Yusuf heard Hamid in the forbidden store. At first he thought it was a burglar or worse, then he heard Hamid's voice. He would have gone out to look, and had even silently unbolted his bedroom door. It was a dark hour. As he stood at the open door of his room, he saw the light of a lamp under the door. The tone of Hamid's mutterings came clearly to him and made him stop. His voice rose and fell in grumbling anxiety and entreaty. There was something uncanny about that whimpering voice in the silent house, both tragic and frightening. He should have kept his mat, he thought, wishing he had not heard anything. When Hamid stopped to listen too, Yusuf slipped the bolt of his room as silently as before and went back to lie down. In the morning nothing was said, although Yusuf caught several glances out of the corner of his eye.

Many traders passed through the town, and if they were coast people or Arabs or Somali, they stopped at Hamid's house for a day or two while they sorted out their affairs and rested. They slept under the breadfruit trees in the clearing and shared the food of the house, repaying their hosts with small gifts and courtesies. Sometimes they traded part of their merchandise before setting off again. The travellers brought news with them and incredible stories of daring and fortitude on the journeys. A few people from the town came to share their company and listen to the travellers, among them an Indian mechanic who was a friend of Hamid. The Indian mechanic always wore a pale-blue turban, and came to Hamid's in a noisy van, causing consternation among the traders at times. He rarely spoke, but Yusuf saw him chuckling in the wrong places sometimes, drawing puzzled and irritated looks from the others. Late at night, they sat in the clearing in front of the house, shivering a little in the mountain chill, lamps burning all around them, and spoke of other nights when animals and men had circled their encampments with malice. If they had not been well armed, or if their nerve had failed them, or if God had not watched over them, their bones would be left on a dusty nyika somewhere, being picked clean by vultures and worms.

Everywhere they went now they found the Europeans had

got there before them, and had installed soldiers and officials telling the people that they had come to save them from their enemies who only sought to make slaves of them. It was as if no other trade had been heard of, to hear them speak. The traders spoke of the Europeans with amazement, awed by their ferocity and ruthlessness. They take the best land without paying a bead, force the people to work for them by one trick or another, eat anything and everything however tough or putrid. Their appetite has no limit or decency, like a plague of locusts. Taxes for this, taxes for that, otherwise prison for the offender, or the lash, or even hanging. The first thing they build is a lock-up, then a church, then a market-shed so they can keep the trade under their eyes and then tax it. And that is even before they build a house for themselves to live in. Has anyone ever heard of such things? They wear clothes which are made of metal but do not chafe their bodies, and they can go for days without sleep or water. Their spit is poisonous. Wallahi, I swear to you. It burns the flesh if it splashes you. The only way to kill one of them is to stab him under the left armpit, nowhere else will do the job, but that is almost impossible because they wear heavy protection there.

One of the traders swore that he had seen a European fall down dead once and another one come and breathe life back into him. He had seen snakes do that too, and snakes also have poisonous spit. So long as the European's body was not ruined or damaged, had not started to rot, another European could breathe life back into him. If he were to see even a dead European he would not touch it or take anything from it, in case it rose again and accused him.

'Don't blaspheme,' Hamid said, laughing. 'Only God can give life.'

'I saw it with my own eyes. May Allah blind me if I tell a

lie,' the trader insisted, looking around at the laughing faces in his audience. 'There lay a dead man and another European lay down beside him, breathed into his mouth, and the dead one shuddered and woke.'

'If he can give life, then he must be God,' Hamid insisted.

'May God forgive me,' the trader said, trembling with anger. 'Why do you say that? I had meant nothing like that.'

'He's an ignorant man,' Hamid said later, after the man had left to continue his journey. 'They're very superstitious where he comes from. Too much religion does that to you sometimes. What was he trying to say? That Europeans are really snakes in disguise?'

Some of the travellers had run into Uncle Aziz's expedition and could report on him. He was last heard of on the other side of the lakes beyond Marungu Hills, in the upper reaches of the great parallel western rivers. He was trading with the Manyema people and doing good business. It was dangerous country, but trade was possible: rubber, ivory and even a little gold, God willing. Messages came from Uncle Aziz himself asking for traders who had sold him supplies and merchandise to be paid in his name, and once a consignment of rubber arrived in the care of a merchant on the homeward journey. There was frequent news from him, and its optimism made Hamid generous with the travellers who brought it.

6

In the month of Shaaban, just before the arrival of Ramadhan and its fierce regime of hunger and prayers, Hamid decided to visit the villages and settlements on the mountain slopes. This was an annual outing, a trip he looked forward to, but he persuaded himself that it was also a way of doing business. Since the customers were not coming to him, he would go

73

to them. Yusuf was invited to accompany him. They hired a van from the Sikh mechanic in the town, the one who visited them in the evenings to hear the stories of the travellers. The Sikh, whose name was Harbans Singh but whom everybody called Kalasinga, drove the van himself. It was as well, since it broke down often and the tyres suffered a puncture every few miles. Kalasinga was not at all daunted by these mishaps, blaming the rough road and the steep incline. He attended to his van cheerfully, fielding Hamid's mockery with good-natured replies and keeping plenty in reserve. They knew each other well. Yusuf had been to Kalasinga's house several times to deliver orders. They thrust and parried at each other with relish, taking pleasure in the bickering. They were both short and plump, and in some ways seemed alike. But where Hamid smiled and grinned as he talked, Kalasinga kept a straight face even in improbable circumstances.

'If you weren't such a miser you would buy a new van and save your customers all this misery,' Hamid said, sitting comfortably on a rock while Kalasinga toiled over his ailing motor. 'What do you do with all the money you steal from us? Send it back to Bombay?'

'Don't make bad jokes, my brother. You want someone to come and kill me. What money? And I don't come from Bombay, you know that. That's the country of these goat-shit banyans. This Gujarati scum, they're the ones with money, and their brothers are the Mukki-Yukki bloodsuckers, these Bohras. And do you know how they make all their money? By moneylending and cheating. Credit to the struggling trader at compound interest and foreclosure at the slightest excuse. This is their speciality. Scum! So I beg you, show some respect and don't mix me up with such insects.'

'But aren't you all the same?' Hamid asked. 'You're all Indians, all banyans and cheats and liars.'

Kalasinga looked sad. 'If you weren't my brother from so many years I would certainly have beaten you for that!' he said. 'I know you're trying to annoy me, so I'll control my anger. I'll not give you the pleasure of seeing me conduct myself in an undignified manner. But please don't push me too far, my friend. It's very difficult for a Singh to take insults quietly.'

'So? Who's asking you to be quiet? I hear that kalasingas have long hairs growing out of their arses. I heard a story of a kalasinga who plucked one of those out and tied up someone who was annoying him.'

'My friend, I'm a patient man. But I have to warn you that once my anger is roused, nothing but blood will satisfy it,' Kalasinga said with a mournful air. He glanced at Yusuf and waggled his head from side to side, asking for sympathy. 'Have you heard what I can be like when I lose my temper?' he asked Yusuf. 'Like a wild roaring lion!'

Hamid laughed delightedly. 'Don't frighten the boy, you hairy kafir. You're nothing but liars, you banyans. A roaring lion! All right, all right, put that spanner down. I don't want my children to be orphans just for a joke. But tell me honestly . . . we're old friends. There are no secrets between us. What do you do with all the money that you make? You give it all to a woman, don't you? I mean, you don't spend it on anything. Your household is a bunch of broken-down cars. You have no one to look after. Everything about you looks poverty-stricken. You don't drink anything except cheap pombe or that poison you manufacture in your workshop. You don't gamble. It must be a woman.'

'Woman! I don't have a woman.'

Hamid pealed with laughter. There were stories about Kalasinga's exploits with women, all of them initiated by Kalasinga himself but embellished by others. In these stories Kalasinga is always slow to rouse, driving women to distraction. But once roused, he won't dismount.

'If you must know, you donkey, I send something to my brothers in Punjab. To help look after the family land. It's all that you want to talk about. What do you do with your money? What money? It's my business!' shouted Kalasinga, thumping the bonnet of his van for emphasis. Hamid laughed joyfully, and was about to begin again, but Kalasinga ducked into the van and started the engine.

Towards evening they stopped near a small settlement on the upper foothills of the mountain. The next day they would trade there before driving on. Kalasinga parked the van under a fig tree, by the bank of a tumbling mountain stream. The banks were knee-high in lush green grass. Yusuf stripped off and jumped into the river. The cold water made him scream, but he persevered for some minutes. Before long he could feel his whole body going numb. Kalasinga told him that the stream was fed by melting ice from the snowcap on the mountain top. The land was lush with trees and grasses here, and as they made camp in the mountain dusk, the air was filled with birdsong and the sound of rushing water. Yusuf walked a little distance along the river bank, stepping on the huge rocks that littered the stream. On the other bank, beyond the open ground, he saw thick copses of banana trees. Soon he came to a waterfall and paused there to look. There was an air of secrecy and magic in the place, but its spirit was benign and reconciled. Giant ferns and bamboos leaned into the water. He saw through the spray that the rock behind the falls had the depth of gloom to suggest a cave, the hiding place of treasures and unfortunate princes on the run from cruel usurpers. When he touched himself his clothes were wet through, and he was soaked to his most intimate garments, but he was happy to stand in the spray and feel it enveloping him. If he listened carefully enough, he felt sure, he would hear a hum rising and falling behind the roar of the falls, the sound of the river God breathing. He stood there silently for a long while. In the end, as the light was rapidly ebbing and shadows of bats and nocturnal birds were crossing the clear sky, he saw Hamid beckoning to him in the distance.

Yusuf hurried towards him, leaping the rocks and splashing along the stream to tell him about the beauty of the waterfall haven. By the time he reached Hamid he was out of breath, and he was only able to stand in front of him, panting and laughing at himself.

'You're wet,' Hamid said, laughing as well and slapping Yusuf on the back. 'Come and eat, and get comfortable before it gets too dark. It gets chilly at night up here.'

'The falls!' Yusuf blurted out, heaving for breath. 'It's beautiful.'

'I know,' Hamid said.

Out of the thickening shadows ahead of them appeared a man. He wore a dark-blue ribbed jersey with leather shoulder-pads and a pair of khaki shorts, the uniform of European employment. As they approached him, he swung out a night-stick from behind his leg, allowing them to see that he was armed. When they were close enough to smell him, Yusuf saw that the man's face was marked with thin diagonal scars, one across each cheek, running from below his eyes to the corners of his lips. His clothes were ragged close up, and smelt of smoke and animal dung. His eyes cast a lurid light, glaring and ghastly.

Hamid raised a hand in greeting and said salaam alaikum. The man grunted and raised his night-stick in reply. 'What do you want?' he asked. 'Go away!'

'We have our camp over there,' Hamid said and Yusuf could see that he was frightened. 'No trouble, brother. The young man went to see the falls, now we're just going back to our camp.'

77

'What have you come for? Bwana does not like you here. Not to camp, not to look at the falls. He doesn't like you here,' the man said flatly, glaring at them with hatred.

'Bwana?' Hamid asked.

The man pointed with his night-stick in the direction from which Yusuf had come. They now saw the shape of a low building, and as they looked one of the windows was suddenly lit up. The man fixed his glaring eyes at them, waiting for them to go. Yusuf thought he saw something tragic in the eyes, as if they had lost their sight.

'But we're camped a long way down there,' Hamid protested. 'We won't even be breathing the same air.'

'Bwana does not like you,' the man repeated sharply. 'Get out!'

'Look, my friend,' Hamid said, slipping into his practised trader manner. 'We'll be no trouble to your bwana. Come and have a cup of tea with us and see for yourself.'

The man suddenly loosed a long stream of words, spoken angrily and in a language Yusuf did not understand. Then he turned on his heel and strode off into the darkness. They looked after him for a moment, then Hamid shrugged and said, *Let's go. His bwana must think he owns the whole world.* When they got back to their camp they found that Kalasinga had cooked some rice and brewed a can of tea. Hamid opened a packet of dates and shared out strips of dried fish, which they singed in the dying embers of the fire. They told Kalasinga about the man with the night-stick.

'Mzungu lives there,' Kalasinga said, farting contentedly without any sign of embarrassment. 'A European man from South, working for government. I fixed his generator for him. It was a big noisy bastard, very old machine. I told him I could arrange for a newer one, but he did not like that. He was shouting and turning red in the face, saying that I wanted a bribe. A small commission, perhaps ... What's wrong with that? This is the custom. But he called me dirty coolie. Dirty coolie, thieving bastard. Then his dogs joined in. Woo! Woo! Many dogs, big hairy ones with large teeth.'

'Dogs,' Hamid said quietly, and Yusuf knew exactly what he meant.

'Yes, big dogs!' Kalasinga said, standing up and opening his arms out, snarling. 'With yellow eyes and silver fur. Trained to hunt for Muslim man. If you understand their angry bark, it says I like the meat of Allah-wallahs. Bring me the meat of Muslim man.'

Kalasinga was pleased with his joke, chortling and slapping his thigh. Hamid called him names, mad infidel, thieving bastard, hairy kafir, but Kalasinga was not discouraged. Every few minutes he would bark and snarl, and then laugh as if he had never heard anything funnier.

'Stop that noise, you dirty coolie. You'll tempt fate too far, and then the European's dogs will descend on us . . . the two-legged one as well. Stop it, hairy banyan!' Hamid said irritably when Kalasinga still would not stop.

'Banyan! I warned you not to call me banyan!' Kalasinga said, looking around for a weapon or a stick, and briefly tempted by the simmering can of tea. 'Is it my fault if you Muslim people are so afraid of dogs? Is this reason to abuse my blood? Every time you say this word it is an insult to my whole family. This is the last time!'

After peace had been restored, they made ready for sleep. Kalasinga spread his mat next to the van, and Hamid lay down close by him. Yusuf spread himself where he could see the sky, a few feet from them, to keep out of range of Kalasinga's wind, but near enough to hear their conversation. They settled down with tired sighs and groans of contentment, and Yusuf began to doze in the friendly silence.

'Isn't it pleasant to think that Paradise will be like this?'

Hamid asked, speaking softly into the night air which was full of the sound of water. 'Waterfalls that are more beautiful than anything we can imagine. Even more beautiful than this one, if you can imagine that, Yusuf. Did you know that is where all earthly waters have their source? The four rivers of Paradise. They run in different directions, north south east west, dividing God's garden into quarters. And there is water everywhere. Under the pavilions, by the orchards, running down terraces, alongside the walks by the woods.'

'Where is this garden?' Kalasinga asked. 'In India? I have seen many gardens with waterfalls in India. Is this your Paradise? Is this where the Aga Khan lives?'

'God has made seven Heavens,' Hamid said, ignoring Kalasinga and turning his head aside as if to address Yusuf alone. His voice was slowly softening. 'Paradise is the seventh level, itself divided into seven levels. The highest is the Jennet al Adn, the Garden of Eden. They don't allow hairy blasphemers in there, even if they can roar like a thousand wild lions.'

'We have gardens like that in India, with seven, eight levels and so on,' Kalasinga said. 'Built by Mogul barbarians. They used to have orgies on the terraces and keep animals in the garden so they could go hunting when they felt like it. So this must be Paradise, and your Paradise is in India. India is a very spiritual place.'

'Do you think God is crazy?' Hamid asked. 'To put Paradise in India!'

'Yes, but maybe he couldn't find anywhere better,' Kalasinga said. 'I've heard that the original garden still exists. Here on earth.'

'Kafir! You'll listen to any childish story,' Hamid said.

'I've read this in a book. A spiritual book. Can you read, you duka-wallah, Muslim dog-meat?'

Hamid laughed. 'I've heard it said that when God sent the

80

Floods to cover the earth at the time of Nabi Nuh, the Garden was beyond the reach of the waters and survived intact. So the original garden may still exist, but it is closed to men by thunderous waters and a gate of flame.'

'Just imagine if it were true that the Garden is on earth!' Kalasinga said after a long silence. Hamid made a teasing remark, but Kalasinga took no notice. The thunderous waters and a gate of flame were details which carried authority. He was brought up in a devout Sikh household in which the writings of the great Gurus had pride of place in the family shrine. But his father was a tolerant man who allowed a bronze statue of Ganesh, a small painting of Jesus Christ the Redeemer and a miniature copy of the Koran a place at the back of the shrine as well. Kalasinga knew the force of such details as thunderous waters and gates of flame.

'Well, I've heard some people say that the Garden is on earth, but I don't believe it. Even if it is here, no one can gain entrance into it, least of all a banyan,' Hamid said firmly.

7

After four days' travel, during which they stopped at every settlement or village which promised business, they reached Olmorog, the government station halfway up the mountain. Their journey had taken longer than planned because the van had broken down so often. Kalasinga was full of justifications during the final stages, but Hamid was too tired to make fun of him. 'Haya, haya, cut out the cackle. Just get us there,' he said. Olmorog was their final destination. After a day here they were to turn back. It had once been the site of a large settlement of the cattle-herding people who painted their bodies and hair with ochre. That was why the agricultural station was built there. It was thought that the example of the station would persuade the nomadic warriors to give up their love of blood and turn into dairy farmers. Nothing like that happened, perhaps because of the impatience of the official who came with the authority of his government to change this corner of the world. In any case, the people were quite happy to leave the agricultural station to itself. They moved their settlement a little farther away and came to Olmorog to trade.

Hamid usually stayed with a man from Zanzibar whose name was Hussein. He ran a store which gave him enough to live on. Just inside the store stood a hand-wound sewing machine, from which he ran off shukas and wrappers for his customers. On the counter against the wall stood bags of sugar and boxes of tea, and other small items of trade. Hussein was a thin tall man who looked used to hardship, as lean and spare as his shop. He lived alone in the back, so when they arrived he made room for them in the storeroom and looked forward to some talk. They sat outside the store in the evening, listening to Hussein talking about Zanzibar. After a while, when he had relieved himself of his need, they talked business and then silently watched the light sink into the mountain.

'Have you noticed how the light up here is green?' Hussein asked after a long time. 'It's no good asking Kalasinga. He never notices anything unless it has grease on it and makes a noise. What's the latest plan, my friend? Last time you came up here you were going to buy a bus and open a route to the mountain villages. What happened to that bright idea?' Kalasinga shrugged but did not reply or even turn around. From a tin mug, he sipped the home-made spirits he had brought with him on the journey. He drank only occasionally in front of them, but Yusuf had seen him take hurried gulps from the large stone bottle when he thought no one was in sight.

'But look, you young man, Yusuf! Did you notice the light?'

Hussein asked. 'You'll drive young women insane with your beautiful looks one day. Come back to Unguja with me and I'll wed you to my daughter. Did you notice the light?'

'Yes,' Yusuf said. He had seen it change as they drove up the mountain, and was as happy to talk about that as about Zanzibar. All of a sudden, as he had listened to Hussein talking about Zanzibar, he had determined that he would go there one day, to see that fabulous place for himself.

'He'll say yes to anything now that you've promised him your daughter,' Hamid said, laughing. 'But it's too late, we've already got him betrothed to our eldest. Didn't I tell you that, Hussein?'

'You're disgusting. She's only ten years old,' Hussein said.

'Eleven,' Hamid said. 'A fine age for a wedding.'

Yusuf knew he was being teased, but he still felt uncomfortable with the talk. 'Why is it green? The light.'

'It's the mountain,' Hussein said. 'When you get as far as the lakes in your travels you'll see that the world is ringed with mountains which give the green tint to the sky. Those mountains on the other side of the lake are the edge of the world we know. Beyond them, the air has the colour of plague and pestilence, and the creatures who live in it are known only to God. The east and the north are known to us, as far as the land of China in the farthest east and to the ramparts of Gog and Magog in the north. But the west is the land of darkness, the land of jinns and monsters. God sent the other Yusuf as a prophet to the land of jinns and savages. Perhaps he'll send you to them too.'

'Have you been to the lakes?' Yusuf asked.

'No,' Hussein said.

'But he's been everywhere else,' Hamid said. 'He certainly doesn't like staying at home, this man.'

'Which Yusuf?' Kalasinga asked. He had chuckled and

smirked during Hussein's description of the light and the lakes
– fairy-tale time, he cried – but they knew he could not resist
stories of prophets and jinns.

'The prophet Yusuf who saved Egypt from famine,' Hussein
said. 'Don't you know that one?'

'What lies beyond the darkness to the west?' Yusuf asked,
making Kalasinga cluck with irritation. He had been hoping
for the story of the famine in Egypt, which of course he knew
but would have liked to hear again.

'It's not known what the extent of the wilderness is,' Hussein
said. 'But I have heard it said that it's the equivalent of five
hundred years' journey on foot. The Fountain of Life is in
that wilderness, guarded by ghouls and snakes as huge as
islands.'

'Is Hell there too?' Kalasinga asked, returning to his
habitual mockery. 'And are all those torture chambers your
God promises you there too?'

'You should know,' Hamid said. 'That's where you're
going.'

'I am going to translate the Koran,' Kalasinga said suddenly. 'Into Swahili,' he added, when the others had stopped
laughing.

'You can't even speak Kiswahili,' Hamid said. 'Let alone
read Arabic.'

'I will translate it from the English translation,' Kalasinga
said, looking grim.

'Why do you want to do that?' Hussein asked. 'I don't
think I've heard you suggest anything more futile. Why do
you want to do this?'

'To make you stupid natives hear the ranting God you
worship,' Kalasinga said. 'It will be my crusade. Can you
understand what it says there in Arabic? A little perhaps,
but most of your stupid native brothers don't. That's what

makes you all stupid natives. Well, maybe if you did understand, you'd see how intolerant your Allah is. And instead of worshipping him, you'd go find something better to do.'

'Wallahi!' Hamid said, no longer amused. 'I doubt that it's proper for someone like you to speak of Him in that unforgivable way. Perhaps someone should teach this hairy dog a lesson. I think next time you come eavesdropping on our conversations at the shop I'll tell the stupid natives what you said. They'll soon set fire to your hairy arse.'

'I will still translate the Koran,' Kalasinga said firmly. 'Because I care for my fellow human beings, even if they are only ignorant Allah-wallahs. Is this a religion for grown-up people? Maybe I don't know what God is, or remember all his thousand names and his million promises, but I know that he can't be this big bully you worship.'

At that moment, a woman came to the shop for flour and salt. She wore a cloth round her middle, and a large ring of beads round her neck and over her shoulders. Her chest was uncovered, revealing her breasts. She took no notice as Kalasinga stirred near her, making noises of desire, slurping hungrily and sighing. Hussein spoke to her in her language, and she grinned delightedly as she replied at length, gesturing and explaining, laughter bubbling out of her as she spoke. Hussein laughed with her, snorting through his nose in explosive whispers. After she left, Kalasinga continued his ode of lust, describing how he would ride and ride until he broke off inside her. 'Oh these savage women, did you smell the cow dung? Did you see those breasts? So plump that they made me hurt!'

'She's nursing. That's what she was talking about, her new baby,' Hussein said. 'You mock us for the intolerance of our God, and for our stupidity in bearing with Him, and then you call people savages.'

Kalasinga ignored the rebuke. Egged on by Hamid, he began to tell stories of his sexual adventures. His emphasis was on the ridiculous. He told the story of the beautiful woman who, after complicated stratagems on his part, agrees to take him home, then turns out to be a man. Or the old lady he negotiates with, taking her to be a pimp, but who turns out to be the prostitute he was paying for. And an affair with a married woman which results in him nearly losing something vital when the cuckolded husband was unexpectedly heard at the door. He acted out all the parts, softening his voice, loosening his body, disjointing his limbs. In between, when he was himself, his beard bristled and his turban straightened as he became the rampant janab single-mindedly in search of action. Hamid hooted and howled with laughter, holding his ribs and panting for air when he was overcome. Kalasinga tortured him when he could, repeating the scenes which Hamid had shown himself unable to resist. Yusuf laughed guiltily at it all because he could see that Hussein did not approve of the dirty talk, but the sight of Hamid writhing in comic agony was too much for him.

Later, when the night was deep into the small hours, their conversation became softer and more gloomy, punctuated by longer and more frequent yawns.

'I fear for the times ahead of us,' Hussein said quietly, making Hamid sigh wearily. 'Everything is in turmoil. These Europeans are very determined, and as they fight over the prosperity of the earth they will crush all of us. You'd be a fool to think they're here to do anything that is good. It isn't trade they're after, but the land itself. And everything in it . . . us.'

'In India they have been ruling for centuries,' Kalasinga said. 'Here you are not civilized, how can they do the same? Even in South Africa, it is only the gold and the diamonds that make it worth while killing all the people there and taking the land. What is there here? They'll argue and squabble, steal this and that, maybe fight one petty war after another, and when they become tired they'll go home.'

'You're dreaming, my friend,' Hussein said. 'Look how they've already divided up the best land on the mountain among themselves. In the mountain country north of here they've driven off even the fiercest peoples and taken their land. They chased them away as if they were children, without any difficulty, and buried some of their leaders alive. Don't you know that? The only ones they allowed to stay were those they made into servants. A skirmish or two with their weapons and the matter of possession is settled. Does that sound as if they've come here for a visit? I tell you they're determined. They want the whole world.'

'Learn who they are, then. What do you know about them apart from these stories about snakes and men eating metal? Do you know their language, their stories? So then how can you learn to cope with them?' Kalasinga said. 'Grumble mumble, what's the good of that? We're the same like this. They are our enemies. That's also what makes us the same. In their eyes we're animals, and we can't make them stop thinking this stupid thing for a long time. Do you know why they're so strong? Because they have been feeding off the world for centuries. Your grumbling won't stop them.'

'There's nothing we can learn which will stop them,' Hussein said flatly.

'You're just afraid of them,' Kalasinga said gently.

'I'm afraid, you're right . . . though not only of them. We'll lose everything, including the way we live,' Hussein said. 'And these young people will lose even more. One day they'll make them spit on all that we know, and will make them recite their laws and their story of the world as if it were the holy word. When they come to write about us, what will they say? That we made slaves.'

'Then learn how to cope with them,' Kalasinga shouted. 'And if what you say is the truth, about these dangers which lie ahead, why do you stay here on the mountain to say it?'

'Where should I go and say it?' Hussein asked, smiling at Kalasinga's rage. 'To Zanzibar? There even slaves defend slavery.'

'Why such gloomy talk?' protested Hamid. 'What is so wonderful about the way we live anyway? Don't we have enough to oppress us without such frightening predictions? Let's leave it all in God's hands. Maybe things will change, but the sun will still rise in the east and set in the west. Let's stop this gloomy talk.'

After another long silence, Hussein asked, 'Hamid, what is that crooked partner of yours up to these days? What stupidity has he got you involved with now?'

'Who?' Hamid asked edgily. 'What are you talking about now?'

'Who! You'll know who one of these days. Your partner! Wasn't that what you said last time? When the time comes, that man will clean you out so thoroughly you won't even be left a needle and thread to mend your shirts,' Hussein said disdainfully. 'He'll make your fortune, you say. There's no risk, he tells you. No doubt about it at all. You can order your silk jackets now, if you wish. Then one of these days the risk will happen and you'll have no comeback. Bad luck, that's business. You know how it is. How many people has he ruined already? He cuts you in above your means, and then when you can't pay up he takes everything. That's his way, and you know exactly what I'm talking about.'

'What's wrong with you today?' Hamid asked. 'It must be living on the mountain with all that green light.' Yusuf could see that Hamid was uneasy and beginning to get angry. He looked gloomy and detached, and glanced once in Yusuf's direction.

'Do you know what I've heard about him, your partner?' Hussein continued. 'That if his partners cannot pay up, he takes their sons and daughters as rehani. This is like in the days of slavery. It is not the way honourable people should conduct themselves.'

'That's enough now, Hussein,' Hamid said angrily, half turning as if he would look at Yusuf. Kalasinga too looked as if he would say something, but Hamid suddenly waved him down. 'And let me make what idiotic mistakes I choose to. You think this . . . what you do . . . what we do . . . is better? How is it better? We labour, we risk everything, we live away from our people . . . and we are still as poor as mice and as frightened.'

'The Lord has told us –' Hussein began, preparing a quotation from the Koran.

'Don't give me that!' Hamid interrupted him, gently, almost beseechingly.

'He'll be caught one of these days,' Hussein insisted. 'All the smuggling and sharp deals will end in no good, and you'll be in the middle of it too.'

'Listen to what your brother's saying,' Kalasinga said to Hamid. 'Maybe we are not rich people, but at least we live by the law and respect each other.'

Hamid laughed. 'Well, what noble philosophers we are! When did you discover the law, you lying scoundrel? Whose law are you talking about? The amount you charge all of us for the simplest task . . . you call that living by the law,' he said. By his manner and his tone he tried to indicate that the moment of tension had passed, that he wished the conversation to change into this more jocular vein. 'Anyway, we don't want to give the young man here a poor impression of ourselves.'

Yusuf was sixteen then, and *young man* sounded noble in his ears, almost as good as being described as tall, or even a philosopher. He made sure his pleasure was evident in his manner, acting a bit of a clown. The three men laughed at his idiocy. And the conversation was safely past the subject of the man who was forced to pawn his son in order to satisfy his creditors. But Yusuf thought he had understood something of what Hussein had said about Hamid. The desperation with which he pined for prosperity, and his nervous concern for Uncle Aziz's journey, spoke of self-mistrust, an expectation of failure. Yusuf remembered the muttering in the forbidden store, and the smell of magendo which rose from the goods kept in there. Hamid's words of entreaty had been prayers.

8

A few days after their return to the town, Uncle Aziz arrived from his travels. As usual, his procession was led by the drummer and the horn player, behind whom came Mohammed Abdalla. They turned up late in the afternoon, during the mellow hour when the sun had waned and the moisture in the breeze and in the leaves was beginning to rise again. Yusuf was the one who saw them, at first only a disturbance in the air above the road where he was strolling alongside the silent track, then a cloud of fine dust and the thud and whine of the drum and horn. He wanted to wait and see what he imagined would be a shambling column of tired travellers, but he thought he should run back to warn the household.

It had been a hard journey, they found out, with many privations and dangers. There had been some nasty moments but no fighting. Two men had been badly wounded, one by a lion and another by snake-bite. They had both been left behind in a small town by the lake, being cared for by a family whom Uncle Aziz had paid well. He had never done business with them before, but he trusted them to take care of the two men, he said. Many of the porters and guards had fallen ill at some stage, nothing unusual or serious, thank God, just the normal usage of a journey into the interior. Mohammed Abdalla had fallen into a gully one night and badly hurt a shoulder. He was healing but still in pain, even though he tried to hide it, Uncle Aziz said. Despite their woes, business had been good, although they were aware all the time of how far away they were from the coast. Uncle Aziz looked as calm as always, if anything leaner and healthier than usual. After he had bathed and changed and perfumed himself, it would have been hard to believe that he had been months on the road.

'The trade was excellent on the upper reaches of the rivers,' Uncle Aziz said. 'We did not spend much time on the river at all, really. We'll return to Marungu next year, before the area is swamped again by traders. The Europeans will close it off soon, the Belgique. I hear they are moving closer and closer to the lakes. They're envious good-for-nothing paupers, with no understanding for business. I've heard about them. Even the German and the English are better, although God knows they are all vicious businessmen. We've brought back valuable goods this time.'

All this was music in Hamid's ears, and in his desire to affirm his alliance with Uncle Aziz he accented his speech with Arabic words. He was full of smiles and groans of admiration as he supervised the stowage of the goods. The sacks of corn which Uncle Aziz had acquired at a give-away price were to be left with Hamid, but the gum, ivory and gold were to travel on the train to the coast. The rubber which had come earlier was already sold to a Greek merchant in the town. In the evening Hamid took Uncle Aziz to the stores, to inspect the goods, then they sat muttering over their books, calculating their gains.

Uncle Aziz did not stay long. It was his intention to return to the coast before the start of Ramadhan, to fast and rest in his own home. The disposal of the goods before the end of the month would allow him to pay his porters off, in time for the new year and all the expenses of Idd. On the day of departure, with Mohammed Abdalla still not his old self, the procession set off for the station. Yusuf had not been invited to accompany it. A short while before they left, Uncle Aziz called him to one side and gave him a handful of money.

'In case you need anything,' he said. 'I'll be back through here next year. You have come through very well.'

THE JOURNEY TO THE INTERIOR

I

Hamid was happy after Uncle Aziz's visit. The stories of the journey had excited him, and put them all in touch with the fearsome great world beyond the horizon. The figures had also made cheerful reading, and the merchandise left behind in Hamid's store gave him a grasp on the good fortune which had attended the enterprise. Hamid did not always wait for night before going into his secret store to gloat over his success, and sometimes he left the door open behind him, releasing into the yard an overwhelming smell of animal skins. Yusuf saw sacks of jute and straw stacked in there, some of which he recognized as the corn which had been delivered by Uncle Aziz's expedition, and some as the bundles the foul-mouthed Bachus had brought up by truck. He saw Hamid pacing around the booty, counting the bags and talking to himself. When he saw Yusuf standing at the open door, a ripple of panic passed over his face, suddenly followed by relief and suspicion. He frowned with a blank inward-looking grimace of concentration, then he laughed in a cunning way and came out.

'What do you want here? Is there no work for you? Have you cleaned the yard? And collected the breadfruit? In that case I have an errand for you in town. Who told you to watch me, eh? You want to see what's in the bags, don't you? You'll know about all that one day,' he said brightly, at the same time padlocking the store door. 'It's been a good trip, we thank God. A good piece of luck for everyone. Did you want something? Why are you looking around?'

93

'I'm –' Yusuf began, but Hamid cut him off, striding away to the front and expecting Yusuf to follow.

'Well, you're not looking for anything, are you? I'd just like to hear what Hussein would say now. Just because he's chosen to live hand to mouth halfway up a mountain, he thinks anyone who tries to get something for himself is sinning. Eh, you were there! It's not that I want great riches, but while I live and trade in this place I might as well make something. If he wants to behave like a sick, dreamy man that's his affair. You heard him, the big idealist. You heard him, didn't you?'

'Yes,' Yusuf said, made uncomfortable by Hamid's aggression. He wondered what really was in the sacks. But he was reluctant to ask since he sensed that Hamid thought he knew. He guessed that they contained something valuable, and were being kept out of the way in Hamid's store.

'Where's the sin in making a better life for your family?' Hamid asked, his voice roused by contempt for Hussein. 'Or in making it possible for them to live among their own people? What's so wrong with that? I'm asking you. All I want is to build a little house for my family, find good husbands and wives for my children, and be able to go to a mosque among civilized people. If it's not too much to ask, I'd also like to sit with friends and neighbours in the evening and drink a cup of tea over friendly talk . . . That's all! Did I say I wanted to kill anybody? Or make a slave out of anyone? Or rob an innocent man? I'm just a small shopkeeper, doing something for himself. Doing a very small something for himself, God knows. These days he's started on the Europeans. How they'll dispossess everyone. How they are born killers without a streak of mercy in them. How they'll destroy us and everything we trust in. When he gets tired of that he tells me my business. I could tell you a thing or two about him, but I just want to live my life in peace. Only that's not good enough for our philosopher

Hussein, living like a fiend among savages. Who has told him he shouldn't do what he likes with his life? But anything you tell him he starts giving you a sermon and quoting suras from the Koran. The Lord has told us! You heard him.'

Hamid reflected on his words, huffing with small indignation. He muttered *Astaghfirullah*, God forgive me, and shivered with the thought that he may have sounded disrespectful about the Book. 'I'm not saying there is ever any harm in quoting from the Book, but he does it out of spite not out of piety. Oh no, I'm not saying there can ever be any harm in God's word. That crazy Kalasinga translating the Koran! It was home-made spirits talking there. I hope God realizes that he's a heathen and a madman, and takes pity on him.' Hamid chuckled happily at the memory.

'The Koran is our religion, and has in it all the wisdom we need to live a good and moral life,' he said, glancing upwards as if he expected to see something there. Yusuf looked up too, but Hamid demanded his attention with an irritable hiss. 'But that doesn't mean we should use it to shame others. It should be our source of guidance and learning. You should read the Book whenever you can, especially now that Ramadhan has started. During this holy month, every good act earns you double the blessing you'd receive at other times. The Prophet was told this by the Almighty himself on the night of Miraj. On that night our Prophet was taken from Makka to Jerusalem on the winged horse Borakh, and from there to the presence of the Almighty, who decreed the laws of Islam. Ramadhan, it was ordered, would be the month of fasting and prayer, a month of self-denial and atonement. How else to express our submission to God if not by denying ourselves the most necessary pleasures of existence: food, water and sensual indulgence? This is what distinguishes us from the savage and the pagan, who denies himself nothing. And if you

95

read the Koran during this period, the words go straight to the Creator, and earn you great blessing. You must set aside an hour every day during Ramadhan for this.'

'Yes,' Yusuf said, retreating. Towards the end of his sermon, Hamid had begun to sound confidential, demanding Yusuf's complicity in his sudden burst of piety. Yusuf thought to escape before the preacher hit his stride, but he was not quick enough.

'Now that I think of it, I haven't noticed you reading very often,' Hamid said, looking stern and suspicious. 'This is not something to play the fool about. You want to go to Hell or what? We'll read together today, after you've said your afternoon prayers.'

By the time afternoon arrived, Yusuf was weak with hunger and exhaustion. He found the first three days of fasting the worst, and if left to himself he would lie silently in a piece of shade through the best part of a day. After the first few days his body adjusted to going for endless hours without food or water, and the daylight agony was at least bearable. He had thought it would be easier to live through the agony in the cooler air in the mountains, but it was not. In the coastal heat he had been able to achieve a kind of dissociation from his numbed body, abandoning it to its exhausted self and arriving at a state of stunned resignation. The cooler air sustained him, did not enfeeble him enough to enable him to slide into mesmerizing stupor. And he knew that humiliation awaited him at the rendezvous with Hamid in the afternoon.

'What do you mean? You can't read?' Hamid asked.

'I didn't say that,' Yusuf protested. What he had said was that he had not finished reading the Koran before he was sent away to work for Uncle Aziz. His mother had taught him the alphabet, and had taught him to read the first three simple suras. When he was seven he was sent to the teacher in the town they had just moved to, to be educated in religion. They learned slowly. The teacher was in no hurry to see the children complete their studies. Once a child had successfully read the Koran from beginning to end, that was one fee less a month for the teacher. It was expected that a child would attend classes for five years before the studies were complete. This was fair to both teacher and pupils. The children did many chores for the teacher, cleaning the house, fetching firewood, running errands. The boys played truant when they could and were often thrashed. Girls were only ever hit on the palm of the hand and were taught to behave decorously. *Respect yourself and others will come to respect you. That is true about all of us, but especially true about women. That is the meaning of honour*, their teacher told them. This was all as it had always been, as far as anyone knew or could remember, and the little boys and girls crowded on the mat in the teacher's backyard chanted their lessons with predictable reluctance and forbearance. In due course Yusuf would have graduated and counted himself honourable among his peers and elders. But he was sent away.

Khalil had taught him figures, and never once suggested that either of them should read the Book. When they went to the mosque on their trips to town, Yusuf managed well enough. His attention wandered during the longer prayers, and he was forced to hum meaninglessly over the noise of other readers when he was required to address the unfamiliar sections of the Book, but he never disgraced himself. Nor was he ever impolite enough to listen too closely to any of his neighbours to check if they were in similar straits. When Hamid and he sat down that afternoon, he knew there would be no chance of humming his way out of this miserable corner. Hamid suggested they should begin by reading *Ya Sin* aloud, taking turns. Yusuf opened the Book and flipped through the pages under Hamid's suspicious gaze.

97

'Don't you know where *Ya Sin* is?' he asked.

'I never finished,' Yusuf said. *Sikuhitimu.* 'I don't think I'll be able to read it.'

'What do you mean? You can't read?' Hamid said, awed and shocked. He rose to his feet and backed away from Yusuf, not fearfully but as if from something catastrophic and vile. 'Maskini! You poor boy! It's not right! Didn't they teach you to read in that house? What kind of people are they?'

Yusuf sighed heavily, shamed by his failure and dishonour. He too rose to his feet, feeling vulnerable squatting on the floor. He was hungry and tired and wished that he did not have to go through the dramas which he knew would follow, but he was not as frightened by his shame as he had feared he would be.

'Maimuna!' Hamid yelled for his wife as if he was in pain. Yusuf had begun to think that Hamid too was feeling the fast, and he would presently sit down and talk quietly about lessons and duty. But he yelled out suddenly, giving way to hysteria. 'Maimuna! Come, come here! Yallah! Come quickly.'

Maimuna was still wrapping a cloth round herself as she came out, her eyes registering the anxiety of Hamid's call despite being bleary with sleep.

'Kimwana, the boy doesn't know how to read the Koran!' Hamid said, turning to her with a distraught look. 'He has no father and no mother, and does not even know the word of God!'

They interrogated him thoroughly, as if they had been waiting to do so for a long time. He did not try to hide anything. What had the Mistress said about it? What did she look like? He did not know what she looked like, had never seen her. Was she not said to be devout? He had never heard that one. Didn't the merchant make him go to the mosque?

No, the merchant had nothing to do with him, left him alone to work in the shop. Had he not thought that without prayers he would go naked to his Maker? No, he had not thought that, or thought about his Maker very much. And without God's word how could he say his prayers? He did not say his prayers, except on Friday when they went to the town. What a dirty business! As their cries of pain rose, their children also came out to witness the scene: the oldest, Asha, who was nearly twelve years old, plump and cheerful like her father; the boy, Ali, who had his mother's curls and her glossy complexion; and the little one, Suda, who cried so much and did not like to be separated from his sister. They all came to join the tragic chorus lamenting his shame. Maimuna raised one hand to her temple, as if looking to still the pounding there. Hamid shook his head with pity. 'Poor boy! Poor boy! What tragedy you have brought to our house,' he said. 'Who could've guessed such things?'

'Don't blame yourself,' Maimuna said, moaning softly between her words. 'How could we have known?'

'Don't feel bad,' Hamid said to Yusuf, when the crescendo of their horror had crested its peak. 'It's not your fault. God would see us as the guilty ones because we had not made sure that you were taught. You've been with us for months . . .'

'But how could your uncle have left you in that state for all these years?' Maimuna asked, looking to share the blame.

For a start he ain't my uncle, Yusuf thought to himself, remembering Khalil and struggling to suppress a smile. He wished he could walk away, leave them to their lamentations, but a feeling of inadequacy kept him where he was. He felt disgusted by their display of shock and horror. It seemed to him a calculated and ridiculous performance.

'Do you know that we who are from the coast call ourselves waungwana?' Hamid asked. 'Do you know what that means?

It means people of honour. That's what we call ourselves, especially up here among fiends and savages. Why do we call ourselves that? It is God who gives us the right. We are honourable because we submit ourselves to the Creator, and understand and adhere to our obligations to Him. If you cannot read His word or follow His law, you are no better than these worshippers of rocks and trees. Little better than a beast.'

'Yes,' Yusuf said, shrinking as he heard the children laugh.

'Are you fifteen yet?' Hamid asked, softening his voice.

'Sixteen last Rajab. Before we went to the mountain,' Yusuf said.

'Then there is no time to lose. To the Almighty you are now a fully grown man, and subject to His laws in full,' Hamid said, growing into his redeeming role. He shut his eyes and said a long muttered prayer. 'Children, look at him. Learn from the sight he presents to us,' he said in the end, flinging out an arm to point at Yusuf. *Shun the weed, I beg you. Learn from my terrible example.*

'Let him go to the Koran school with the children,' Maimuna said sharply, giving Hamid a very direct look. 'You don't have to go on at him as if he has killed someone.'

2

That was the indignity they forced on him. Every afternoon during that month of Ramadhan, Yusuf went with the children of the house to the teacher for lessons. He was by far the eldest pupil there, and the other children teased him with manic persistence. It was as if this was required of them, and they had no choice but to perform. The teacher, who was an imam at the only mosque in the town, treated him with compassion and kindness. Yusuf learned quickly, putting in extra time at home every day. To begin with it was the shame that drove him, but then he began to take pleasure in his growing skill. The teacher encouraged him lugubriously, as if he had expected no less. Yusuf went to the mosque every day, and submitted and humbled himself to the God he had neglected for so long. The imam sent him on small errands in front of the other worshippers, a token of his trust and approbation. He sent him to fetch a book from which he intended to read to his congregation, or to fetch the rosary or the incense burner. Sometimes he fed Yusuf questions, encouraging him to demonstrate his new learning, and once he asked him to climb to the roof and call the faithful to prayer. Hamid looked on with delight at first, talking to other people about the miraculous conversion and taking it that God could not have failed to notice the part he and his wife had played in the rescue. Even after Ramadhan was over Yusuf's ardour did not appear to relent. In two months he read the Koran from beginning to end, and was ready to start again. The imam invited him to attend on him at a funeral service and at a birth ceremony. Yusuf neglected his duties at home and in the shop to go to school and the mosque, and late into the evening he pored over the books which the imam had given him. After a while Hamid began to worry about this new piety. It was obsessive and abject, he thought. There was no need to take such things too far.

Kalasinga, to whom he confided these thoughts on occasions when he called round for a chat, felt otherwise. 'Let the boy gain what virtue he can,' he said. 'These feelings in us do not last very long. Soon the world tempts us away to sinning and filth. Yet religion is a beautiful thing, pure and true. You wouldn't know about this kind of spiritual matter, but we eastern people are expert. You're just a stupid trader with your five-times-kiss-the-ground and starve-to-death-in-Ramadhan.

You don't understand meditation or transcendence or anything like that. It's good that he thinks there's more worth
troubling for in his life than bags of rice and baskets of fruit,
but a pity that he can only turn to the teachings of Allah.'

'But it's too much for the boy, no?' Hamid said, ignoring
Kalasinga's provocation.

'He's not such a boy,' Kalasinga said. 'He's almost a young
man. You want to spoil him, neh. With those good looks of his
you could make him into a blasted weakling.'

'He's an attractive boy,' Hamid agreed after a moment.
'But manly. And you know, he's completely uninterested in
his looks. If anyone mentions his beauty, he goes away or
changes the subject. Such an innocent! Anyway, what was all
that you were saying about religion and virtue? If I don't
know about such matters do you think a grease-monkey like
you does? You worship gorillas and cows, and tell childish
stories of how the world came into being. You're no better
than these heathen people around us. I feel sorry for you
sometimes, Kalasinga, whenever I think of your hairy arse
sizzling in hell-fire after the day of judgement.'

'I'll be in Paradise screwing everything in sight, Allah-
wallah, while your desert God is torturing you for all your
sins,' Kalasinga replied cheerfully. 'To that God of yours
almost everything is sinful. Anyway, maybe the young man
just wants to learn. He's fed up of being cooped up in this
rubbish compound of yours. If he has a brain in his head it
must be turning into pulp by now. All you ask him to do is sit
around listening to your lying stories or collect that useless
breadfruit for the market. Even a monkey would turn to
religion under that kind of torture. Send him to me and
I'll teach him to read in English alphabet, and teach him
mechanic work. At least it will be a useful skill instead of
this shopkeeper business.'

Hamid did what he could to distract Yusuf with work, and even revived the idea of the garden in the backyard, but he also mentioned to him the offer that Kalasinga had made. It was in this way that Yusuf came to spend several afternoons a week in Kalasinga's workshop, sitting on old tyres with a board on his lap, learning to read and write in rumi. In the morning he did his work at home, in the afternoon he went to Kalasinga, and in the early evening he went to the mosque until isha prayers. He delighted in his hectic new life at first, but within a few weeks he was telling lies about the mosque and staying longer at Kalasinga's. By then he could write slowly on the board and could read from the book which Kalasinga gave him, although the words meant nothing to him. He learned many other things too. How to change tyres and clean cars. How to charge a battery and rub down rust. Kalasinga explained to him the mysteries of the engine, and Yusuf grasped something of this but was happier watching him magically coax the tangle of pipes and bolts into life. He heard about India, where Kalasinga had not been for many years, but dreamt to return, and South Africa, where he had lived as a child. *It's a madhouse in South. All kinds of cruel fantasies have come true there. Let me tell you something about those Afrikander bastards, though. They're crazy. I don't mean just wild and cruel, I mean round the loop. Hot sun has turned their Dutch brain to soup.* Yusuf helped push cars and learned how to brew tea in an old tin on a Primus. He was sent to the supplies shop for spares, and often came back to find that Kalasinga had used the opportunity to have a quick drink. When he was in the mood, Kalasinga told him stories about saints and battles and love-smitten gods, and statuesque heroes and mustachioed villains while Yusuf sat on a box and applauded. He played the parts himself, sometimes calling upon Yusuf to stand in for a silent prince or a cowering offender. Often he could not remember important details, so he adapted and perverted to hilarious effect.

In the evenings, Yusuf sat on the terrace with Hamid and any of his friends or guests who might have called round. He was required to be there, to serve coffee and fetch glasses of water, and at times to be the butt of their jokes. They sat on mats, forming a circle around the lamp on the floor. When the mountain nights were chilly or when it rained, he brought out armfuls of shawls for the guests. Yusuf, a little withdrawn from this huddle as fitted his age and station, listened to their tales of Mrima and Bagamoyo, and Mafia Island and Lamu, and Ajemi and Shams, and a hundred other magical places. Sometimes they dropped their voices and leaned nearer to each other, and shooed Yusuf away if he strained too near. Then he saw the eyes of the listeners dilate with excitement and surprise, and their faces would explode with laughter at the end.

One night a man from Mombasa came to stay with them, and he told them a story of an uncle of his who had recently returned after fifteen years in the country of the Rusi, a people no one had heard of before. He had gone there in the service of a German officer who had been stationed in Witu, until the English chased the Germans out of there. The officer had then gone back to Europe as a diplomat in his country's embassy in a city called Petersburg, in the country of these Rusi. The stories the merchant told about his uncle did not bear belief. In this city of Petersburg, the sun shone until midnight, he said. When it was cold all the water turned to ice, and the ice over rivers and lakes was so thick that you could drive a heavily laden cart over it. The wind blew all the time, sometimes beating into sudden storms of ice and stones. In the night you could hear cries of fiends and jinns in the wind. They made their voices sound like women or children in distress. Anyone who dared to go out to their aid never returned. In the deepest weeks of winter even the sea froze, and wild dogs and wolves rampaged through city streets and would eat any living thing they found, people, horses, anything. The Rusi people were not civilized, not like the Germans, his uncle said. One day, in their travels across these lands they entered a small town to find every human being in it – man, woman and child – blind drunk. *Sikufanyieni maskhara*, dead to the world. Their savagery made his uncle suspect that he was in the country of Gog and Magog, whose borders formed the limit of the land of Islam. But even in this he had a surprise waiting for him, perhaps the biggest surprise of all. So many of the people who lived in Rusi were Muslims! In every town! Tartari, Kirgisi, Uzbeki! Who had heard of these names? His uncle's surprise was shared by these people too, who had never heard of a black man in Africa being a Muslim.

Mashaallah! They marvelled, and pressed the merchant from Mombasa for more details. Well, his uncle visited the city of Bukhara, and Tashkent and Herat, old cities where the inhabitants had built mosques of unimaginable beauty and gardens which were like paradise on earth. He slept in the most beautiful of the gardens in Herat, and in the night he heard music of such perfection that it almost ravished his reason. It was autumn, feverfew was everywhere in bloom and on the vines bunches of sweet grapes were ready for harvesting, grapes so sweet that you could not imagine that they might have grown out of the earth. The land was so pure and bright that the people there never fell ill or aged.

You're telling us tales, they cried. It can't be true that such places exist.

It's true, the merchant said.

Can it be true? they asked, desperate to believe. You're just telling us another piece of make-believe. Confusing our senses with more fairy tales.

I said the same to my uncle, the merchant replied. Though more politely. How can such stories be true?

What did your uncle say? they asked.

He said, I swear it.

So there must be such places, they sighed.

Later on in their journey, the merchant said, they crossed a wild sea with enormous waves called Kaspian. On the other side he saw jets of black oil rushing out of the ground, and metal towers that stood in the water like sentinels of Satan's kingdom. Spumes of fire filled the sky, like gates of flame. From there he travelled over mountains and valleys into country that was the most beautiful he had seen in all his travels, even more so than Herat. It was covered with orchards and gardens and rushing streams and was inhabited by people of learning and civilization whose nature made them obsessively fond of war and intrigue. So there was never any peace in their countries.

What was this land called? they asked him.

The merchant paused for a long time. Kaskas, he said at last, hesitantly. Then his uncle went down to the land of Shams and back all the way to Mombasa, he said quickly, before anyone could interrogate him further about names.

3

Yusuf told the children the stories he heard among the men in the evening. They came to his room when they tired of their games and poked about wherever they wanted. Since he had been forced to go to the imam's school with them, they had lost their inhibitions with him. He had enjoyed the privacy of his own room at first, but as his loneliness increased it began to seem like a prison and he thought fondly of Khalil and the time they had spent together. Sometimes the younger children fought each other on his mat, squealing with excitement, or threw themselves at Yusuf in mock battles. It was Asha who prompted him to tell the stories, watching his face intently as he talked. The others leaned against him, or held his hand, but Asha sat where she could see him. If she was called away, she insisted that he did not continue until she returned. One afternoon she came on her own to hear the end of a story he had had to leave unfinished the previous day. She sat in front of him on the mat, listening intently.

'You're lying,' she cried when he finished, tears in her eyes.

In his confusion he made no reply, and she leaned forward suddenly and hit him on the shoulder. He reached roughly for her, expecting her to fight and wriggle away as the others did, but she came willingly into his arms. She curled up against him with a long sigh, and he felt the heat of her breath on his chest. As his panic subsided, he felt her plump body softening too, and they lay silently against each other for several minutes. He felt himself stirring and was ashamed that she would notice.

'Someone will come,' he said at last.

At that she jumped away from him and then laughed. She was only a child after all, he thought. Nothing like that had even occurred to her. Who would think ill of it? They expected him to look after the children, and she was one of them. So then he opened his arms again and she came to lie in them with a little cry of pleasure.

'Tell me again about the gardens in that city,' she said.

'What city?' he asked, afraid to move.

'Where the music rose in the night,' she said, laughing though her eyes clung to him watchfully. She wriggled beside him, making him stir again.

'Herat,' he said. 'At night in the garden the traveller heard the voice of a woman singing and it ravished his senses.'

'Why?' she asked.

'I don't know. Perhaps because her voice was lovely. Or he was not used to the sound of a woman's voice in song.'

'What was his name?'

'A merchant,' he said.

'That's not a name. Tell me his name,' she said, rubbing herself against him while he stroked her soft, plump shoulder.

'His name was Abdulrazak,' he said. 'It wasn't really the uncle who said those words. The uncle was quoting a poet who had lived in Herat many centuries ago and who wrote verses about its beauty.'

'How do you know?'

'Because his nephew said.'

'Why do we have so many uncles?' she asked.

'They ain't our uncles,' he said, laughing and holding her tighter.

'Will you be a merchant?' she asked, her voice rising dangerously before she burst into noisy chuckles.

Whenever she came to him alone she lay in his arms like that, and he held her silently at first, afraid to move suddenly or touch her in a way that would frighten her. Her plump buttery smell revolted him slightly, but he could not resist the soft warmth of her body as it rubbed against his. She kissed his hands while she lay beside him, and sometimes she sucked the ends of his fingers. He moved his legs so she would not see how much she stirred him, but he could not be sure what she saw or whether she understood what they were doing. In the many silent hours he had to himself he hated himself, and feared what would happen to him if they were discovered. He rehearsed ways to end her visits but could not make himself say anything.

It was Maimuna who first became suspicious. Asha was too insistent in chasing away her brothers from Yusuf's room, and they went to complain to their mother. She descended on them at once and chased Asha away. To Yusuf she said nothing but stared angrily at him for a long moment, standing at his door. Her manner towards him cooled after that, and became watchful whenever he was near the children. Asha dropped her eyes in his presence, and never came to his room again. Hamid required him more often at his side, but did not seem as appalled at him as Maimuna had been. He wondered what Hamid had been told, but from the teasing remarks he made he guessed with apprehension that marriage had entered his thoughts in earnest.

4

Soon enough and at the agreed time, a year after his previous trip, Uncle Aziz arrived with a new expedition. This was a huge one compared with the previous year's. The porters and guards now numbered forty-five, not large in comparison with the bloated caravans of the last century which were like travelling villages with their own petty princes, but a large enough strain on the merchant. To get so many porters to accompany him, Uncle Aziz had had to mortgage a share of his profit to other merchants. They carried a greater volume of merchandise, for which Uncle Aziz had been forced to borrow a large amount of money from Indian creditors on the coast, which was not his usual practice. They had iron implements: hoes and axes from India, American knives and German padlocks. And cloths of different kinds: calico, kaniki, white cotton, bafta, muslin, kikoi. Also buttons, beads, mirrors and other trinkets which would be used as gifts. When Hamid saw the procession and heard about the creditors, he developed a bad cold. His eyes watered and his sinuses congested almost at once. A powerful pounding gradually emptied his head of all but its own thick echoes. He was still a partner to the enterprise, and if it failed, all his possessions and goods would belong to the creditors.

Mohammed Abdalla was still the leader of the expedition. His right shoulder had not healed properly, despite having been painfully reset by a famous mganga. The pain prevented him from swinging the cane with his accustomed grandiose freedom, and as a result his walk lost some of its haughtiness and menace. The steep tilt of the head and the thrown-back shoulders now seemed like an exaggeration, and therefore affected and ridiculous. In the past, his aggression had looked like indiscriminate malice, now it seemed the posturing of a vain man. He even spoke a little differently, sounding burdened and preoccupied at times. Uncle Aziz spoke kindly to him when before he would have ignored him and left him to his work.

The increase in the number of porters meant that Mohammed Abdalla had to hire an overseer to assist him. He was a tall and powerful-looking man from Morogoro called Mwene who rarely spoke in the first few days of joining the expedition. His reputation for ferocity had earned him the name of Simba Mwene, Lion Mwene, and he glowered and prowled among the men as if to show that the name was well earned. This time Yusuf was to go on the journey. Uncle Aziz himself had spoken to him, cheerful and full of smiles, and told him that he needed someone along that he could trust. 'You're too old now to stay here,' he said. 'You'll only get into mischief and mix with bad company. I need someone with a sharp mind to keep an eye on my affairs.' Yusuf was confused by the compliment, but understood that Hamid had asked for him to be taken on the journey. He had overheard them talking about him. Some of it he had missed because of Uncle Aziz's habit of breaking into Arabic and Hamid's attempts to do the same. But he had heard Hamid say to Uncle Aziz on the terrace that he was a tense and difficult boy who needed to see something of life.

'Tense and difficult boy,' he had repeated. 'Either take him on the journey or get him a wife. He's old enough, seventeen this last month. And look how grown-up he is. There's nothing for him to do here.'

On the eve of departure, a storm blew. It began with powerful winds in the morning which blew clouds of dust and dry thickets across roads and open spaces. By the middle of the day the dust was thick enough to dim the light of the sun, and to cover everything in a layer of grit. Late in the afternoon the wind suddenly died, and a great silence descended on them, the loudest noises muffled by the thick suspension of dust. When they tried to speak, their mouths filled with grit. Then the wind came again, this time bringing rain in squalls that lashed at the houses and trees, and tore into anyone who was still in the open.

Within minutes the rain had settled into a steady frenzy, broken at intervals by the crack of a shattered tree or the rumbling of distant thunder. Porters and goods were scattered, and from the shouts and cries of alarm it was likely that some were hurt. When everything turned dark in the hours of day, the porters groaned God's name and wailed for mercy, driving Mohammed Abdalla into a rage.

'Why should God be merciful to ignorant animals like you?' he shouted, his words only audible to those nearest to him. 'It's only a storm. Why are you behaving like this? Oh a snake has eaten the sun!' he mimicked, swinging his hips in a ridiculous parody of effeminacy. 'Oh it's bad luck! An omen of disaster! Oh our road will be dogged with fiends! Why don't you chant a song to chase away the bad magic? Or eat a disgusting powder some magician has prepared for you? Don't you know any spells? Why don't you slaughter a goat and read its stomach? You people are obsessed with fiends and omens. And you call yourselves men of honour, and give yourselves such airs. Go on, give us a song to chase the bad magic away.'

'I'll put my trust in God,' Simba Mwene cried. 'Not everyone here is afraid.'

Mohammed Abdalla gave him a long look, standing streaming in the rain. It was as if he was carefully digesting what Simba Mwene had said and how he looked when he spoke. Then he smiled with careful malice and nodded. Mohammed Abdalla seemed more like his old self during the storm, stomping through the chaos with relish. 'Haya, haya,' he said, shouting at the porters. 'Unless you want me to dog your arses with a few lashes of my stick, you'd better get yourselves a lot calmer. Look at the seyyid. He has more to lose than any of you. All you have are your miserable lives, of no use to anyone. He has his wealth, and the wealth other people have entrusted to him. He has your well-being as well as his own to keep in mind. He has the gift for business which God has granted him. He has a beautiful house to return to. He has these things to lose yet do you see him squawking all over the yard like a pregnant chicken? Fiend! I'll give you a hundred fiends and a thousand afreets if you don't stop this racket and get on with securing all the packs and supplies. Haya!'

The rain did not relent until the depths of night, by which time houses had collapsed and animals had been swept away and drowned in pools frothing with the storm's rage. The roofs of the outhouses had blown off and one of the breadfruit trees in the clearing had cracked to the ground. It was a miracle that none of the pigeon houses were damaged, Hamid said. The hurricane lamps in the yard were kept lit until the early hours while porters and guards worked to recover what they could. They chattered cheerfully, occasionally breaking out into their howls of mockery at each other or a shouted exchange of abuse. They exclaimed about the chaos and destruction around them, but they did not seem distressed by it.

In the morning, when all was ready, Uncle Aziz gave the signal. 'Haya,' he said. 'Take us to the country.' The mnyapara led off, squaring himself despite the pain in his shoulder and lifting his head with the defiant arrogance of the well bred. It was harder for him to carry himself with the old dignity, he knew that, but he was imposing enough, he prayed, for the hired riff-raff and dusty savages they passed. As a mark of the greater distinction of this expedition, the drum and siwa were accompanied by two horn players, a small orchestra. It was the siwa which struck up first, its long venerable notes making everyone stir with secret nostalgia, and then the other players joined in, lifting the travellers' hearts as they marched out into the country.

Hamid stood on the terrace to see them go, looking frightened and anxious. Yusuf thought of what Hussein had said about Hamid being out of his depth, and wondered if Hamid himself was thinking the same thought. Yusuf imagined the hermit on the mountain watching from his great height and shaking his head at their folly. Hamid's two little sons stood beside him, but neither Asha nor Maimuna was there. Nor was Kalasinga, whom Yusuf had hoped would turn up to see them go. He had gone to see him, to tell him about the journey, and Kalasinga had rhapsodized the value of travel and loaded him with eccentric advice. *Don't forget to put a drop of oil in your ear once a week to prevent insects and worms laying eggs in there.* Yusuf imagined him, until the last moment, dramatically chugging towards them on the muddy road and then leaping out of his van to salute them as they marched past. At important moments, Kalasinga always saluted. And perhaps he was wise to stay away, Yusuf thought as he remembered the porters' laughter at his turban and his woven beard.

They did not travel far on that first day's journey, satisfied to get well clear of the town. The porters grumbled of their tiredness after such a chaotic night, but Mohammed Abdalla kept them going with shouts and threats. At mid-afternoon they made camp, to take stock of their circumstances and compose themselves for what lay ahead. The storm had dampened and settled the earth, so that the land looked plump and turgid with sap. Bushes and trees glistened in the clear light, and from coverts came sounds of furtive cracks and urgent scurrying as if the earth itself was stirring to life. They camped near a small lake, the verges of which were churned with the footmarks of animals.

At first Yusuf tried to hide himself among the porters, keeping a distance from Uncle Aziz for reasons he did not examine. But quite early on the march Mohammed Abdalla sought him out and sent him towards the back of the column where the merchant acknowledged him with a pat on the neck and a friendly smile. He soon understood, from the errands Uncle Aziz sent him on, that this was to be his place. After they stopped on that first afternoon, he saw to the merchant's needs. He spread his mat and fetched water for him, and then settled nearby to wait for the food which was being prepared. Uncle Aziz seemed oblivious to the raucous high spirits of the company, his eyes calmly gazing at the countryside, as though every feature of the landscape had set itself out for his attention and scrutiny.

Once the camp had settled, the mnyapara came to join Uncle Aziz, sitting opposite him on the mat. 'When you look

114

on this land,' Uncle Aziz said, reluctantly taking his eyes away from the countryside, 'it fills you with longing. So pure and bright. You may be tempted to think that its inhabitants know neither sickness nor ageing. And their days are filled with contentment and a search for wisdom.'

Mohammed Abdalla chuckled. 'If there is paradise on earth, it is here, it is here, it is here,' he sang satirically, making Uncle Aziz smile.

Soon they began to talk in Arabic, their arms pointing directions as they debated the virtues of different routes. Yusuf wandered through the camp, past the neatly stacked piles of merchandise and the clumps of men gathered round their small fires and their belongings. In the brief hours they had been there, the encampment had taken on the appearance of a small village. Some of the men called to him, welcoming him to share their tea or inviting him to something less polite. The largest gathering was around Simba Mwene, who reclined against sacks while the crowd around him leaned forward to listen to his stories of the Germans. He spoke admiringly of their sternness and implacability. Every infringement was punished, however much the victim begged for mercy or promised to reform, he said.

'With us, if a culprit shows repentance we find it hard to punish him, especially if the sentence is severe. People will come to beg and plead for him, and we all have loved ones who'll mourn. But with the German it's the opposite. The more severe the punishment, the more firm and unforgiving he is. And his punishment is always severe. I think they like giving punishment. Once he has decided your sentence, you can beg until your tongue swells, but the German will stand there in front of you, his face dry and without shame. When he gets tired of you, you know that you'll have no choice but to take your punishment. That's how they can do all the things we see them do. They let nothing distract them.'

As the dusk deepened, the air was filled with the bellows and yells of the animals which came to the water to feed and drink. Yusuf found it hard to sleep, troubled by fear and discomfort. It was incredible that they were there on a chilly hillside at the dead of night while hungry animals roared and brayed within leaping distance. Yet everyone except the guards who were barricaded behind the stacks of goods seemed asleep. Perhaps they weren't asleep, Yusuf thought, merely lying in their own agitated silences.

5

Each day the land changed on them as they descended from the high mountain ground. The settlements grew less clustered as the country dried out. Within days they were down on the plateau and their column raised clouds of dust and grit with every step. The scattered scrub took formidably gnarled and twisted forms, as if existence was a torture. The songs and spirits of the porters also dried up as they contemplated the unkind country they were entering. They came to life when they saw huge herds of animals in the distance, arguing bitterly among themselves as they debated their identities. In those first days, Yusuf's stomach turned to water and his body ached with exhaustion and fever. Thorns tore into his ankles and arms, and his flesh was covered with insect bites. He wondered how anything could survive on a land so brutally severe. At night the cries of the animals startled him from sleep into nightmare, so that often in the morning he could not be sure if he had slept through the night or had lain cowering with fear. Yet they ran into people and settlements strung out on the plain. The people looked as wizened as the scrub, every feature of their bodies attenuated to the bare necessities. Uncle Aziz instructed that every settlement they passed should be given a small gift, to create goodwill and obtain information.

Yusuf began to understand why they called Uncle Aziz the seyyid. Despite everything, he managed to look untroubled, said his prayers five times a day at the appointed hours, and almost never wavered from his appearance of amused detachment. At most he frowned at delays, or stood rigid with impatience while a mishap was put right. He did not speak often, and usually only with Mohammed Abdalla, with whom he had long conferences at the end of each day's journey. But Yusuf felt that he was aware of everything of importance that happened during the day's journey. Now and then Yusuf saw him chuckle to himself as he watched the antics of the porters, and once he called him to his mat after he had said the evening prayer and put a hand on his shoulder. 'Do you think of your father?' he asked him. Yusuf was speechless. Uncle Aziz waited for a few moments and then slowly smiled at Yusuf's silence.

The mnyapara took Yusuf under his wing. He summoned him whenever he came across something that he thought Yusuf should see, and explained to him the wiles and lures of the land they were passing through. The porters told Yusuf that the mnyapara would be tupping him before the journey was much advanced. 'He likes you, but who wouldn't like such a beautiful boy? Your mother must have been visited by an angel.'

'You've found yourself a husband, pretty one!' Simba Mwene said, laughter rolling out of him as he made a lovelorn face for the benefit of the company. 'And what are the rest of us to do? You're too beautiful for that ugly monster. Come and give me a massage later tonight and I'll show you what love is.' It was the first time Simba Mwene had spoken to him like that, and Yusuf frowned with surprise.

Simba Mwene had become popular with the porters and guards, and a small group always gathered round him like a court. The chief courtier was a short, round-looking man called Nyundo. He led the laughter and the praise, and followed Simba Mwene faithfully whenever he could. When Mohammed Abdalla and Simba Mwene stood together, Nyundo placed himself out of the mnyapara's eye-line and mimicked him, provoking the other porters to laughter and glaring at those who did not find his antics amusing. Yusuf knew that Mohammed Abdalla watched Simba Mwene and spoke about him to Uncle Aziz. Yusuf was required to sit with them on the mat now when they held their evening conferences, although he slipped away whenever he could, to listen to the stories the porters told among themselves. It exasperated Mohammed Abdalla that Yusuf could not understand Arabic, but he translated a summary of what was interesting in their conversation.

'Take a good look at that big mouth,' he said one evening, watching a noisy group sitting around Simba Mwene. 'I've got a fine big thorn right into him, and will make him squirm if he gets any ideas. He has murdered a man, that's why he's on the journey. To earn enough to compensate the people he has injured, or to perish himself if God wishes it. It was on my word that he was given this chance to redeem himself. Otherwise the relatives of the murdered man would have delivered him to the Germans for vengeance. And the Germans would have strung him up sooner than spit at him. They like that kind of thing. Bring them a murderer and their eyes light with happiness as they get the gallows ready. He came to me with this story and I agreed to take him. Now take a good look at him. I have a feeling about this Simba Mwene. There is a violence in his eyes, a madness. He wants trouble. It looks like a kind of hunger or eagerness to do things, but I think he is hankering for pain. The journey will shake it out of him. There's nothing like a few months among the savages for finding the weakness in a man.'

Mohammed Abdalla also taught him about the business they were engaged in. 'This is what we're on this earth to do,' Mohammed Abdalla said. 'To trade. We go to the driest deserts and the darkest forests, and care nothing whether we trade with a king or a savage, or whether we live or die. It's all the same to us. You'll see some of the places we pass, where people have not yet been brought to life by trade, and they live like paralysed insects. There are no people more clever than traders, no calling more noble. It is what gives us life.'

Their trade goods were mostly cloth and iron, he explained. Kaniki, marekani, bafta, all kinds of cloth. Any of it was better than the stinking goatskin the savages wore when left to themselves. That is if they wore anything at all, for God made heathens shameless so that the faithful can recognize them and resolve how to deal with them. On this side of the lake the market was flooded with cloth, although there was still demand for iron, especially among the farming people. Their real destination was the other side of the lake, the country of the Manyema, in the very depths of the dark and green mountain country. There, cloth was still the most common item of exchange. The savage did not trade for money. What could he do with money? They also had some clothes, sewing needles, hoe blades and knives, tobacco and a well-hidden supply of powder and shot, which they were taking with them as a special gift to the more difficult sultans. 'When all else fails, powder and shot never does,' the mnyapara said.

Their direction was to the south-west until the lake, country-side that traders knew well but which was already under the shadow of European power. There were very few of the dogs themselves actually there, so the people still lived as they wished, but they knew that the Europeans would come in any day. 'They are without doubt amazing, these Europeans,' Mohammed Abdalla said, looking to Uncle Aziz for confirmation.

'Trust in God,' the merchant said soothingly, his eyes bright with amusement at the mnyapara's intensity.

'The stories we hear about them! The fighting they have done in the south, the fine sabres and the wonderful, precise guns they make. We are told they can eat metal and have powers over the land, but I can't believe this. If they can eat metal, why shouldn't they be able to eat us and the whole of the earth? Their ships have sailed beyond all known seas, and are sometimes the size of a small town. Have you ever seen one of their ships, seyyid? I saw one in Mombasa some years ago. Who taught them to do these things? Their houses, I hear, are built with marble floors that shine and gleam so softly that a man is tempted to pull his cloth up a few inches lest it should get wet. Yet they look like skinless reptiles and have golden hair, like women or a very bad joke. The first time I saw one, he was sitting in a chair under a tree in the middle of a forest. I whispered the Almighty's name, thinking I was in the presence of evil. Then after a moment I knew that the ghostly creature was one of the famed breakers of nations.'

'Did he speak?' Yusuf asked.

'Not words known to the human ear,' said Mohammed Abdalla. 'Perhaps he rumbled. I saw fumes of smoke coming out of his mouth. It could be that they are jinns, for God made them out of fire.'

Yusuf understood that the mnyapara was making fun of him and saw a smile on the corners of Uncle Aziz's mouth. 'If the jinns built the pyramids, why shouldn't they be able to build ships as big as towns?' the merchant asked.

'But who can tell why they have come all this way?'
Mohammed Abdalla said. 'As if the earth itself had cracked
open and thrown them out. Perhaps when they've done with
us, the earth will open again and suck them back to their land
on the other side of the world.'

'You're beginning to talk like an old woman, Mohammed
Abdalla,' the merchant said, stretching himself on the mat
and getting ready for a nap. 'They're here for the same reason
you and I are.'

6

Whenever they could, they camped near a settlement so they
could barter for food and not use up their provisions. The
further they moved into the country, the more they had to
pay for flour or meat. On the eighth day of their journey they
camped near a small clump of trees. For the first time since
they started, orders were given to construct a stockade for fear
of animals. The porters grumbled and protested, as they did
about any work at the end of a day's journey, saying that the
copse was infested with snakes. Simba Mwene, cutlass in
hand, cut a path into the tangled wood and shamed the
others into following. They chopped down bushes and dragged
out dead branches to make a barrier about four feet high.
They were now approaching the village of Mkata at the
crossing place on the river just ahead of them. The merchant
had heard rumours of a caravan which was attacked by the
villagers near the river and did not want to take any risks. He
sent two men ahead of the column in the morning with gifts
for the sultan of Mkata. The merchant addressed the humblest
village elder as sultan, and spoke to him with deference.

His gift of six cloths and two hoes was returned with the
message that the sultan of Mkata wanted all the goods the

merchant possessed put at his disposal. Then he would himself select gifts appropriate to his station, especially if the gifts were intended as tribute, requesting the favour of passage through his land. Uncle Aziz laughed at the sultan's demand and doubled the gift. By this time the column had stopped within half a mile of the village, and curious children were peering at them from a distance. The messengers returned with word that the sultan of Mkata was still not satisfied. He had told them to say that he was a poor man, and did not want to be forced into actions he would later regret. The merchant doubled his gift again. 'Tell the sultan that we're all poor,' he said. 'But let him remember that most of the occupants of Heaven are also the poor, while most of the occupants of Hell are the covetous.'

The rest of the day passed with this exchange of messages until honour and greed were satisfied. It was late afternoon by the time they reached the river, and as they stood in the open ground by the bank, they saw a woman who had gone into the water being attacked by a crocodile. The villagers and the travellers ran to the place where the struggle was taking place and where the water was foaming, but they could not save her. The villagers mourned her loss with abandon, weeping in the shallows and on the river bank, and gesturing angrily towards the farther bank where the crocodile had retreated. Her relatives threw themselves in the water in their grief and had to be pulled out by the others, some of whom were now watching the water warily for more crocodiles.

It was a large river but shallow at Mkata. Its wide muddy banks attracted crowds of animals and flocks of birds. Throughout the night they heard noises in the water and in the bushes, and some of the porters frightened each other by crying out as if they had been attacked. The sultan of Mkata slaughtered two goats and invited the merchant to bring a company over to eat with him. He was sombre throughout the meal and made no effort to be hospitable, helping himself to what he wanted and leaving his guests to eat if they wished. The sultan was a thin man with cropped grey hair, his eyes veined and reddened in the firelight. He spoke Kiswahili with difficulty and with a confusing accent, but Yusuf understood much of what he said if he attended. 'You've brought calamity with you,' he said. 'The woman taken by the animal today was protected against water and crocodiles. It has not happened before that someone like her should have been taken, not in all the years that I have lived. Nor have I heard of it in the times before us.' He spoke to them endlessly about the woman, his eyes roving over them in the leaping light. None of the other villagers spoke to them, though their voices hummed and swelled at the edges of the firelight. Yusuf saw that Uncle Aziz leaned forward politely while the sultan spoke, and now and then nodded in sympathy or agreement. 'Many people have passed here to take the crossing,' the sultan continued. 'But only you have brought this evil on us. If you do not take it away when you go, our lives will be adrift and without reason.'

'Trust in God,' the merchant said gently.

'We will have to see what can be done tomorrow to restore what you have shattered,' the sultan said as he released them.

'Filthy savage bastard!' Mohammed Abdalla said. Two torch-bearers flanked the company and everyone looked sharp. 'Keep your wits about you or you'll end up without your zub before the night's out. Our kind host wants to make a sacrifice to his filthy spirits, and it could well be that he has in mind a handful of your manhoods thrown to the crocodiles in the middle of the night. May God protect us from evil.'

'Who knows if it isn't as good as any other medicine?' Uncle Aziz said to Yusuf later, smiling to see his leap of interest at the blasphemy.

123

That night Yusuf dreamt that he was visited by the huge dog of his nightmares again. It spoke lucidly to him, opening its long mouth in broad grins, and flashing its yellow teeth at him. Then it straddled his open belly in search of his deepest secrets.

At dawn their encampment erupted in screams and desperate growlings, and they discovered that hyenas had attacked one of the sleeping porters and taken off most of his face. Blood and slimy viscous fluids ran off the raw stump of what was left. The man thrashed dementedly on the ground, in unimaginable pain. People rushed from everywhere to watch, among them children who wriggled furiously through the crowd to get a close look. The sultan too came to see, and afterwards stood apart for a few minutes before he returned to announce himself satisfied that what had been desecrated had now been put right. The animals had been sent to take away the evil the caravan had brought to their town the previous day, and the travellers could now go. Only they did not wish them to come through the town again. Looking at Yusuf, he said he had thought it would be the young man who would be given to them. He would have been fitting return for the loss of the woman in the water, the sultan said. For she was well loved.

Two men sat with the wounded porter, weeping as they held him down, while the rest of the caravan was forded across the river by the villagers. When it was time to take the wounded man across, the sultan refused to let him go. The merchant offered one gift after another but the sultan would not be placated. The wounded one was theirs. The land had given him to them.

The man died suddenly that afternoon, in the middle of his endless groans, his wound covered with matter that had leaked from his brain. They buried him at once at a place some distance from the village. It was where they buried their own unwanted or evil dead, the sultan said, those whose restless spirits they did not want wandering through their lives. As the last of the travellers crossed the river at dusk the sultan and the villagers congregated under the trees by the river bank, noisily speeding their departure. Hippo and crocodile eyes were already alert, resting lightly on the water, and wild bird-calls shrilled from the other bank, which was now deep in shadow.

More guards were set that night, and large fires were lit to give the men courage. The merchant sat for a long time on his mat, silently saying prayers for the man they had lost. From a small Koran, which he pulled out of his box, he read *Ya Sin* for the dead by the light of a lamp hung on the branch of a tree. The mnyapara and Simba Mwene went among the men, talking roughly to them at times and trying to shake them out of their panic. Yusuf went to sleep at once, but dreams came to trouble him. Twice he woke up with a cry on his lips, and looked around in the dark to see if anyone had noticed. The column was ready to leave by first light, with the mnyapara shouting to everyone to look sharp. 'Did a snake bite you last night?' he said quietly to Yusuf. 'Or were you having filthy dreams? Look sharp, young man. You're not a boy any more.'

As he helped Uncle Aziz prepare for departure, the merchant stopped him with a soft cough. 'You were troubled again last night,' he said. 'Did the words of the sultan worry you?'

Yusuf was silent with surprise. Again! Troubled again! He felt as if he had been found out in a weakness beyond remedy. Did they all know of the dogs and beasts and shapeless voids which came to prise his self from him in the night? Perhaps he cried out often and the men laughed at him.

'Trust in God,' the merchant said. 'He has given you a gift.'

Across the river, the land was fertile and more populous. The appearance of the green landscape cheered them at first. The bushes shook and shuddered with birds, whose sharp tireless songs sawed through the cooler hours of the day. Ancient trees towered over them, and filtered a gentle light to the shrubs in the arbours underneath. But the glossy shrubs hid barbed creepers and were tangled with poisonous vines, and the most inviting shades were full of snakes. Insects bit them day and night. Clothes and flesh were torn by thorns, and strange ailments befell the men. And almost every day now they had to pay ever increasing tributes to the sultans to be allowed to pass. The merchant kept out of the negotiations if he could, waiting alone in an uninviting silence while Mohammed Abdalla and Simba Mwene haggled for passage. Sometimes it looked as if the sultans were enjoying provoking the mnyapara and his overseer too much to want to come to an agreement. To Yusuf it seemed that the people were eager to show their dislike of the visitors.

The town of Tayari, their first destination, was only a few days' journey away, and the people here understood the havoc they could cause to a march by some selective awkwardness, and so expected to be well paid for their goodwill. Food was plentiful and could be had for a steep price. The merchant bought chicken and fruit every other day, knowing that the porters would steal from the villagers if denied, and that would only lead to argument and war.

The warrior people from the other side of the mountain raided here, to blood their spears and simis, and capture cattle and women. On the seventh day of their journey from the river, they arrived at a village which had been attacked two days before. They felt and saw a disturbance before they arrived at the village, plumes of smoke in the middle of the day and black birds wheeling in the sky. When they reached

126

the wrecked village, they saw only a few wounded and mutilated survivors huddled in the shade of trees. The roofs of all the dwellings had been set on fire. The survivors lamented the loss of their loved ones, many of them taken away by the raiders. Some of their young men had fled during the attack, taking a few of the children with them. Who knew if they would ever be able to come back? Yusuf could not bear to look on the incredible horror of the wounds, swollen now with disease. He wanted life to end at the sight of such pain. He had never seen or imagined anything like it. They found bodies everywhere, in the burnt-out huts, near the bushes, under trees.

Mohammed Abdalla wanted them to leave as quickly as possible, for fear of disease or the return of the raiders. Simba Mwene went to the merchant to ask that they should bury the dead, standing too close to him at first and making him step back. 'The ones left can't manage the task in their state,' Simba Mwene said.

'Then leave them to the animals,' Mohammed Abdalla cried, hardly able to control his rage. 'This is nothing to do with us. Most of the bodies are putrid and half eaten already . . .'

'We shouldn't leave them like this,' Simba Mwene said, his voice low.

'They will give us diseases,' Mohammed Abdalla said, keeping his eyes on the merchant. 'Let their brothers come and do this disgusting job. They are only hiding in the bushes. When they come back they will turn on us with their superstitions and say we defiled their dead. What has this to do with us?'

'We are their brothers, from the blood of the same Adam who fathered all of us,' Simba Mwene said. Mohammed Abdalla grinned with surprise but did not speak.

'What is your concern?' Uncle Aziz asked.

'For the decency of the dead,' Simba Mwene said, glaring.

The merchant laughed. 'Very well,' he said. 'Bury them.'

'May God squirt hyena shit in my eyes!' the mnyapara said. 'And may God cut me into a thousand little pieces if this does not look ill thought and dangerous! Since this is your wish, seyyid . . . but I cannot understand the necessity.'

'Since when have you been afraid of superstition, Mohammed Abdalla?' Uncle Aziz asked gently.

The mnyapara gave the merchant a quick, wounded look. 'All right, make it quick,' he said to Simba Mwene. 'And no risks or heroics. These are savages who do this to each other all the time. And we haven't come here to play at being saints.'

'Yusuf, go with them and see how base and foolish is the nature of men,' said Uncle Aziz.

They dug a shallow pit at the edge of the village, cursing that fate should have decreed their presence at this gruesome ceremony. The villagers watched them as they laboured, spitting in their direction from time to time, casually, as if they meant no offence. Then the moment the men dreaded arrived as they lifted and shoved the broken bodies into the pit. The wails of the villagers rose inconsolably as the pit was filled in. When the task was done, Simba Mwene stood beside the grave, staring at the villagers with loathing.

THE GATES OF FLAME

Three days later the column reached the river on the outskirts of Tayari. Even from a distance Yusuf could see that it was a large town. The men shrugged off their loads and rushed into the river with excited cries. They splashed water at each other and lunged into mock fights like children. A few of them would end their journey here, and their anticipation of release infected everyone else. After they had refreshed and cleaned themselves the porters returned to their loads with lingering smiles. Not long now! The mnyapara and Simba Mwene strode up and down the column, straightening out the loads and hectoring the men into shape. The drummer and horn players began to warm up their instruments with short mischievous outbursts which the siwa players marked with deep remonstrating replies. Their playing grew more measured as order resumed, so that by the time they entered the town, the travellers were striding to the deep rising music of the march. Idlers and passers-by stood by the road to watch. Some of them waved and clapped, shouting indistinct words between cupped palms. The land around the town was parched, waiting for the rains. Uncle Aziz, at the back of the column as usual, took no notice of the bystanders. Now and then he put a handkerchief over his nostrils to keep out the dust, and as they strolled together behind the great stifling cloud the men raised, he spoke to Yusuf.

'Look at their happiness,' he said, unsmiling. 'Like a mindless herd of beasts approaching water. We're all like that, small-minded creatures misled by our ignorance. What is their excitement for? Do you know?'

Yusuf thought he knew, because he felt something like that himself, but he did not speak. Later, after they had found a house to rent, with a yard in which the men could sleep and where the goods could be kept under guard, Uncle Aziz said to Yusuf, 'In the days when I first started to come to this town it was run by the Arabs of the sultan of Zanzibar. They were Omanis, or if not Omanis then they were servants to Omanis. Gifted people, the Omanis. Very able. They came here to build little kingdoms for themselves. All the way from Zanzibar to this place! And some went even further, into the deepest forest beyond Marungu to the great river. And there they set up their kingdoms too. Well, the distance was nothing. In their own lifetimes their noble prince had come all the way from Muscat to make himself master of Zanzibar, so why not them? Their sultan Said made himself rich on the fruit of those islands. He built palaces which he stocked with horses and peacocks and rare beauties purchased from around the world . . . from India to Morocco, and from Albania to Sofala. He sent out for women from everywhere and paid well for them. It is said he produced a hundred children with them. I would be surprised if he himself knew the number accurately. Can you imagine the bother of keeping that crowd in order? He must have worried about all the little princelings who would grow up one day wanting a piece of flesh to dig their teeth into. He himself had the blood of a murdered relative or two on his hands. If their sultan could do all this, and deserve nothing but honour for it, why not them?

'The lords who came here divided this small town into districts, under the power of one or the other of them. First there was Kanyenye, which belonged to an Arab whose name was Muhina bin Seleman El-Urubi. And the second part of the town was called Bahareni, and the Arab it belonged to was Said bin Ali. And the third was called Lufita, which belonged to Mwenye Mlenda, a man from Mrima on the coast. The fourth part was called Mkowani, to an Arab Said bin Habib Al-Afif. And the fifth was Bomani, and the Arab's name was Seti bin Juma. The sixth was Mbugani, and the Arab who owned it was Salim bin Ali. And the seventh part was called Chemchem, it belonged to an Indian whose name was Juma bin Dina. The eighth part is N'gambo, and the Arab's name was Muhammad bin Nassor. And the ninth was Mbirani, to an Arab Ali bin Sultan. And the tenth part was Malolo, to an Arab whose name was Rashid bin Salim. And the eleventh was Kwihara, whose owner was an Arab called Abdalla bin Nasibu. The twelfth part was Gange, to an Arab Thani bin Abdalla. And the thirteenth was Miemba, it belonged to a former slave of an Arab whose name was Farhani bin Othman. And another part was called Ituru, to an Arab called Muhammad bin Juma, the father of Hamed bin Muhammad, who was also called Tipu Tip. You've heard of him, I suppose.

'Now there's talk that the Germans will build their railway all the way to here. It's they who make the law and dictate now, although it has been that way since the time of Amir Pasha and Prinzi really. But before the Germans came, no one travelled to the lakes without going through this town.'

The merchant waited to see if Yusuf would say anything, and when he did not, he continued. 'You'll be thinking: how did so many of these Arabs come to be here in such a short time? When they started to come here, buying slaves from these parts was like picking fruit off a tree. They didn't even have to capture their victims themselves, although some of them did so for the pleasure of it. There were enough people eager to sell their cousins and neighbours for trinkets. And the

markets were open everywhere, down in the south and on the
ocean islands where the Europeans were farming for sugar, in
Arabia and Persia, and on the sultan's new clove plantations
in Zanzibar. There were good profits to be made. Indian
merchants gave credit to these Arabs to trade in ivory and
slaves. The Indian Mukki were businessmen. They lent money
for anything, so long as there was profit in it. As did the other
foreigners, but they let the Mukki act for them. Anyway, the
Arabs stole the money and bought slaves from one of the savage
sultans near here and made the slaves work in the fields and
build comfortable houses for them. This is how the town
grew.'

'Listen to what your uncle is saying,' Mohammed Abdalla
said, as if Yusuf's attention had wandered. He had joined
them during Uncle Aziz's account, and his eager interruption
marked the detachment of the merchant's delivery. He ain't
my uncle, Yusuf thought.

'Why was he called Tipu Tip?' Yusuf asked.

'I don't know,' Uncle Aziz said, shrugging with indifference.
'Anyway, when the German Amir Pasha came to these parts,
he went to see the sultan of Tayari. I forget the sultan's name.
He was created sultan by the Arabs, someone they could
influence and sway. Amir Pasha treated the sultan with utter
contempt, deliberately, to provoke him to war. This was their
method. He demanded that the sultan fly the flag of the
Germans, that he swear loyalty to the German sultan and
that he hand over all the arms and cannon he possessed,
because he was sure to have stolen them from the Germans in
the first place. The sultan of Tayari did everything he could
to avoid a fight. He liked fighting well enough usually and
was always at war with his neighbours. His Arab allies sup-
ported him when it suited them, but everyone had heard of
the merciless way these Europeans made war. The sultan of

Tayari flew the flag of the Germans as he was asked, he swore loyalty to the German sultan and sent gifts and food to the camp of Amir Pasha, but he was reluctant to give up the guns. By this time he had lost the support of the Arabs, who saw that he had betrayed them. He had given away too much. So when Amir Pasha left, they began to intrigue to remove him.

'There wasn't much longer to wait. After Amir Pasha came Prinzi, the German commander, and he made war at once and killed the sultan and his children and any of his people that he could find. He placed the Arabs under his heel at first and then chased them away. The foreigner ground them down so thoroughly that they could not even force their slaves to work on their farms any more. The slaves just hid or ran away. The Arabs were left without food or comforts and had no choice but to leave. Some have gone to Ruemba, some to Uganda and some have retreated to their sultan in Zanzibar. There's still the odd one left who doesn't know what to do. Now the Indians have taken over, with the Germans as their lords and the savages at their mercy.'

'Never trust the Indian!' Mohammed Abdalla said angrily. 'He will sell you his own mother if there's profit in it. His desire for money knows no limits. When you see him, he looks craven and feeble, but he will go anywhere and do anything for money.'

Uncle Aziz shook his head at the mnyapara, admonishing him for his impetuosity. 'The Indian knows how to deal with the European. We have no choice but to work with him.'

2

They did not stay long in Tayari. The town was a bewildering maze of narrow alleys which suddenly opened into small clear yards and squares. The air in the dark streets smelt intimate and tainted, like that inside crowded rooms. Rivulets of waste water ran inches from the thresholds of houses. At night, while they slept in the yard of the house they had rented, cockroaches and rats crawled over them, nipping at calloused toes and tearing into sacks of provisions. The mnyapara hired new porters to replace the ones who had contracted to go no farther and they set off again in a few days. They made good time after leaving Tayari. A light rain sped them on, making the men break into song as their bodies cooled. Even the ones who were ailing from the wear and tear of the journey found their old strength returning. There were some whose illnesses had such a hold on their bodies that neither songs nor jokes could make their frequent scuttering into the bushes less agonizing, but their fellows now smiled ruefully over their shrieks of pain rather than falling silent.

After a few days they knew they were close to the lake. The light ahead of them looked thicker, softer with the burden of water below. The thought of the lake made everyone happier. At the villages and settlements they passed, people stood to watch them with knowing smiles, which none the less broadened at the sight of their cheerfulness. Some of the men became exuberant in their pursuit of women in the villages, and one was badly beaten, requiring the merchant to intervene with gifts to restore goodwill. In the evenings after they had made camp and built a stockade of bushes against attack from animals, the men sat in groups and told stories. The mnyapara warned Yusuf against sitting with the men, telling him that his uncle disapproved. *They'll teach you evil,* Mohammed Abdalla said, but Yusuf took no notice. He felt himself growing stronger with each day on the march. The men still teased him but with increasing friendliness. When he sat with them in the evening, they made room for him and included him in their talk. Sometimes a hand stroked his thigh, but he knew to avoid sitting next to it after that. If the musicians were not feeling too tired, they played their full-throated, reedy tunes while the men sang and clapped in time.

One evening, overcome by the joy which had overtaken everyone, the mnyapara stepped into the firelit circle and danced. Two steps forward, a graceful stoop, then two steps back while his cane whirled over his head. The horn player added an embellishment, a phrase on a rising note like a sudden yell of glee, making Simba Mwene laugh with his face turned to the night sky. The mnyapara twirled to the new phrase and came to a stop with a heroic pose, to the hilarity of the men.

Yusuf saw the mnyapara wince as his dance came to an end, and knew that he was not the only one who had noticed. But the smile did not leave Mohammed Abdalla's face, which was streaming with sweat. 'You should've seen me as I was before,' he cried, heaving a little as he waved his cane at the men. 'We used to dance with naked blades in our hands, not sticks. Forty, fifty men dancing at the same time.'

He stroked himself briefly before stepping out of the firelight to the shouts and whistles of the men. He had hardly taken a couple of steps when Nyundo leapt to his feet, cane in hand, and began to mimic the mnyapara's dance. The musicians gleefully struck up again while Nyundo pranced in the firelight, two steps forward, two tottering steps back, then exaggerating the stoop so that it looked obscene. After a few wild turns and frantic whirls of his stick, he came to a sudden stop, legs apart, and stroked himself slowly in the crotch. 'Who'd like to see something? Not like it was before, but it's still something. And it still works,' Nyundo cried. While everyone laughed at this satirical display, the mnyapara stood at the edges of the light, watching them.

The lakeside town lay in soft impossible light, violet with an edge of crimson from the great cliffs and hills which formed the banks. Boats were pulled up along the water's edge and a row of small brown houses lined the bank. The lake stretched away in all directions, making the men lower their voices with the feeling the sight stirred in them. The travellers waited outside the town as was their custom, until permission was granted for entry. A shrine stood nearby, surrounded by snakes and pythons and wild animals. Only if the spirit allowed it could a person reach the shrine safely and leave in peace. Mohammed Abdalla told them this as they waited, pointing to a grove not far from their resting place. 'That's where their God lives. Savages believe anything if it's crazy enough,' he said. 'It's no good saying to them that this or that is childish. You can't argue with them. They only tell you endless stories about their superstitions.' They had passed through the town on their last journey, he said, and it was from here that they had crossed to the other side. This was also where they had left two injured men on their return journey. It was during the worst of the dry season when they stopped before, and they had thought it would be safer to leave the wounded men here than carry them on a fly-infested journey all the way to Tayari. Yusuf thought how those words had sounded on Hamid's terrace, how solicitous and civilized. He remembered that Uncle Aziz had said the two men were left in a town by the lake, with people he had never done business with before but whom he trusted to take care of the men. The straggling line of houses along the lakeside, and the sweet stench of rotting fish which reached them even at the town's edges, gave that explanation a different meaning. When Yusuf glanced at the mnyapara, and saw the calculation and watchfulness in his eyes, he knew with shamed certainty that the two men had been abandoned here.

Nyundo had been sent into the town as the messenger, because he said he could speak the language of the people here. Uncle Aziz said he remembered the sultan could speak Kiswahili, but he agreed it would be more courteous to address him in his own language first. Nyundo returned from the sultan of the town with words of welcome. The sultan was pleased with the gifts, Nyundo reported, but he would like most of all to see his old friends again. Before they entered, though, he wanted to acquaint them with a great sorrow which had befallen all of them. The sultan's wife had died four nights ago.

The merchant expressed his sadness and asked that his condolences and those of the whole caravan be conveyed to the sultan. He also sent more gifts with the messenger, asking that they be allowed to express their sorrow in person. While they waited again, the men talked about customs of honouring the dead, especially if the dead happen to be wives of sultans. For a start they don't always bury their dead, one of the men said. Sometimes they throw them into the bush while they are still alive, so the wild beasts can have them. They walk them to the bush and leave them for the hyenas and leopards to carry them away. They think it brings bad luck to touch a corpse, even if it is the corpse of your own mother. In some places they kill all strangers at such times. And suppose the sultan is too distraught to do business. And who knows what ritual and magic and sacrifices they do? Some of them don't bury the dead for weeks. They put them in a pot or under a tree. The men looked towards the grove nearby. 'They've probably got the stinking corpse in there,' one of them said.

At last Nyundo returned with permission for them to enter. The merchant instructed that the men should march silently, without music or noise, as a mark of respect for the sultan's bereavement. It was a small town, two or three dozen huts clustered in groups of threes and fours. The air hummed with the stink of rotting fish. Along the water's edge were wooden platforms on stilts, covered with thatched awnings. Pieces of canvas and matting were stretched across some of them, and large dugout canoes were pulled up out of the water and into the shade of the platforms. Children playing in the shade ran out to watch the column march silently in.

The men gathered where they were directed and waited for the merchant to complete his negotiations. After a few moments, some of the men began to drift away, looking for the townspeople who were obviously keeping out of sight. In the silence, their cries of greeting as they made contact reached the others easily, prompting more of them to stream away. The sultan sent another message that he would now see the merchant and his men, but the angry-looking old man who came to deliver this summons ordered that only four people would be admitted to the sultan. In his grieved state of mind the sultan could not bear the sight and noise of a crowd. The mnyapara and Nyundo accompanied Uncle Aziz to the sultan's residence, as did Yusuf. *Bring the scholar so he can learn how to greet the owners of the land*, Uncle Aziz said. They approached a group of huts, close to the water, which was more numerous than any of the others, and were led to a large building with a covered porch. Inside, it was gloomy and smoky from the fire which glowed close to the door. The only light came through the doorway, and as they were ushered to one side, the room brightened a little. The sultan was a large man, dressed in a brown cloth tied round his middle with a band of woven straw. The taut rolls of his upper body glistened in the poor light. He sat on a backless chair, elbows on thighs, both hands clasping a thick carved stick planted between his spread-out legs. His attitude made him seem eager and attentive. Standing on his right and on his left were two young women, naked to the waist, each holding a drinking gourd. Behind him stood another woman, also half naked and waving a woven fan across the sultan's shoulders. Behind her, deep in the shadows, stood a young man. Six elders sat on mats on the floor on either side of the sultan, some of them bare chested. The smoke in the chamber made Yusuf struggle for breath and made his eyes water, and he wondered how the sultan and his attendants could bear it so comfortably.

'He says you're welcome,' Nyundo translated after the sultan had said a few smiling words. 'This is a bad time you have come, he says. But a friend is always welcome in his house.' At a signal from him, the woman on his right put the gourd to the sultan's lips, and he took several deep draughts. The woman stepped towards the merchant and Yusuf saw that her breasts were marked by small scars. She smelt of smoke and sweat, a familiar and stirring aroma. 'He says you will now have some beer,' Nyundo said to the merchant, unable to hide a smile.

'I am grateful, but I must decline,' the merchant said.

'He asks why?' Nyundo said, grinning. 'It's good beer. Is it because you think there's poison in it? He's already tasted it for you. Don't you trust him?' The sultan then said something else and the elders laughed among themselves, cackling with long-toothed merriment. The merchant looked at Nyundo, who shook his head. His gesture was ambiguous, perhaps he had not understood or thought it best not to translate.

'I'm a trader,' Uncle Aziz said, looking at the sultan. 'And I am a stranger in your town. If I drink beer I'll begin to shout and get into fights, and this is not how a stranger on business should behave.'

'He says it's because your god won't let you. He knows about that,' Nyundo said, as the sultan and his people laughed again among themselves. Nyundo took a long time before translating the sultan's next remark. The grin had disappeared from his face and he spoke carefully to give the impression that he was striving for a faithful delivery. 'He says what kind of cruel god is it which doesn't allow men to drink beer?'

'Tell him a demanding but just God,' the merchant said quickly.

'He says very well, very well. Perhaps you drink your beer in secret. Bring me your news now,' Nyundo said as the sultan pointed the visitors to mats on the floor. 'Have you been trading well? What have you brought with you this time? He says you can see he's not asking for tribute, can't you? He has heard that the big man has said that it is no longer allowed to ask for tribute. So he doesn't want to make the mistake of asking for anything in case the big man comes to hear of it and comes to punish him. He says do you know which big man he's talking about?' The sultan's body shook with short, squelchy gasps of laughter as he asked this. 'The German, he's the big man. From what he has heard this is the new king now. He came through near here not so long ago and told everyone who he was. They have heard that the German has a head of iron. Is it true? And he has weapons which can destroy a whole town in one blow. My people want to trade and live their lives in peace, he says, not make trouble for the German.' The sultan added something else which made his attendants laugh again.

'May we have your assistance to make a crossing?' the merchant asked when chance presented itself.

'He asks who you are going to see across the water,' Nyundo said. The sultan was leaning forward with a critical air, as if he expected the answer to prove the merchant foolish or reckless.

'Chatu, a sultan in Marungu,' Uncle Aziz said.

The sultan leaned back and made a soft, snorting noise. 'He says he knows about Chatu,' Nyundo said. They watched as the sultan motioned for more beer. 'He says he has told you that his wife passed away recently. He says he still hasn't been able to bury her and his heart is filled with unrest.'

After a moment the sultan continued. He could not bury his wife without a shroud, he said. The fire had gone out in him since her death, and he could not think where a shroud might come from. 'He says give him a shroud,' Nyundo said to the merchant.

'Would you deny a man a shroud to bury his wife?' said the young man who had been standing in the shadows at the back. He stepped forward to face the merchant and spoke to him directly without need of Nyundo. His left leg was swollen with disease, and as he walked forward he dragged the leg behind him. His face was unmarked, and his eyes shone with zeal and understanding. Yusuf was able now to separate the peculiar smell of living, putrefying flesh from the astringency of the smoke-filled hut. Several of the sultan's elders also spoke after the young man, making long contorted faces of disbelief. The women sucked their lips and murmured with disgust.

'Certainly I would deny no one a shroud,' said Uncle Aziz, and told Yusuf to fetch five rolls of white bafta cotton.

'Five!' said the young man, taking charge of the negotiations. One of the elders rose to his feet in consternation and spat in the merchant's direction. Yusuf caught a bit of the spray on his bare arm. 'Five rolls of cloth for a sultan as important as him. You won't be crossing the water like that. Would you give five cloths to your sultan to bury his wife? Stop fooling now! His people love him and you offend him like this.'

The sultan and the elders laughed when this was translated

for them. The sultan's body trembled and shook with the force of his pleasure. 'He's his son,' Nyundo whispered to the merchant. 'I heard him say.'

'Merchant, don't you laugh?' the young man asked. 'Or does your god not let you do that either? You'd better do your laughing while you can, because I don't think you'll be getting many jokes out of Chatu.'

They settled at a hundred and twenty rolls of cloth. The sultan also demanded guns and gold, but the merchant smiled and said they did not do that kind of trade. Not any more, the young man said. In the end, the sultan gave permission to the merchant to speak to the boatmen and negotiate his own price with them. 'We've just been robbed,' Mohammed Abdalla whispered angrily.

'We left two of our men with you when we visited last year,' the merchant said smilingly. 'They were unwell and you agreed to look after them until they recovered. How did they fare? Are they well?'

'They left,' the young man said calmly, but his face had a look of contempt and defiance.

'Where did they go?' Uncle Aziz asked gently.

'Am I their uncle? They left,' he said angrily. 'Go look for them out there. Do you think I don't know you people?'

'I left them in the care of the sultan,' Uncle Aziz said. Yusuf thought he could tell from his voice that the merchant had already given up the two men.

'Do you want to go to Marungu or not?' the young man asked.

The boatman they were taken to was called Kakanyaga. He was a small sinewy man, who looked away from them towards the water as he listened quietly to their needs and asked· questions about numbers and weight. They returned with him to where their goods and the porters were waiting, so he could judge for himself. They would cross in four of their large canoes, he said. He then stated a price for himself and his boatmen and strolled away, to allow them time to consider. But the price was so reasonable, and Mohammed Abdalla was so keen to leave, that they summoned the boatman back before he had gone a few paces.

They would leave in the morning, the boatman said. And the goods they had agreed were to be given to them before they left.

'Why not leave straight away?' Mohammed Abdalla asked. He had been made uneasy by the amount of beer he had seen the sultan consuming. Who knows what a drunken savage may dream up?

'My men have to prepare,' the boatman said. 'Are you in such a rush to get to Chatu? If we leave now we will be travelling through the night. It's not safe on the water at certain hours.'

'There are bad spirits out at night, are there?' the mnyapara asked. The boatman heard the mockery but did not reply. They would leave in the morning, he said.

'You speak our language well,' said Uncle Aziz, smiling pleasantly. 'And so does the son of your sultan.'

'Many of us worked for a Mswahili trader, Hamidi Matanga, who used to travel in these parts and even on the other side,' the boatman said reluctantly, then refused to say more despite Uncle Aziz's invitation.

'Last time we were here I remember that your sultan spoke a little Kiswahili too, but he seems to have forgotten it,' the merchant said, still smiling. 'Time cheats all of us like that. Tell me, the two wounded men we left behind when we visited last year . . . What happened to them? Did they get better?' As he spoke, he passed to the boatman a small packet of tobacco and a bag of nails which he had asked Yusuf to fetch for him.

The boatman waited for some moments before answering, looking from the merchant to the mnyapara and Simba Mwene, who was now with them, and at last at Yusuf. His eyes sparkled slightly before he spoke, hinting at some mischief. 'They left. I don't think they got better. They were here in that hut, smelling bad. They brought disease to us. Animals died and the fish went away. Then a young man died without reason. His age. The same age as him,' he said, looking at Yusuf. 'That was too much. The people said the men must leave.'

After the boatman left, Simba Mwene said, 'They do magic here.'

'Don't blaspheme,' Mohammed Abdalla said sharply. 'They're just ignorant savages who believe their own childish nightmares.'

'We shouldn't have left them here. It was my responsibility, my mistake,' Uncle Aziz said. 'But that knowledge doesn't help them or their relatives much now.'

'What knowledge was necessary, seyyid, to guess that these beasts would sacrifice anything to carry on their ignorant way of life? I would've done the same. Why don't you ask them to do magic and bring our two men back?' the mnyapara asked Simba Mwene scornfully.

Simba Mwene winced. 'We'd better watch out for the young man,' he said, glancing at Yusuf. 'That's what I meant. Make sure he comes to no harm. You remember the way they spoke of him at Mkata, and the way the boatman looked at him.'

'What will they do? Feed him to their hungry demons? You take these stinking fishermen too seriously, I think. Let them try anything!' cried Mohammed Abdalla, shaking his cane with anger. 'What can you be thinking of? I'll lash the bastards to the threshold of Hell. I'll vomit on them. I'll give them magic up their smelly arses, the filthy savages.'

'Mohammed Abdalla,' Uncle Aziz said sharply.

'Everyone look sharp,' the mnyapara said, making no sign that he had heard the merchant but none the less dropping his voice. 'Simba, explain to the men about magic and evil diseases. You know how to do this. It means something to you. And tell them not to go too far into the thickets when nature calls otherwise a spirit or a magic snake may nip their arses. And tell them to keep away from the women. Young man, stay with the seyyid at all times and don't fret.'

'Mohammed Abdalla, you'll give yourself indigestion with all your shouting,' Uncle Aziz said.

'Seyyid, this is an evil place,' the mnyapara said. 'Let's get away from here.'

4

A fight broke out between two of the porters before they left the next day. One of them had stolen a hoe from the trade goods to pay for the company of a woman. The other porter had reported his theft to the mnyapara, who announced in front of everyone that the first porter's share of the journey would be cut by the value of two hoes. The mnyapara used many filthy words as he passed this sentence. It was not the first time the porter had stolen to trade for a woman and Mohammed Abdalla made a show of having to restrain himself from swinging the cane at him. The other men made the porter's humiliation greater by adding their own jeering rebuke. As soon as he could, once the ceremony of humiliation was over, the wounded porter threw himself at the informer, and the two were given the space and encouragement to beat each other thoroughly. A large crowd formed to watch, rolling over the open spaces by the water as they followed the fight, shouting their excitement and cheering. In the end, the

145

merchant sent Simba Mwene to stop the fight. 'We must see to our affairs.' he said.

It was late in the morning by the time they were ready to leave. As the moment for boarding the boats approached, their high spirits had an edge of anxiety. The boatman, Kakanyaga, disposed the loads himself and instructed Uncle Aziz and Yusuf to board his canoe. 'The young man will bring us luck,' he said. The boatmen paddled steadily in the rising heat, their bare backs and arms glistening. They kept the canoes in close formation, close enough to throw snatches of song at each other and laugh at the replies. The travellers sat silently for the most part, troubled by the immensity of the water and the strong men in whose hands their lives lay. Most of them were not swimmers, even though their homes were by the sea. Their feet would cross a lifetime of mountains and plains but still retreat hurriedly from the hissing tides which washed their shores.

After they had been travelling for nearly two hours, the skies quickly darkened and a strong wind sprang up, apparently out of nowhere. 'Yallah!' Yusuf heard the merchant say softly. Kakanyaga called the wind by its name, shouting it out to the men who were with him and to the other boats. They all knew from the yells of the boatmen and the intensity of their strokes that they were in danger. The waves rose higher and swept into the flimsy craft, drenching the men and their goods and releasing torrents of nervous complaints, as if what mattered most to them at that time was to keep dry. Some of the porters began to cry out and call to God, pleading for time to change their ways. Kakanyaga in the lead boat changed direction and the other canoes followed. The boatmen paddled furiously, encouraging each other with cries which sounded close to panic. The waves were now powerful enough to lift the craft out of the water and drop them down again. To Yusuf it seemed suddenly obvious how frail dugout canoes were, as likely to roll over in rough water as a twig in a gutter. Snatches of prayers and weeping intermittently rose, muffled by the roaring air. Some of the men vomited over themselves with terror. Through it all Kakanyaga was silent except for deep grunts of effort which escaped him as he paddled on one knee while sweat and lake water streamed off his back. Then at last they saw an island in the distance.

'The shrine. We can make a sacrifice there,' he called out to the merchant.

The sight of the island made the men row more furiously, amid hysterical cries of encouragement from their passengers. When they knew they were safe, the boatmen broke into shouts of triumph and cries of thanksgiving. Their passengers did not begin smiling until the canoes were pulled up out of the water and all the goods unloaded. After which they huddled from the wind and spray behind bushes and rocks, heaving great sighs and muttering about their luck.

Kakanyaga asked the merchant for a black cloth, a white cloth, some red beads and a small bag of flour. Anything else the merchant wanted to give would also be welcome, only it must not be anything made of metal. Metal scorches the hand of the spirit of this shrine, Kakanyaga said. 'You will have to come too,' he said. 'The prayer is for you and your journey. And bring the young man. The spirit of this shrine is Pembe, and he likes youth. Repeat his name to yourself when we enter the shrine, but don't say it aloud unless you hear me say it.'

They walked a short distance through sharp-leaved bushes and grasses, accompanied by the mnyapara and some of the boatmen. In a clearing bounded by dark shrubs and tall trees they saw a small canoe propped up with stones. Inside it were gifts of other travellers who had made offerings here.

Kakanyaga made them repeat words after him which he translated for them. 'We have brought you these gifts. We beg you to give us peace on this journey, so we can go and return safely.'

Then he placed the gifts in the boat and circled it once in one direction and once in the other. The merchant gave Kakanyaga the bag of tobacco he had brought, and the boatman put that too in the shrine. By the time they returned to the boats, the wind had dropped.

'Like magic,' Simba Mwene said, laughing at the mnyapara

Mohammed Abdalla gave him an unfriendly look and shook his head disbelievingly. 'It could have been worse. They might have wanted us to eat something disgusting or copulate with beasts,' he said. 'Haya, let's load up.'

The sun was setting as they caught sight of the other shore, and the slanting rays lit up the red cliffs so that they looked like a wall of flames. It was near midnight when they reached land, and the night sky was blanked out by clouds. They pulled the canoes out of the water, but Kakanyaga would not allow anyone to sleep on land. Who knew what walked the land in the dark? he said.

5

In the morning Kakanyaga and his boatmen left as soon as the canoes were unloaded, at first light, leaving the travellers and their packs on the beach. Soon people began to appear and ask them their business. Who had brought them there? How far had they come? Where were they heading? What were they after? Yusuf and Simba Mwene were sent to find the chief men of the town, which looked bigger than the one they had come from across the water. They were directed to the house of a man called Marimbo, whom they found only recently risen from sleep. He was a thin old man, his face deeply lined and loose fleshed. His house looked no different from others nearby, and the woman who had guided them to it walked up to the door and knocked on it unhesitatingly, without deference or ceremony. Marimbo was pleased to see them, curious and hospitable. Yusuf could see that he was watchful despite his good humour, and guessed that much of life's business had gone through his hands. Nyundo had come with them to translate, but they had no need of him.

'Chatu!' Marimbo said, and a small knowing grin escaped him before he carefully suppressed it. 'Chatu is a difficult man. I hope you mean business. He's not someone to trifle with. His town is only a few days away, but we never go there unless he summons us. He can be fierce if he thinks he's wronged, but he is a watchful father to his people. Agh, I would hate to live there. My friends, let me tell you, they don't like strangers in Chatu's town.'

'He sounds like a clown,' Simba Mwene said.

Marimbo laughed, sharing the joke watchfully.

'Does he trade?' Simba Mwene asked.

Marimbo shrugged. 'He has ivory. He'll trade if he wants to.'

He agreed to supply a guide and to store any of their goods upon their return. 'I have dealt with traders many times before,' he said. 'Don't give me any of your cloths. Where would your trade be without these cloths? This is how you've bought your way across this land. Give me two guns, so I can send my sons hunting for ivory. Have you any silk? Give me silk. The guide I'll give you knows the country well. It's not a good time now that the rains have come, but if you pay him well enough, you can trust him completely.'

The land was heavily wooded on this bank and rose steeply. Though there were more people in Marimbo's town, more of

149

them looked ill. At night, swarms of mosquitoes descended on the men, stinging with such violence that some of their victims cried out with pain and exasperation. There was nothing to keep them in the town once they had concluded their arrangements with Marimbo. He took knives and hoes, and a pack of white cotton cloth in return for looking after their goods. They would settle fully with him on the way back. The frenzied attentions of the mosquitoes made everyone happy to leave. Uncle Aziz too was eager to go. Their merchandise was now seriously depleted after all the tributes they had had to pay during the journey, and they had hardly done any trade. But there was enough left to make it worth while, Uncle Aziz said. This was what they had travelled all this way for, to these lands of Marungu behind the red cliffs.

Early the following day they set off for Chatu's country. The guide Marimbo had found for them was a tall quiet man. He did not talk or smile at them, but waited on one side while they made their packs ready. They travelled on narrow country paths, beating uphill through lush vegetation. Strange plants whipped into them and lacerated their faces and their feet. Clouds of insects circled their heads. When they stopped to rest, the insects alighted on them and sought out orifices and tender flesh. At the end of their first day in Marungu several of them had fallen ill. They were tormented by mosquitoes in such numbers that in the morning their faces were bloodied and scarred with bites. They pressed on the next day, anxious to get out of the overpowering forest through which they were travelling. All night they had heard crashes and growls in the bushes, and had huddled together in fear of buffaloes and snakes. *Don't go too far for a piss*, Simba Mwene teased. The mnyapara hectored the men to keep up, swishing his cane at the stragglers and breaking through the forest din with his abuse. The rising ground made progress difficult.

Simba Mwene and Nyundo kept up with the guide, shouting out warnings whenever new horrors were approaching. Nyundo was the only one who could understand the guide, and he made as much mischief as he could out of this, irritating the mnyapara and making the others laugh. The guide said little and sat beside Nyundo at the end of the day's march.

By the third day, the afflicted men were desperately ill and others were showing signs of decline. The worst ones could neither eat nor prevent their bodies from evacuating. Their fellows carried their stinking bodies in turn, ignoring their delirious groans as much as was possible and trying to evade the black blood that oozed out of them. On the steep inclines the men could only move a few feet at a time, dragging their burdens on hands and knees. On the fourth day two of the men died. They buried them quickly and waited an hour while the merchant silently read a sura from the Koran. All of them were now tormented by festering sores, which the insects dug deep into to lay their eggs and draw fresh blood. In their terror the men were certain that the guide was leading them to their deaths and watched him as well as they could in their wretchedness. The mnyapara berated the guide often, staring at Nyundo with unconcealed disgust as he made the translation. This was not the way they had come last year. Where was he taking them? Stop your clowning and ask these questions properly.

The other route is not safe after the rains, Nyundo translated.

When two more men were found dead on the fifth morning, eyes turned to the guide, who was waiting with Nyundo for the start of the day's journey. Mohammed Abdalla strode to the guide and hauled him to his feet, then to the cheers and encouragement of the porters and guards he lashed him with his cane again and again while the man cowered under the blows and begged for mercy. Nyundo tried to intervene, but Mohammed Abdalla hit him two swift blows of the cane across his face, making him retreat with a cry of alarm. *My eyes.* The mnyapara returned to the guide, who in the end rolled on the ground, howling and weeping as each new blow cut into his bare flesh. Still the mnyapara flogged the guide, and other men began to press near, sticks and thongs in their hands.

Simba Mwene came hurrying to the mnyapara and held his arm, then tried to shield the screaming guide with his body. 'He's had enough! He's had enough now,' he pleaded. Mohammed Abdalla was heaving for breath, his face and arms covered with sweat as he struggled to land more blows around Simba Mwene's body.

'Let me beat the dog!' he cried. 'He's trying to kill us in this forest.'

'He said one more day. We'll be out of this hell by to-morrow . . .' Simba Mwene said, herding the mynapara away.

'He's a lying savage. And that clown Nyundo, instead of keeping an eye on him . . . This man has been lying to us all the time. We didn't come this way last year,' Mohammed Abdalla said. Suddenly, he broke free from Simba Mwene and returned to the fallen man to deliver another frenzy of lashes. When Simba Mwene rushed up to him again, Mohammed Abdalla turned to him with glaring eyes.

'What you're doing is not just,' Simba Mwene said, retreating.

The mnyapara stared speechlessly, his face streaming. The merchant detached himself from the crowd of men and spoke briefly and softly to Mohammed Abdalla, holding him by the arm. He then signalled for Yusuf and told him to arrange the burial of the two men who had died that morning. And read

Ya Sin for them, he said. All day they heard the groans of the guide ahead of them as they beat through the thinning forest. Nyundo struggled silently behind the guide, his face puffing angrily from the blows he had received. The men laughed and shook their heads, embarrassed at their levity but finding the guide's pain irresistible. The way that mnyapara beat him! they said. Lo, that Mohammed Abdalla is an animal, a killer! As for Nyundo, he should've known the mnyapara would get him one day.

In mid-morning on the sixth day they reached open ground. They rested until the afternoon and then set off for Chatu's town. As their column approached, travelling past cultivated fields and small barns, they saw people racing away from them. Though they were exhausted, the musicians beat out their tunes to announce the approach of the column, and each man walked as upright as he could. Mohammed Abdalla swaggered behind the musicans, putting on his usual show in case the riff-raff were watching from the bushes.

They were met by a deputation of elders from the sultan, accompanied by a huge laughing crowd of townspeople. The elders led them to a large clearing surrounded by long, low houses with roofs of thatch. The large house behind thick mud walls is Chatu's residence, the elders said. Rest here and the people will come to sell you food.

'Ask if we may be allowed to greet the sultan,' the merchant said to Nyundo.

'He asks what for?' Nyundo said after speaking to the chief of the elders. He was a short man with grizzled grey hair whose eyes roved over Nyundo's wounded face as they talked. He spoke with angry, aggressive dignity, and an unmistakable edge of dislike. Nyundo told the merchant that the elder's name was Mfipo.

'We passed near your town the last time we came through

here and heard a great deal about your sultan. We've come back to bring him gifts and to trade with him and his people,' Uncle Aziz said.

Nyundo had trouble with this and asked the help of the guide. The crowd pressed in on them to hear these exchanges, but drew back when Mfipo glared at them. 'Mfipo asks what have you brought for him?' Nyundo said after several exchanges. 'They had better be rich gifts, because Chatu is a noble ruler. He doesn't want any of your trinkets, he says.' Nyundo grinned after he said this, making it clear that Mfipo had said more.

'We would like to present our gifts to him,' the merchant said after a long silent look. 'It would give us great pleasure.'

Mfipo looked contemptuously at the merchant and then laughed briefly. He spoke slowly, giving Nyundo time. 'He says we have need of rest and medicine, not of trade. He'll send the healer to us. Let the young man bring the gifts for Chatu. He means him, Yusuf. He wants him to go to Chatu. If Chatu is pleased he may summon you too. I think that's what he said.'

'Everyone wants Yusuf,' the merchant said with a smile.

Mfipo ignored further attempts to address him and strode away. After he had taken a few steps he turned round and beckoned the guide. The merchant and the mnyapara exchanged brief glances. The people of the town brought food to trade with the travellers, and disposed themselves comfortably among them, asking questions and joking with them. The words they spoke were impenetrable, unless Nyundo was available and willing, but they managed to understand enough. They spoke of the size of their town and the power of their ruler. If you have come here to make any mischief you'll regret it, they said. What mischief? the men said. We're traders. Men of peace. Our zeal is only in making trade. We leave trouble to the deranged and the lazy. Mohammed Abdalla bought timber and thatch to build a temporary shelter for the sick and for the merchandise. He supervised the construction in the fading light, making the crowd laugh with his shouts and his antics. Afterwards he ordered that all the packs be piled neatly in the middle of the shelter and that they be constantly guarded.

When the merchant had washed himself and prayed, he called Yusuf to him and instructed him on the gifts he should take to Chatu. *If we trade well here, this will make our whole journey worth while*, he said. Mohammed Abdalla thought they should wait until the morning, put a good strong guard on for the night and sit tight. Only two of their guns were armed, perhaps they should arm a couple more of the ones packed away. The merchant shook his head. He was keen that the gifts should be sent before nightfall, in case the sultan was offended by their lack of courtesy. Yusuf could see that Uncle Aziz was worried, or perhaps a little excited. Let's see if that Mfipo was barking for himself or for his master, he said. Simba Mwene, who was to go with Yusuf, hurriedly put together the merchandise and selected five porters to carry it across the clearing to Chatu's residence. Nyundo would also have to go as their voice. His good humour was on the mend with his new importance, but the men teased him that he was making up the translations as he went along. He frequently felt the weals on his face, stroking the broken flesh absent-mindedly.

They entered the walled courtyard of Chatu's residence without being challenged. Inside the courtyard they waited for someone to approach and direct them, and soon two young men came to them and said they were Chatu's sons. People were sitting outside the houses and some glanced at them without great interest. Children ran about, engrossed in their games.

'We've brought gifts to the sultan,' Yusuf said.

'And the greetings of the seyyid. Tell them that too,' Simba Mwene added firmly, as if faulting Yusuf.

The two young men escorted them to one of the houses, distinguished from the others by the wide terrace at the front of it. Several men were sitting on low benches on the terrace. Mfipo and the other elders were among them. As they approached, a slim man rose from a bench and stood smiling, waiting for them. When they were near enough he stepped off the terrace and came towards them with an outstretched hand and words of welcome. It was as if he was pleased to see them. The friendliness and the easy charm were not what Yusuf had expected from everything he had heard about Chatu. He escorted them to the terrace and listened with an appearance of discomfort to the fulsome greetings from the merchant which Simba Mwene conveyed through Nyundo. At times he looked surprised at what Nyundo said, even sceptical.

'He says you honour him too much,' Nyundo said. 'As for the gifts, he thanks me for my generosity. Now he says please sit down and don't make a noise. He wants me to tell him my news.'

'Don't be a fool,' Simba Mwene growled at him. 'We haven't come here to play. Just tell us what he says and never mind the jokes.'

'He says sit,' Nyundo said defiantly. 'And don't shout at me, otherwise you can talk to him yourself. Anyway, he wants to know what has brought us among them.'

'Trade,' Simba Mwene said, and then glanced at Yusuf, inviting him to elaborate.

Chatu turned his full smiling gaze at Yusuf, leaning back to get a fuller view of him. Yusuf could not speak for a moment, held by Chatu's comfortable scrutiny. He tried to smile back, but his face resisted, and he knew he must look foolish and frightened. Chatu laughed softly, his teeth gleaming in the sinking light. 'Our merchant will explain what he has to trade,' Yusuf said at last, his heart light with anxiety. 'He has only sent us to you to convey his respect, and to ask that you allow him to call on you tomorrow.'

Chatu laughed delightedly when this was translated for him. 'How well spoken you are, he says,' said Nyundo, affecting Chatu's light air. 'I changed all the words to make you sound wiser than you are, but there's no need to thank me. About the merchant, he says anyone can call on him whenever they want. He's nothing but a servant to his people, he says. He wants to know if you are a servant to the merchant or if you are his son.'

'A servant,' Yusuf said, savouring the humiliation.

Chatu turned away from him and addressed Simba Mwene for a few minutes. Nyundo struggled with this and spoke for only a few moments to Chatu's minutes. 'He will see the merchant tomorrow, if all is well. The guide has told him about our journey through the forest. May our companions recover quickly, he says. Oh, and now listen to what he's saying. He says look after this beautiful young man. That is what he said. Look after this beautiful young man. Do you want me to ask him if he has a daughter he wants betrothed? Or maybe he wants you for himself. Simba, we'll be lucky to get this one back to the coast without someone stealing him from us.'

Simba Mwene delivered an enthusiastic report to the merchant, and infected both him and the mnyapara with his eagerness. How friendly he was, and so reasonable. *We will trade well here*, the merchant said. *I've already heard that they have a lot of ivory to sell.* Most of the men were stretched out on the ground, exhausted. Before long the travellers' camp had fallen

157

silent, and the guards were making themselves comfortable against whatever support they could find. Yusuf fell asleep at once but woke up suddenly in the midst of clamour and flashing lights. He had been struggling up a steep mountain, menaced by jutting rocks and prowling beasts. As he cleared the cliff's edge, he saw before him thunderous waters and beyond that a high wall with a gate of flame. The light was the colour of plague, and the birdsong was a prophecy of pestilence. A shadowy figure appeared beside him and said gently, *You have come through very well.* At least there was no slavering dog rummaging into him, he thought wryly to himself, conscious of the tremors of terror subsiding within him. He was ashamed of the fear which rose in him at these silent hours of their travels, and as he peered at the sleeping men around him, he tried not to remember that they were so near the edges of the known world.

He was asleep again when Chatu's men fell upon them from all sides. They slaughtered the guards at once and captured their weapons, then clubbed the sleeping men awake. There was no resistance, so complete was the surprise. The travellers were herded into the middle of the open clearing by jeering and jubilant men. Torches were lit and held high above the milling crowd of captives, who were instructed to squat on the ground with their hands on their heads. The packs of merchandise they had brought on their shoulders were taken away into the darkness by laughing men and women. Until first light, their captors circled them gleefully, mocking them with their antics and beating some of them.

The travellers shouted words of encouragement to each other, and the voice of Mohammed Abdalla rose above the groans and wails, yelling at the men and calling on them to be steadfast. Some of the men were weeping. Four among them had been killed and several injured. In the light Yusuf saw that the mnyapara was hit. Moist blood covered the side of his face and his clothes. 'Cover the dead,' Mohammed Abdalla said. 'Make them decent, may God have mercy on them.' When he saw Yusuf he smiled. 'At least our young man is still with us. It would only have brought bad luck to lose him.'

'The luck of the Devil,' someone shouted. 'Look what luck he's brought us so far. Look at how everything has turned out for us. We've lost everything.'

'They'll kill us,' cried another man.

'Trust in God,' said the merchant. Yusuf shuffled without rising to bring himself closer to Uncle Aziz. The merchant smiled and patted him on the shoulder. 'Don't be afraid,' he said.

As it became lighter, the townspeople came to look at the captives, laughing and throwing stones at them. They kept an eye on them all morning, neglecting their affairs and watching the knot of huddled men as if they expected them to do something strange or unexpected. The prisoners were forced to relieve themselves where they sat, to the great excitement of the children and the dogs. Late in the morning, Mfipo came to summon the merchant before Chatu. His talk was sneering and loud. 'He wants him too,' Nyundo said, pointing at the mnyapara. 'And the two who went last night.'

Chatu was sitting on his terrace again, surrounded by elders. The courtyard was full of people, jubilant with smiles. Chatu rose to his feet but did not approach the prisoners. His face was solemn. He beckoned Nyundo, who approached with reluctance. 'He says he will speak slowly so that I will understand everything he tells me,' Nyundo announced to the others. 'I'll do my best, brothers, but forgive me if I get it wrong.'

'Trust in God,' the merchant said gently.

Chatu looked at him with dislike and then began to speak. 'This is what he says,' Nyundo began, pausing after every few words until Chatu spoke again. 'We did not ask you to come, and we have no welcome for you. Your intentions are not generous, and by coming among us you only bring us evil and calamity. You have come here to do us harm. We have suffered from others like you who have preceded you, and have no intention of suffering again. They came among our neighbours and captured them and took them away. After their first visit to our land only calamities have befallen us. And you have come to add to them. Our crops do not grow, children are born lame and diseased, our animals die from unheard-of diseases. Unspeakable events have taken place since your presence among us. You have come and brought evil into our world. This is what he says.'

'We have only come to trade,' the merchant said, but Chatu did not wait for this to be translated.

'He doesn't want to hear you, bwana tajiri,' Nyundo explained hastily, struggling to keep up with Chatu's words. 'He says we will not wait until you have made slaves of us and swallowed up our world. When your like first came to this land you were hungry and naked, and we fed you. Some of them were ill and we cared for them until they were well. Then you lied to us and cheated us. Those are his words. Listen to him speak! Who's telling lies now? He says do you think we are beasts that we should go on accepting treatment like that? All these goods you brought with you belong to us, because all the goods produced by the land are ours. So we are taking them away from you. That's what he said.'

'Then you will be robbing us,' said the merchant. 'Tell him that before he begins again. Everything that we brought with us is rightly ours, and we came here to trade those goods for ivory and gold and whatever else of value –'

Chatu interrupted to demand a translation, which when it came was greeted with howls of derision from the crowd. Then Chatu spoke again, his face angry and scornful. 'He says only our lives belong to us now,' Nyundo said.

'We're grateful that he allows us that,' the merchant said with a smile. Nyundo did not convey this. Chatu pointed at the merchant's money belt and instructed one of his men to tear if off him.

A sigh issued from the gathered multitude as Chatu glared at the merchant. After a moment he spoke again, slowly and menacingly, allowing his anger and loathing to fill his mouth. 'He says that enough calamities have descended on them. He doesn't want our blood on their land. Otherwise he would have made sure we will not trouble any other people in this world. But he says that before we can leave, he wants to teach one of your servants some manners. That is what he said.' At a signal from Chatu the guide who had come with them through the forest moved out from the crowd and touched Mohammed Abdalla on the chest, making the mnyapara wince with involuntary disgust. When Chatu gave a sign two men held Mohammed Abdalla while others beat him with sticks. Blood spurted out of his nostrils as his body jerked under the force of their blows. The crowd's glee drowned any noise the mnyapara made, making his convulsions seem like mute play-acting. They went on beating him even after he fell on the ground and lay still. When they stopped, spasmodic ripples ran over the mnyapara's body.

Yusuf saw that tears were running down Uncle Aziz's face.

Chatu spoke again. The crowd groaned with disappointment, and some of the elders shook their heads in dissent. Chatu spoke again, raising his voice against the murmur of dissent. As he spoke, he kept his eyes on Nyundo but pointed at the merchant. 'He says now take your evil caravan and go away from here,' Nyundo said. 'His people don't like it, but he says he does not want to bring any more calamity on the land. He says when he looks on young people like him, he hopes that we cannot all be evil kidnappers and hunters of flesh ... and that makes him feel mercy. Go now, he says, before he changes his mind and takes back his gesture of kindness. The young man has brought us luck at last.'

'Mercy belongs to God,' the merchant said. 'Tell him that. Tell him carefully. Mercy belongs to God. It is not for him to give or withdraw. Tell him that carefully.'

Chatu stared at the merchant in disbelief while the elders and those who were near enough to hear Nyundo's softly spoken words laughed and jeered. 'He says that's a brave tongue you've got in your mouth. He's telling you again, in case it was wagging without your direction. Take your men and leave. That's what he's saying, bwana. And I think he's getting angry again.'

'Not without our goods,' the merchant said. 'Tell him that if it is our lives he wants he can have them. They are worthless. But if we are to have our lives we also demand our goods. How far would we get if we were unable to trade? Tell him we will not go without our goods.'

6

The merchant described to the men what had happened at the sultan's palace: the bad words Chatu spoke against them, the beating of Mohammed Abdalla, the confiscation of all their goods, their expulsion from the town, and the merchant's refusal to leave. He invited anyone who wished to leave to do so. The men shouted and swore their loyalty to the merchant and vowed to accept the fate that God decreed. Simba Mwene told them how Yusuf's youth had saved them from worse, which provoked cheers and filthy remarks. Then they sat quietly, as they were required by their captors, and were forced to reflect on their empty stomachs and their ailing companions. There was no shade to hide from the sun, and as the day passed the grumbling became intense. They built awnings for the wounded with their clothes, holding them up with sticks and string.

The mnyapara had recovered his mind, although he was feeble and shaking with the beginnings of fever. He lay groaning on the ground, muttering words which no one bothered to try to understand. His eyes flew blearily open every few minutes, and he looked around him as if he had no knowledge of where he was. The men waited on the decision of the merchant, arguing among themselves about what was best. Shouldn't they go while they were still safe? Who could tell what Chatu would do next? What were they to do now? If they stayed in the town they would starve, if they left without their goods they would starve. Or someone was sure to take them captive.

'Look how stupid the human body is,' Uncle Aziz said to Yusuf, his distant indestructible smile beginning to hover again on the corners of his face. 'Look at our valiant bin Abdalla and how his body turns out so absurdly frail and untrustworthy. A weaker man would never recover from a beating like that, but he will. Only matters are worse than that, for our nature is also base and treacherous. If I had not known different, I would have believed the claims of that angry sultan. In us he sees something he desires to destroy, and he tells us stories so that we can agree to gratify him. If only we could leave our bodies to themselves, and be sure that they will know how to look to their well-being and pleasure. Yusuf, you can hear the men complaining. What do you think we should do? Perhaps a dream came to you in the night and you can interpret it to our salvation, as the other Yusuf did,' Uncle Aziz said with a smile.

Yusuf shook his head, unable to say that he could not see any hope for them.

'Then in that case it's best that we stay here and starve. Will that shame the sultan with his cruelty?' the merchant asked, drawing a wince of sympathy from Yusuf.

'Simba,' the merchant called, beckoning Simba Mwene nearer. 'What do you think? Should we leave without our goods or should we stay here until we get them?'

'We should leave and then return to make war,' Simba Mwene said without a moment's pause.

'Without weapons or the means to buy them? And how would such a war end?' the merchant asked.

In the afternoon Chatu sent them some ripe bananas and boiled yam, and some dried game meat. Some of the towns-people brought them water to drink and to clean themselves. Later Chatu sent for the merchant, who went accompanied by Nyundo, Simba Mwene and Yusuf. There were no crowds in Chatu's courtyard this time, but the elders still sat on the terrace, comfortable and at ease, having forsaken their cere-monial poses. Perhaps they always sat there, Yusuf thought, like the old men at the shop. Chatu spoke quietly, as if he had arrived at these words after long reflection. 'He says that two years ago a group of our people came through here,' Nyundo said, leaning forward to hear the sultan's softly spoken words. 'Some of them pale skinned like you, bwana tajiri, and others darker. They had come to trade, they said. Like you did. He says he gave them gold and ivory and some fine leather. Their merchant said they did not have enough goods to pay, and they would go and come back with the rest. Since then he has not seen them. This merchant is our brother, he says. So our goods will now pay back our brother's debt. This is what he says'.

The merchant made to speak, but Chatu began to talk
again, forcing Nyundo to attend. 'He says he doesn't want to
know what you think about this. He has wasted enough time
with you. Do you take him for a khoikhoi? A khoikhoi will let
strangers steal from him while he dances under the moon. He
just wants you to go before something bad happens. Not
everyone here is happy with this solution, he says, but he
wishes to bring this matter to an end. After careful thought,
this is what he has decided. He will give you some goods to
trade, enough to get us out of his land. Now he wishes to
know if you have anything to say in reply.'

The merchant was silent for a long moment. 'Tell him his
decision shows him to be a ruler of wisdom, but his judgement
is not just,' he said in the end.

Chatu smiled when this was translated to him. 'What has
brought you here all the way from your home? A search for
justice? This is what he asks. If that is the case, he says, then
you have found it. I am taking your goods so I can give
justice to my people for the goods they lost to your brother.
Now you go and seek this brother who stole from me and get
your justice from him. I think that is what he said.'

They resumed the next day, arguing about the amount of
goods the merchant would be allowed to take, about the value
of what had been taken, about what was owed to Chatu. The
elders sat around them offering what wisdom they could,
which Chatu genially disregarded. The younger men wanted
the three guns they had taken from the guards given to them
at once so they could go hunting, but Chatu ignored them
too. None of the women approached, although Yusuf could
see them wandering around the courtyard after their own
affairs. Nyundo struggled to deliver everyone's words and
both sides watched him suspiciously. The merchant asked that
while they were still held in Chatu's town, until the men had

165

recovered well enough to travel, could they be allowed to move freely and perhaps do some work for the townspeople in return for food? Chatu agreed on condition of Yusuf being left with him as a hostage. That night, while Yusuf slept on the terrace of one of the houses in Chatu's courtyard, two of the travellers escaped undetected to look for help.

Yusuf was well treated in Chatu's house. The sultan himself spoke to him, though Yusuf could not understand more than a few words. Or he thought he understood, so many of the words sounded familiar. From the look on Chatu's face and from what words Yusuf understood, he guessed the subjects of his questions and answered along those lines: how far they had travelled, how many people lived in his land, what made them travel these distances. Yusuf spoke solemnly about these matters, but neither the sultan nor any of his elders appeared to understand what he was saying either. When the merchant came for another round of haggling on the following day, he looked searchingly at Yusuf and then smiled.

'All is well with me,' Yusuf said.

'You've come through very well,' Uncle Aziz said, still smiling. 'Come and sit with me so we can hear the sultan's stories about you.'

Yusuf was not allowed to leave the walled courtyard, nor was he expected to approach the terrace, where Chatu and the elders spent so much of the day, unless he was called. Did the elders not have work they liked to do, or farms to look after or even gaze at with admiration and pleasure? Perhaps the presence of the caravan in their town had required them to abandon everything else. Yusuf too sat all day in the shade waiting for time to pass, watching the women as they worked. To a visitor it might have seemed that all any of them ever did with their days was sit in the shade staring ahead of them.

The women teased him, shouting remarks at him with wide

smiles, though neither the remarks nor the smiles felt entirely kind. They sent the younger girls over with small gifts and propositions. Yusuf took them to be propositions, anyway, and translated them to himself to pass the time. Come and see me this afternoon while my husband is taking his nap. Do you want a hand-bath? Have you got an itch you'd like me to scratch? Sometimes they hooted with laughter as they shouted at him, and one of the old women blew kisses and wiggled her bottom whenever she passed by. The girl who brought him food stared unashamedly at him, sitting a few feet away while he ate. She spoke to him now and then, frowning and intense. He kept his eyes away from her barely covered chest. She drew his eyes to the beads she wore round her neck, lifting them up slightly for his admiration.

'Beads. I know what they are,' Yusuf said. 'I don't understand why people like beads so much. In some of the places we've passed people sell a whole sheep for a handful of them. They're only trinkets. What can you do with beads?'

'What's your name?' he asked her another time but failed to make her understand. He thought her lovely, with a slim pointed face and smiling eyes. Often she sat near him without speaking, and he felt he should be more manly but did not want to show her disrespect. Whenever he made a sign that he needed something, it was she who was called for. Even Chatu started to tease him about it when Uncle Aziz came to haggle. 'He says he hears that our young man has already married one of their girls, and we will have to add this to our debt,' Nyundo said, grinning at Yusuf. 'You've been working fast, you filthy devil. He says let him stay with us and give Bati sons. What is this trading to do with a healthy young man like him? He says let him stay here and Bati will teach him about life.'

Bati, that was her name. Yusuf saw now that whenever Bati

approached him, people watching exchanged looks and smiled. On his fourth night in Chatu's courtyard the girl came to see him after dark. She sat by his mat, humming softly while her hand ran over his face and hair. He stroked her without speaking, overwhelmed by the comfort and pleasure he felt at these caresses. She did not stay long and left suddenly, as if she had remembered something. All of the next day he could not keep his mind away from the girl. And every time he caught sight of her he could not hide a grin. The women clapped and called out when they saw them, laughing at the comedy.

Uncle Aziz visited Chatu again that day and made sure to have a conversation with Yusuf. 'Keep yourself ready,' he said. 'We'll be leaving one night soon. We'll try and get our goods back and then break out. There's danger.'

That night the girl came to him again and sat beside him as she had done before. They caressed each other and finally lay on the ground. He sighed with pleasure, but she sat up almost at once, ready to leave. 'Stay', he said.

She whispered something, putting the palm of her hand over his mouth. In his elation he had raised his voice, and he saw her smiling in the dark. Someone coughed in a nearby house and Bati ran off into the darkness. Yusuf lay awake for a long time, living again the brief moments of pleasure and looking forward to the morning when he would see her. He was surprised how eager his body had been for her, and how much it ached that she had left so suddenly. He thought of Chatu and of the merchant, and guessed that they would be angry about what he was doing. The thought filled him with anxiety, which he allayed by relieving himself of the urgent passion Bati had aroused. Then he turned away from himself in search of sleep.

In the morning he saw her leaving the courtyard with some

of the women, on their way to the farms. She looked over her shoulder at him, and the women laughed at her display of how everything was between them. *It's love*, they cried. *When will the wedding be?* Or at least that was what Yusuf took them to be saying.

7

In the middle of the morning a column entered the town. It was led by a European who marched his men directly to the clearing in front of Chatu's residence. A large tent was quickly pitched, and a flag-pole erected. The European, who was a tall balding man with a large beard, was dressed in a shirt and trousers, and fanned himself with a wide-brimmed hat. He sat behind a table which his men placed for him and immediately started to write in a book. His column was made up of dozens of askaris and porters, all dressed in shorts and baggy shirts. People gathered round the encampment, but were kept at a distance by the askaris, who were well armed. When the merchant heard the news of the column's arrival he hurried to meet the European, and although he was stopped by the guards at first, he made sure the European saw him. When the European finished his writing, he looked towards the man dressed in a flowing white kanzu and beckoned him nearer. His chief askari, who spoke Kiswahili fluently, stepped forward to translate. The merchant told his story hurriedly, pleading for the return of his stolen goods. After he had heard the story the European yawned and said he would rest now. When he woke up, he wanted Chatu presented to him.

The merchant and Chatu waited in the clearing for the European to wake. The big man is here now, Uncle Aziz's men taunted Chatu. He'll make you eat shit, you thief. Chatu asked Nyundo if he had ever seen Europeans before. He had heard that they could eat metal. Was that true? Anyway, when he was summoned he had come rather than bring more tragedy on his head. 'He asks do you know what kind of people they are?' Nyundo said to the merchant.

'Tell him he'll see soon enough,' the merchant said. 'But he'll be giving me back my property before this day is out.'

Yusuf stood with his fellow travellers, who teased him happily about his holiday at the sultan's house. At last the European came out of his tent, his face red and creased with sleep. He washed himself thoroughly as if he was on his own and not surrounded by hundreds of people. Then he sat at the table and ate the food which his servant placed before him. When he finished he beckoned for the merchant and Chatu to come nearer.

'Are you Chatu?' he asked.

The chief askari translated the European's words for Chatu, and Nyundo translated the askari's words for the merchant. The sultan nodded at the interpreter and turned quickly to look at the European again. He had never seen anything as strange looking as the shining red man with hair growing out of his ears, he would say later.

'You, Chatu. Have you become a big man? Is this what you think?' the interpreter asked after the European had spoken again. 'How is it you're robbing people of their possessions? Aren't you afraid of the law of the government?'

'What government? What are you talking about?' Chatu said, raising his voice at the interpreter.

'What government? Do you want to see what government? And you'd better not shout when you speak to me, my friend. Have you not heard of other big-mouthed people like you that the government has silenced and put into chains?' the interpreter asked sharply. Nyundo translated these words in a shout, making the merchant's men cheer.

'Has he come to take slaves?' Chatu asked angrily. 'This big man of yours, has he come here for slaves?'

The European spoke impatiently, his face reddening with irritation. 'Stop this useless talk,' the interpreter said. 'The government does not deal in slaves. It's these people who have been buying slaves, and the big man has come to stop them. Go and bring these people's goods before there is trouble.'

'I didn't take their goods without reason. One of their brothers took my ivory and gold,' Chatu complained, his voice rising querulously again.

'He has heard all this,' the interpreter said, taking matters fully in his own hands. 'And he does not want to hear any more of it. Bring all the goods which belong to these people. This is what the big man says . . . otherwise you'll soon know what the government can do.'

Chatu looked round the encampment, undecided what to do. Suddenly the European stood up and stretched. 'Can he eat metal?' Chatu asked.

'He can do anything he wants,' the interpreter said. 'But right now if you don't do what he says he'll make you eat shit.'

The merchant's men broke into shouts of jubilation and mockery, yelling abuse at Chatu and praying that God should damn him and his town. All the goods which remained were brought out. The European instructed that the merchant and his men should now leave, and return to wherever they had come from, leaving their three guns behind. There was no need for guns now that the government had brought order to the land. The guns were only to bring war and capture people. Go now, the big man has business with this chief, the interpreter said. The merchant would have preferred to search the houses for the missing goods, but he did not argue. They packed hurriedly, made cheerful and triumphant by their release. Yusuf looked through the crowd around them as they rushed at the preparations, hoping to catch sight of Bati for the last time. Before night had fallen they were out in the country. They retraced their painful journey to Marimbo's town on the lake, tumbling down the steep paths with a haste which was close to panic, and trusting to Simba Mwene's memory of their earlier route. He was the only one for whom their first passage through the forest had not receded into a feverish nightmare.

The men made up a song about Chatu the python which had been swallowed by a European jinn with hair growing out of his ears, but the forest muted their voices and emptied them of resonance. The merchant lamented that they had been unable to settle matters between themselves and the sultan. 'Now that the European has arrived there, he will take the whole land,' he said.

They stayed in Marimbo's town for several weeks, resting and making what trade they could, and hoping that the two men who had escaped from Chatu's town would turn up. There was little for the men to do. At first, in the joy of their escape, they were cheerfully idle, paying for dances and cele-brations and orgies of food. In the evening they played cards and told stories, slapping at the clouds of mosquitoes which hovered to torment them. Some of them chased the women of the town. They bought beer from the townspeople and drank it secretly, but in their inebriation they wept and wailed in the night streets and abused the fate that had decreed their miserable state. The mnyapara recovered from his beating, except for a wound on his calf which had not healed, but the pain and humiliation had weakened and silenced him, and he did nothing to control the men. Simba Mwene distanced himself from all of them, hiring himself to a fishing boat as a day-labourer. Before long squabbles broke out among the men. Threats were exchanged and knives flashed. Marimbo complained to the merchant about the extravagant behaviour of his people, but accepted another gift in return for continued forbearance. Yusuf saw that a weariness had descended on Uncle Aziz. His shoulders rounded and drooped, and he sat for hours without speaking. Watching him in the gloom of an evening, Yusuf suddenly saw him as a small soft animal which had lost its shell and was now stranded in the open, afraid to move. When he spoke to Yusuf his voice was still gentle and amused, but his words had neither edge nor wit. Yusuf began to fear their abandonment on this edge of nowhere. When the setting sun shone on them in the evenings sometimes, he felt that he was burning.

'Is it time we travelled?' Yusuf asked the mnyapara one day. They sat on a mat together and Yusuf tried to keep his eyes away from the glistening wound on the mnyapara's leg. He looked at the sky and felt dizzy at the profusion of brilliant stars. They seemed like a wall of bright rocks hurtling down on them.

'Speak to the seyyid,' Mohammed Abdalla said to him. 'He doesn't hear me any more. I've told him we should leave before we all rot in this hell, but a great weight is on him. He doesn't hear me.'

'What will I say? I daren't speak to him,' Yusuf said, although he knew he would.

'He has a place in his heart for you. Speak to him and listen to his replies. But then tell him we must leave. You're not a boy any more,' Mohammed Abdalla said roughly. 'Do you know why he feels kindly to you? Because you are quiet and steadfast, and at night you whimper at visions none of us can see. Perhaps he thinks you're blessed.' Yusuf smiled at the mnyapara's pun. Blessed was the polite word for madman. Mohammed Abdalla grinned back at him, pleased that he had understood his joke. After a moment he reached for Yusuf's thigh and squeezed it gently.

'How you've grown on this journey,' he said, looking away. Yusuf saw that Mohammed Abdalla had an erection under his cloth and immediately rose to leave. He heard the mnyapara chuckle to himself and then clear his throat. Yusuf went to the lakeside to watch the fishermen bringing in their last catch.

He waited until the middle of the morning, when the air had warmed and the day's burden was not yet heavy on them. 'Has the time come for us to leave, Uncle Aziz?' he said, sitting a few feet away and leaning forward to show respect. For a start he ain't your uncle! It was the first time since his bondage that he had addressed him as Uncle, but the circumstances were exceptional.

'Yes, we should have left days ago,' the merchant said and then smiled. 'Have you been concerned? I saw you keeping an eye on me. It is a kind of heaviness which has kept me here. Indolence or weariness . . . I've been hearing about these dogs of ours behaving badly, so perhaps it's time we took them out of here. We'll call the mnyapara and Simba soon, but now sit with me and tell me what you make of everything.'

They sat in silence for some minutes. Yusuf felt the reel of his life running through his hand, and he let the reel run without resistance. Then he rose and left. For a long time after, he sat silently with himself, numbed by guilt that he had been unable to keep the memory of his parents fresh in his life. He wondered if his parents still thought of him, if they still lived, and he knew that he would rather not find out. He could not resist other memories in this state, and images of his abandonment came to him in a spate. They all condemned him for self-neglect. Events had ordered his days and he had held his head above the rubble and kept his eyes on the nearer horizon, choosing ignorance rather than futile knowledge of what lay ahead. There was nothing he could think of to do which would unshackle him from the bondage to the life he lived.

For a start he ain't your uncle. He thought of Khalil and smiled despite the gloom and the sudden sense of self-pity he felt. That was how he would become, if he kept his wits. Like Khalil. Nervous and combative, hemmed in from all sides and dependent. Stranded in the middle of nowhere. He thought of his ceaseless banter with the customers, and his impossible cheerfulness, and knew that it only disguised hidden wounds. Like Kalasinga, a thousand miles from home. Like all of them, stuck in one smelly place or another, infested by longing and comforted by visions of lost wholeness.

8

The merchant said that the only way to break even on the journey, let alone make any profit, was to travel a different route through more populated areas. With so many sick among their number it would be a slow journey, but in any case speed was the least of their concerns. They had lost nearly a quarter of the men they had started with, and nearly half of their goods, what with tributes and Chatu's robbery.

They travelled on a southward route, going round the southern edge of the lake. The mnyapara took charge once again, but his old vigour had gone. Both he and the merchant relied on Simba Mwene more than they had done before. Trade was plentiful in the lands they travelled through, but the goods they carried had no great value here, and the produce of the area was not as valuable as ivory. In some places they were able to buy rhino horn, but for the most part they had to be content with hide and gums. After a few days a pattern began to develop as they looped and circled for business, going out of their way in search of settlements and towns. The sights which had filled Yusuf with wonder and fear on their outward journey now receded into a nightmare blur of dust and weariness. They were bitten by insects and cut and grazed by thorns and bushes. One evening a troop of baboons descended on them and made off with whatever they could carry. At every stop after that they built a stockade, for without their guns they feared even worse attacks from the animals which prowled around them at night. Everywhere they went they heard stories of the Germans, who had forbidden the people to ask for tribute, and had even hanged some people for reasons no one understood. Simba Mwene keenly led them away from all reported German stations.

It took them five months to make the return journey, moving slowly and sometimes having to work on farms in order to get food. In the town of Mkalikali, north of a large river, they were forced to stay for eight days until they finished building a stockade for the sultan's livestock. The sultan insisted on it before he would agree to sell them food for the journey.

'Your caravan trade is finished,' the sultan of Mkalikali said. 'These Mdachi! They have no mercy. They have told us they don't want you here because you will make us slaves. I tell them no one will make us slaves. No one! We used to sell slaves to these people from the coast. We know them, and we're not afraid of them.'

'The Europeans and the Indians will take everything now,' the merchant said, making the sultan smile.

At Kigongo they were required to labour on the elders' farms before they could sell their hoes. While they were there, the merchant became ill. He refused to be carried and after three days in Kigongo he insisted they leave. He could not bear to stay any longer among thieves who took so much from them every day in return for so little, he said. Because of his illness they rested frequently, and Yusuf walked beside him to assist him when he tired. When they reached Mpweli they knew they were getting close to the coast. They rested for several days there, and Uncle Aziz was welcomed by an old friend who ran a shop in the town. He listened with tears in his eyes to the tales of their trials and ill luck. Have you made enough to repay the Indian? he asked the merchant. Uncle Aziz shrugged.

After Mpweli they hurried for the coast, and arrived outside their town in six days. The elation of the men was tempered by weariness and failure. The clothes they wore were nothing but rags, and hunger had given their faces a gaunt and tragic look. They made camp by a pool and washed as well as they could, and then the merchant led them in prayers, asking God to forgive them for any wrong they may have done. The following morning they marched into town, led by one of the horn players, who insisted on playing despite everything. His reedy tunes, for all their attempt at jauntiness, sounded strident and mournful.

THE GROVE OF DESIRE

Later Yusuf could not remember the moment of their arrival.
The days after their return were crowded with mobs of people
circling the house and the clearing, clamouring to be heard.
The porters and guards were there too, telling tales of their
heroic survival and grumbling about their luck as they waited
to be paid off. A village of tents and camp-fires arose in the
large yard by the merchant's house, visited day and night by
the curious and by street-traders selling them food and coffee.
Ramshackle kiosks appeared by the side of the road, and the
aromas of grilled meat and frying fish drew knots of people to
them. Flocks of scavenging crows abandoned their affairs to
lurk on nearby trees, their sharp, bright eyes restlessly on the
lookout for an unguarded morsel. Mounds of rubbish dotted
the edges of the encampment, and thin rivulets of sluggish
slime oozed out of them as the days passed.

The merchant received a stream of visitors on the terrace in
front of the shop. The old men who usually sat there graciously
made space but silently resisted eviction. They too wanted to
stay close to the drama of the merchant's return. The manner
of the merchant's visitors was solicitous, and they spent many
idle hours with him, listening to his account of the journey
with sudden exclamations or small cries of commiseration.
While they chatted and drank coffee, the agitated crowds
wheeled around them. At times, one or other of the visitors
took out a notebook and jotted something down, or strolled
round to the stores by the side of the house. Mohammed

Abdalla was installed in one of the stores, still recovering from exhaustion and fever, and suffering strange pains which had begun after the beating in Chatu's town. A length of cloth hung over the open doorway to his room, billowing languidly when there was any breeze. The visitors stopped to greet him and wish him well before going on to glance into the other stores.

'They've come to pick the seyyid's bones,' Khalil said to Yusuf.

There were bristles of grey in his hair and his lean face was more pointed than Yusuf remembered it. He had greeted their return with frenzied delight and glee, overwhelming Yusuf with his joy, jumping around him, squeezing him, slapping him on the back. 'He's back,' he told his customers. 'My little brother is back. Only look how big he's grown!' In the days which followed the early chaos, he drew Yusuf back into the shop with insistent demands that he come and do some real work for a change. Uncle Aziz smiled indulgently, and Yusuf understood that this was also the merchant's wish. He liked to have him within call and summoned him often to perform small courtesies to his guests, which he rewarded with casual tokens of his approval. Khalil talked at Yusuf incessantly, breaking off to deal with the customers, whom he invited to admire the returned traveller. 'Look at those muscles. Who'd have thought that feeble kifa urongo would turn out like this? I don't know what they fed him there behind the hills, but it's swelled him up nicely for one of your daughters.' At night, while the encampment hummed with murmurs and bursts of laughter or song, they spread their bedding on a corner of the terrace. Every night Khalil said, 'All right, now bring me news from the journey. I want to hear everything.'

Yusuf felt as if he was waking from a nightmare. He told Khalil that so often on the journey he felt he was a soft-fleshed animal which had left its shell and was now caught in the

179

open, a vile and grotesque beast blindly smearing its passage across the rubble and the thorns. That was how he thought they all were, stumbling blindly through the middle of nowhere. The terror he had felt was not the same as fear, he said. It was as if he had no real existence, as if he was living in a dream, over the edge of extinction. It made him wonder what it was that people wanted so much that they could overcome that terror in search of trade. It was not all terror, not at all, he said, but it was the terror which gave everything shape. And he had seen sights which nothing in him could have predicted.

'The light on the mountain is green,' he said. 'Like no light I've ever imagined. And the air is as if it has been washed clean. In the morning, when the sun strikes the peak of snow, it feels like eternity, like a moment which will never change. And in late afternoon near water, the sound of a voice rises deeply to the skies. One evening, on a journey up the mountain, we stopped by a waterfall. It was beautiful, as if everything was complete. I have never seen anything as beautiful as that. You could hear God breathing. But a man came and tried to chase us away. Night and day, everywhere throbbed and buzzed and shook with noise. One afternoon near a lake I saw two fish eagles calmly roosting on a branch of a gum tree. Then suddenly both of them whooped with great energy, two or three fierce yells with neck bent back and the open beak pointing at the sky, wings pumping and body stretched taut. After a moment, a faint reply came back across the lake. A few minutes later, a white feather detached itself from the male bird, and in that great silence it drifted slowly to the ground.'

Khalil listened without speaking, occasionally making a *hem* in support. But when Yusuf stopped, because he guessed that Khalil had dropped off to sleep, a question came out of the dark to prompt him. Sometimes Yusuf himself was struck dumb by the memory of the huge red land, teeming with people and animals, and the image of the cliffs which had risen out of the lake like walls of flame.

'Like the gates of Paradise,' Yusuf said.

Khalil made a soft incredulous noise. 'And who lives in this Paradise? Savages and thieves who rob innocent traders and sell their own brothers for trinkets,' he said. 'They're without God or religion, or even simple everyday mercy. Just like the wild beasts who live there with them.' Yusuf knew that this was how the men prompted each other to tell the story of Chatu once again, but he kept silent. Whenever he thought of their stay in Chatu's town he also thought of Bati and the feel of her warm breath on his neck. It shamed him to think how Khalil would laugh at him if he knew.

'How was that devil Mohammed Abdalla? The savage sultan really taught him a lesson, eh? You were there! But before that . . . what did he do before that?' Khalil asked. 'After every journey people come back with terrible stories. You know his reputation with the men, don't you?'

'He treated me kindly,' Yusuf said after a moment. In the silence he had seen the mnyapara dancing in the firelight, bursting with vainglory and arrogance, and trying to hide the pain in his shoulder.

'You shouldn't be so trusting,' Khalil said irritably. 'He's a dangerous man. Anyway, did you see any wolf-men? You must have. No? Perhaps they wait deeper in the forest. I know they're famous in that country. Did you see any strange animals?'

'I didn't see any wolf-men,' Yusuf said. 'They were probably hiding from the strange wild beasts which were tramping across their land.'

Khalil laughed. 'So you're not afraid of wolf-men any

181

more. How you've grown! We should get you a wife now. Ma Ajuza is still waiting for you, and she'll be sniffing your zub again next time she sees you, grown-up or not. She's been pining for you all these years.'

Ma Ajuza's jaw dropped with melodramatic amazement when she saw him in the shop. For a long moment she stood still, robbed of words and volition. Then she smiled slowly with pleasure. He saw how heavily she moved and how weary her face looked. 'Ah, my husband has come back to me,' she said. 'Thank you, God! And how beautiful he looks. I'll have to watch the other girls now.' But there was no zest in her teasing, and her voice carried a hint of apology and deference, as if she feared he might be displeased with her.

'You're the one who looks beautiful, Ma Ajuza,' Khalil said. 'Not this feeble young man who doesn't recognize true love when he sees it. Why didn't you choose me, zuwarde? I would have given you plenty of tobacco to sniff. How are you feeling today? And the family?'

'We're all as we are. We thank God that this is what He has chosen for us,' she said, her voice rising with self-pity. 'Whether He makes us poor or He makes us rich, or weak or strong, all we can say is alhamdulillah. We thank You. If He doesn't know what's best for us then who does? Anyway, be quiet now. Let me talk to my husband. I hope you didn't play around with any other women while you were away. When are you coming home to live with me? I have a feast waiting for you.'

'Don't provoke him, Ma Ajuza,' Khalil said. 'He's a wolf-man now. He'll come to your house and eat you.'

Ma Ajuza managed a small ululation at that, which made Khalil swivel his hips in lascivious joy. Yusuf saw that Khalil gave generous measures of everything Ma Ajuza asked for, and saw him add a small cone of sugar as well. 'Will I see you tonight at the usual time, then?' Khalil asked. 'I need a massage.'

'First you steal from me, then you want to interfere with me,' Ma Ajuza cried. 'Keep away from me, mtoto wa shetani.'

'You see, she still loves only you,' Khalil said to Yusuf, clapping him on the shoulder to give him courage.

2

The door in the garden wall was kept shut with so many strangers about, and only Khalil and Uncle Aziz went through it, and the old gardener Mzee Hamdani. Yusuf saw the crowns of the taller trees over the wall and heard the birdsong at dawn, and longed to wander again in the grove of desire. In the mornings he saw Mzee Hamdani pick his way fastidiously through the clearing, circling the tents and the mounds of rubbish without appearing to look at them. He glanced neither right nor left and made straight for the door in the garden wall. In the afternoons he left just as silently. It took Yusuf a few days to find the courage to position himself in such a way that Mzee Hamdani could not miss him. The old man made no sign that he saw him. Yusuf was hurt at first, but then he smiled to himself and retreated.

The men in the clearing began to leave one by one. Uncle Aziz was still negotiating with creditors and merchants, but the men were becoming bored and troublesome. They came to him with their chits, on which the terms of their original agreement with the merchant were written. Mohammed Abdalla and Simba Mwene attended as witnesses while the merchant himself made the entry in his ledger. They took what the merchant gave them, and took another chit for what the merchant owed them. There was to be none of the promised share of the profit, Uncle Aziz explained to each of them. As it was, he was likely to have to find money from somewhere to pay his creditors. The men did not believe him but only said so among themselves. Big merchants were notorious for defrauding the men who travelled with them. To the merchant they grumbled and wheedled, pleading for more. Nyundo asked that his valuable services as a translator be taken into account, and the merchant nodded, altering his chit accordingly. After the men had signed the ledger saying they were paid, their chits were marked by Mohammed Abdalla and Simba Mwene, neither of whom could write. Some of the men delayed accepting their chits, storing up disputes for later, but in the end they all had to agree to what the merchant offered or go without. The families of those who had died on the journey were sent what their deceased relatives would have received. Uncle Aziz sent enough white cotton for a shroud, even though the body was already buried hundreds of miles away, and added something from his pocket. 'For the funeral prayers,' he would say to the man to whom the money was entrusted.

Uncle Aziz held back the money for the two men who escaped from Chatu's town and did not turn up again. If he sent the money to their families, and then the men turned up, the disputes could go on for a lifetime. If he did not, sooner or later a relative would turn up to claim it, and curse him for treachery. But that was the lesser evil, the merchant said.

As the men departed, so did the street-traders and the food kiosks, leaving only the crows to sift through the rubbish which was left behind. 'Don't forget us for your next trip,' the men said to Mohammed Abdalla as they left. They said so out of kindness, for it was plain that the mnyapara was ill and tired, oppressed by his weakness. 'Did we not work well for you? It was only that God did not bless our journey. So don't forget us, mnyapara.'

'What next trip do you want to go on? There will be no next trip,' the mnyapara said, his haughty face cruel with malice and mockery. 'The European has taken it all.'

The last to receive payment were Mohammed Abdalla and Simba Mwene. They accepted their share with mutters of gratitude, barely glancing at what they had been given. Then they sat politely with the merchant on the terrace, unsure if they were of any further use to him but reluctant to remove themselves too quickly in case they gave offence. As they both rose to leave, the merchant put out a hand and held back Simba Mwene. For a moment, Mohammed Abdalla stood perfectly still, his eyes on the ground. Then he walked calmly away.

Khalil nudged Yusuf as they watched the dismissal of Mohammed Abdalla. Khalil's face was glowing with triumph, as if he had engineered the coup personally. 'That gets rid of the filthy dog,' he whispered. 'Now he'll have to go back to his wilderness and torture his animals. Go away from here, you dog!'

Yusuf was surprised by the intensity of Khalil's dislike, and looked at him expectantly, waiting for an explanation. But Khalil turned away and began to rearrange the boxes of rice and beans on the shop counter. His eyes blinked rapidly, and his mouth twisted at the corners as if he was struggling to control himself. The veins on his taut face were swollen, making him look vulnerable. He lifted his eyes anxiously towards Yusuf and attempted a smile. Yusuf made another interrogative face, but Khalil pretended not to notice. Then he broke into song, clapping his hands gently as he unconcernedly surveyed the road for customers.

That same afternoon Mohammed Abdalla sat on the terrace, his pack beside him, ready to travel. He was waiting for the merchant to rise from his siesta. Yusuf was alone behind the shop counter, but there were no customers. Khalil had gone to lie down in the back of the shop. Mohammed Abdalla beckoned Yusuf and invited him to sit beside him on the bench. 'What will become of you?' he asked roughly. Yusuf sat silently, waiting to hear out what Mohammed Abdalla wanted to say to him. After a moment, Mohammed Abdalla made a derisive snorting noise and shook his head. 'Nightmares! Whimpering in the dark like a sick child! What was it that you saw in your nights which was worse than the evil we passed through? Otherwise you did well, for such a beautiful boy. You put up with everything and kept your eyes open, and did all that was asked of you. After another journey you would have become as sturdy as metal. But there will be no more journeys now the European dogs are everywhere. By the time they've finished with us they will have fucked us up every hole in our bodies. Fucked us beyond recognition. We'll be worse than the shit they'll make us eat. Every evil will be ours, people of our blood, so that even naked savages will be able to despise us. You'll see.'

Yusuf kept his eyes on Mohammed Abdalla but sensed that Khalil had appeared from the back of the shop. 'The seyyid . . . he's a champion merchant despite this trip,' Mohammed Abdalla continued. 'You should've seen him the last time we were there in Manyema. He doesn't mind taking risks and he's afraid of nothing. Nothing! There's no foolishness in him, because he sees the world as it is. And it is a cruel bad place, you know that. Learn from him! Look sharp, look sharp . . . and don't let them make a shopkeeper out of you like that plump fool you used to live with. That Hamid with the big buttocks and the empty shop! Muungwana, he calls himself, a man of honour, when he's nothing but a plump little bun, strutting about like his plump white pigeons. He won't have much honour left by the time the seyyid has finished with him

186

this time. Or that little woman over there. That one. Don't let them make you into something like him.' Mohammed Abdalla raised his cane and pointed it towards the shop counter where Khalil was standing watching. He glared at Khalil as if he dared him to protest. When he said no more, Yusuf rose to leave. 'Look sharp,' Mohammed Abdalla said with a grin.

<h2>3</h2>

Simba Mwene accompanied Uncle Aziz to town, where he went to talk to his creditors and make arrangements for repayment. Although he was not admitted to their discussions, he understood something of what was going on, he said. When he came back, he told Khalil and Yusuf what he had learned of the merchant's business. The losses had been steep, and all the creditors had to bear a share, but a heavy burden still fell on the merchant. 'But he's too sharp to be caught out on his own, and the Indian has lost a lot of money too, so he has no choice but to help out. We have to go on the train on another journey. To a place where our bwana has some valuable goods. But only the bwana and I will be going,' Simba Mwene said smugly, smiling at Yusuf.

'Where? What valuable goods? In Hamid's shop?' Yusuf asked.

'He doesn't know anything,' Khalil said. Simba Mwene had lost some of his intimidating airs since the men had left and he found Khalil's exuberance difficult to deal with sometimes. 'He's talking big, that's all. He's used to showing off in front of ignorant porters and those wild people over there, so he thinks he can fool us. Do you think the seyyid will trust him with anything valuable?'

'I think you know the place, Yusuf. Do you know what valuable merchandise he has in that store in Hamid's shop? If you don't know, you'd better not ask,' Simba Mwene said with a grin, ignoring Khalil.

'What merchandise?' Yusuf asked, frowning with puzzled ignorance to encourage Simba Mwene to talk. 'There were only sacks of dried maize in there.'

'Perhaps there's a secret cellar where a jinn has stored gold and jewels for the seyyid,' Khalil said. 'And now our loud-mouth Simba is going to fetch the treasure and save the seyyid's business. Only he has the magic ring, only he knows the magic words which will open the thick brass doors.'

Simba Mwene laughed. 'Do you remember the story Nyundo told us on the journey? A jinn stole a beautiful young princess from her home on the night of her betrothal . . . Do you remember that one? And abducted her to an underground cellar in the forest which he filled with gold and jewels and all kinds of rich foods and comforts. Every ten days the jinn visited the princess and spent the night with her, then he went off on his jinn business. The princess lived down there for years. One day a woodcutter stubbed his toe on the handle of the trapdoor leading down to the cellar. He opened the door, descended the stairs into the cellar and there found the princess. He loved her immediately, and the princess loved him too and told him the story of her many years of imprisonment. He saw the great luxury in which she lived and she showed him the beautiful vase which she was to rub if she required the jinn to come urgently. After staying with the princess for four days and four nights, the woodcutter tried to persuade her to come with him, but she laughed and told him there was no escape from the jinn, who had stolen her from her home when she was ten years old and would know how to find her wherever she went. The woodcutter was overcome with love and envy, and in a fit of rage the woodcutter picked up the vase and hurled it against the wall.

'In an instant the jinn was with them, his naked sword in his hand. In the confusion, the woodcutter escaped up the stairs, but he left his sandals and his axe behind. The jinn now understood that his princess had been entertaining another man, and with one blow he cut off her head.'

'And the woodcutter?' Khalil asked eagerly. 'What happened to the woodcutter? Get on with it.'

'The jinn found him easily because of his sandals and axe. He showed them to people in a nearby town, saying he was a friend, and they led him to the woodcutter's house. Do you know what he did to him? He took him to the top of a huge barren mountain and turned him into an ape,' Simba Mwene said with relish. 'Why could he not visit the princess for the nine days when the jinn was not there? Can you tell me that?'

'Because it was his fate,' Khalil said without hesitation.

'So Uncle Aziz has a secret cellar in Hamid's . . .' Yusuf began, wanting to return their talk to the contraband in Hamid's store. He saw a look of surprise cross Khalil's face. *For a start he ain't your uncle.* He considered forcing himself to say the seyyid but could not do it. 'Anyway, what is the valuable merchandise in Hamid's store?'

'Vipusa,' Simba Mwene whispered. Rhino horn. 'But if you say anything to anyone we're all in trouble. The Mdachi government has forbidden trade in vipusa so it can have all the profit. That's why the price is so high and our bwana is sitting comfortably waiting to sell the merchandise to the Indian. We won't be bringing the vipusa back here. That's my job, to take them over the hills all the way to the border, juu kwa juu, and deliver them to a certain Indian near Mombasa. Our bwana has different business to see to, so he will leave all this to me.'

Simba Mwene delivered this with an air of importance, as a possessor of secrets. He glanced at both of them in turn to see

189

the effect of his words, and Yusuf saw Khalil's look of awe and knew that he was mocking Simba Mwene.

'The seyyid certainly picked a brave man for the job, a real lion,' Khalil said.

'It's a dangerous road,' Simba Mwene said, smiling and taking Khalil's mockery in his stride. 'Especially along the border. Even more so now that there's talk of war between the English and the Germans.'

'Why are vipusa so valuable?' Yusuf asked. 'What are they used for?'

Simba Mwene thought for a moment, and then gave up the possibility of constructing a reply. 'I don't know,' he said. 'Medicine, perhaps. Who knows the way of the world? All I know is that the Indian buys it, and I don't care where he puts it after that. It can't be that he eats it. I think it must be medicine.'

When Simba Mwene left them, to return to the storeroom he had occupied since Mohammed Abdalla's departure, Khalil said, 'The seyyid will be calling on those who owe him, to call his debts in. He always keeps something in hand. That's his way. Even when it looks as if his affairs have gone badly, he travels here, he travels there, and soon all is well again. He may even call on your Ba. They'll fix everything between them and you'll no longer be rehani. Your Ba will pay his debts and the seyyid will pay his, and then you'll be free. What will you do then? Go back to live on the mountain like the hermit from Zanzibar? But I don't think anything like that will happen. You Ba is probably completely poor now, just like my marehemu Ba was, and couldn't repay his debt in this world or the next. So no mountain retreat for you . . . But the seyyid won't even ask him, I don't think. He likes you. Look at that noisy Simba and all his airs! He is sent on the dangerous job because the seyyid does not care if anything should happen to him . . . otherwise he would've sent you.'

'Or you,' Yusuf said, out of friendship and loyalty.

Khalil smiled, then shook his head at him. It was a rueful gesture, lamenting Yusuf's ignorance. 'The Mistress,' he said. 'How will you talk to her without Arabic? And if you think I'm going to leave my shop for you to ruin . . . If the seyyid can't pay all his debts this shop may be his only livelihood. He'll find something else for you. He likes you.'

Yusuf shivered. 'But he still ain't your uncle,' Khalil said, making to hit Yusuf on the back of the head. Yusuf easily parried the blow.

Uncle Aziz invited them to eat with him on the eve of his return to the interior. At the appointed hour immediately after the sunset prayers, Khalil led Simba Mwene and Yusuf into the garden. The gloom and silence were serene, lightly touched by the sound of water. A fragrance filled the air, a music which ravished the senses. At the far end of the garden, lights hung on posts illuminated the terrace and carved a golden pavilion out of the deepening gloom. The reflection turned the water channels into paths of dull metal. Rugs were spread on the terrace, and from them issued vapours of sandalwood and amber.

The moment they were seated, the merchant appeared from the courtyard, dressed in the thinnest cotton, which flowed and rippled as he strode towards them. He wore a cap embroidered with golden silk. They all rose to greet him, but he smilingly waved them down and seated himself among them. Yusuf saw that this was the seyyid again, the man who had so casually taken him away from his parents and his home, and who had strolled the hard lands to the lakes with smiling equanimity. Even in their worst time in Chatu's town, a graceful and invincible assurance had issued from him and embraced all of them. On their journey back and since their return, anxiety had dispersed this air and laid him open to the bickering and demands of the men who had travelled with him. But he was the seyyid again, composed and untroubled, with a smile of magnanimous amusement hovering barely out of sight.

He began to reminisce about the journey, but lightly as if he had not been there himself and was recalling someone else's account. By gesture and looks he invited Simba Mwene to confirm the details, and nodded with gratified recognition as the memory was recalled. Yusuf guessed that Simba Mwene understood what was happening, but knew from his delighted laughter and from the way his voice deepened and rose that he found the merchant's flattery irresistible. After a while, Simba Mwene was in steady spate and required only small encouragement to move from story to story, as if they were once again round a fire in the heart of the country.

The courtyard door opened very slightly, and Khalil rose smoothly as if at a signal. He disappeared inside and after a moment came out with a platter of rice. Repeated trips brought out platters of fish, of cooked meats, of vegetables, of bread and a large basket of fruit. The first appearance of the food halted their conversation and they waited in polite silence as Khalil made his trips. Yusuf tried not to look at the food but could not keep his gaze away from the rice glistening with ghee and dotted with sultanas and nuts. In the silence in which they sat, Yusuf heard the voice that had used to chase him away from the garden, and the recognition warmed him to the memory. At last Khalil came out with a brass jug and bowl, and a towel draped over his forearm. He poured water for them one by one so they could wash their hands. Simba Mwene also rinsed his mouth and noisily spat the water out into the garden. Bismillah, Uncle Aziz said, inviting them to eat.

Simba Mwene became more uninhibited with his talk as

they ate, and addressed the merchant with freedom. He was inclined to put the blame for the failure of the journey on the mnyapara, he said. 'If he had not beaten that man in the forest, then Chatu would not have been so much against us,' he said, his voice turning hard. 'He treated everyone like they were servants and slaves. Such ways may have done well enough before, but no one will put up with them now. What could Chatu have thought? He must have taken us for kidnappers and traders in flesh. You shouldn't have let him have so much freedom, bwana. Eh, he was a hard man, not an ounce of pity in him. But I think Chatu was harder than him.'

Uncle Aziz nodded quietly and did not contradict. Simba Mwene went on talking, his rising voice drowning the quiet rustle of the bushes and trees and filling the garden with clamour. Yusuf wondered that he could not hear himself talking, but he continued like a man intoxicated. The merchant's eyes rested pitilessly on him, and Yusuf could see that he was weighing Simba Mwene against the vipusa hidden in Hamid's store. In the end, Uncle Aziz spoke to Khalil in Arabic, and he began to return the ravaged platters to the house, inclining each one towards the guests first before taking it away.

'Did you see the look on the seyyid's face as that loud-mouth spat the water into the garden? Or when he was talking about what went wrong with the journey?' Khalil whispered later, chortling with joy. They were lying on their mats on the terrace in front of the shop, heads close together. 'He knows he can't trust him, but he has no choice. So many problems for your uncle! And that Simba Mwene barking away like a blind hyena.'

'He's no fool,' Yusuf said. 'There were times on the journey when he was the only one with his wits about him.'

'His wits about him,' Khalil laughed. 'What kind of talk is

193

that? Where did you learn to speak like that? It must come from hanging around nobility in your travels. You could still end up being a hakim in your old age. You say he's no fool. Then why does he act like one? Unless he's up to something. Unless he means to make mischief and wants the seyyid to know. In their time the seyyid and Mohammed Abdalla would have wrapped that Simba in spinach leaves and eaten him for lunch. But now Mohammed Abdalla is finished and the seyyid has you, and you make him feel that he's behaving badly. You make him feel something different too, I think. You look at him all the time. Anyway, until he knows that his smelly rhino horns are safe, your uncle won't be sleeping easy for a few nights,' Khalil said, pleased with his summary.

'What is this . . . I look at him,' Yusuf asked, frowning angrily. 'Why shouldn't I look at him? I look at you.'

'You look at everyone, at everything,' Khalil said, taking any challenge out of his voice. 'Who doesn't know this? And anyone can see that your miserable eyes are open and that you desire nothing to escape them. So if I can see that, what do you think a clever one like the seyyid sees? Eh, my brother, he feels your eyes cutting into him. Can't you see that? What is this I look at him! Don't forget I saw you shitting yourself over mangy dogs that are scared of flies, and you saw something in them. Wolf-men, perhaps. Did you hear that beast talk about the devil Mohammed Abdalla, though? Those evil days are gone! What a loud-mouth! And did you see how much food he put away?'

In the morning Khalil kissed Uncle Aziz's hand reverently as he bid him goodbye, then stood beside him nodding quickly as he listened to his final instructions. Uncle Aziz beckoned to Yusuf and asked him to accompany him part of the way to the station. He signalled Simba Mwene to start and followed a few feet behind.

'We'll talk when I return,' Uncle Aziz said to Yusuf. 'You have grown up well, and now we have to find something of meaning for you to do. You have a home here with me. You know that, I think. Make it your home, and we'll talk when I come back.'

'Thank you,' Yusuf said and struggled to suppress the shiver which he could feel swelling in him.

'I think Hamid was right. Maybe it's time we found you a wife,' Uncle Aziz said with a large smile, his eyes rummaging over Yusuf's face. His smile turned into brief pleasant laughter. 'I'll keep my eyes open on my travels, and bring back stories of any beauties I hear about. Don't look so frightened,' he said.

Then he gave Yusuf his hand to kiss.

4

They visited the town at the first opportunity. Khalil wanted to go to all the places they knew before. He had not been to town in all the years Yusuf had been away, he said, although every Friday he thought about the trips they used to make together. 'Where could I go on my own? Who do I know?' he said. At the mosque Yusuf could not resist showing off his knowledge of the Koran, and later told Khalil the story of his discovery and shame. 'Knowing the Koran will always help you,' Khalil said. 'Even if you're lost in the deepest cave or the darkest forest. Even though you can't understand the words.' Yusuf told him about Kalasinga and his plans to translate the Koran, so that Waswahili could see what a cruel God they worshipped. Khalil wondered angrily how Yusuf could sit quietly and listen to such blasphemy from an unbeliever. What should I have done? Stoned him to death? Yusuf asked. They visited the street where they had seen the Indian wedding procession and had heard the man singing to the guests. At times they played in the streets like two children, throwing rotten fruit at one another and running through crowds of strangers. By the time they reached the beach it was already night, but the sea shone with silvery luminescence and crested frothily as it raced for their feet. On their way back they stopped at a café and ordered mutton and beans and quantities of bread, and a pot of sweet tea all to themselves. They agreed that neither of them had tasted beans as delicious as the plateful they shared in that café.

With Mzee Hamdani Yusuf bided his time. The old gardener looked no more aged than before, but Yusuf saw that he walked more deliberately and avoided company even more fiercely than he used to. He waited until he saw him struggling with the buckets of water one hot day, and only then came forward to help. Mzee Hamdani was too surprised to protest and perhaps after all the journeys he had already made in that heat from the water tap to the garden, he was even a little relieved to have a rest. And when Yusuf gave him a sheepishly triumphant smile for the small success of his stratagem, the old gardener's eyes did not turn blank. He filled the gardener's two buckets with water every morning and lined them up inside the wall for his use. In the light of day he saw how the garden had grown. The young orange trees along the far wall had strengthened and swelled, and the pomegranates and palms were as plump and sturdy as if they would be there for all eternity. White blossom covered the sour cherry, which had grown to a round and moderate shape. But among the clovers and grasses he saw tall nettles and clumps of wild spinach, and the lavender blossoms struggled to be seen between the bedraggled lilies and irises. The edge of the pool into which the water channels flowed was scummy with algae, and the channels themselves were sluggish with silt. All the mirrors in the trees had been removed.

He went into the garden from early morning, often before Mzee Hamdani himself arrived. He weeded the grasses and thinned out the lilies, and began clearing the channels. The old gardener accommodated him silently, only approaching to correct him irritably when he made a mistake. Yusuf saw that Mzee Hamdani spent longer than he used to at his prayers. His songs had become lugubrious and plaintive, aching notes held for long moments instead of rising and falling with the solemn ecstasy of his old qasidas.

Khalil called for him when he needed help, or when Ma Ajuza came to the shop. Otherwise he treated his desire for the garden with tolerant amusement. If he discouraged him it was only by making jokes to the customers at his expense. He became fidgety when Yusuf was still in the garden in late afternoon and came to call him out. 'I'm sweating to put food in your belly, you ignorant Mswahili, and you want to play in the garden all day. Come and sweep the yard and then give me a hand with the sacks. Everyone who comes here asks about you. The old men want to hear everything about the journey. The customers want to greet you. Where's your little brother? they ask. Little brother! The big oaf is playing in the garden, I tell them. He thinks he's a nephew of a rich merchant and likes to lie under the orange trees and dream of Paradise.' But Yusuf guessed that the Mistress did not want him in the garden as evening approached. Perhaps that was when she herself liked to come into the garden, and his presence there prevented it.

Late one afternoon, as he paused from widening one of the four channels into the pool, he saw a small dark stone protruding out of the shallow bank he had cut. He bent down casually to pick it up and saw that it was not a stone but a tiny leather pouch. It was frayed and roughened by the soil, and the water had darkened the leather, but it was intact enough for him to see that it was a hirizi, an arm amulet which was sure to contain words of prayer for the benefit of the wearer. The stitching was frayed in one corner and through the crack he saw the tiny metal casket inside the pouch. He shook the amulet and heard it rattle, so whatever it contained was still firm and had not rotted underground. With a tiny twig he scraped more dirt away from the crack and saw a hint of design on the metal casket. He remembered stories of the magical powers of amulets, and how jinns can be summoned from their lairs in the upper air by rubbing one. He tried to insert a fleshy tip of his little finger into the crack, to see if it could reach the metal. A raised voice made him look up and he saw that the door into the courtyard, through which Khalil had gone in and out on the night of their dinner with Uncle Aziz, was ajar. Even in the failing light he could see a shape standing there. The voice was raised again, and this time he recognized it as that of the Mistress. A crack of light appeared in the doorway as the figure moved away, and then the door was shut.

When Khalil went into the house to fetch their food that evening, he was a long time coming out. Yusuf imagined that he was the subject of angry complaints from the Mistress for having overstayed in the garden. If she did not want him in the garden at a certain hour, all that was required was to tell him so. I don't want him in the garden at such and such an hour. That was all, and he would be sure not to be there. The secrecy and the whispering made him feel like a child. It irritated him that he should be thought to desire any disrespect by sullying her honour with his sinful gaze. He wondered what angry prohibitions Khalil would bring out with him. Would he be banished from the garden? What else could she decree against him? His finger had been working at the crack in the amulet and a little more of the silver casket was now visible. He felt its cool touch and wondered if he should summon the jinn now to come and save him, or keep him back for whatever new catastrophe lay ahead. For some reason he saw Chatu as the growling jinn, and the thought cheered him. A memory of the courtyard in which he had spent those days of captivity came to mind and he remembered again the feel of the girl's warm breath on his neck.

Khalil looked angry when he came out. He put the plates of cold rice and spinach in front of them and began to eat without speaking. They ate by the light of the shop, which was still open. Afterwards Khalil rinsed his plate and went into the shop to count the day's takings and begin restocking the shelves. When he finished eating, Yusuf also cleaned his plate and went into the shop to help. Khalil was only waiting for him to finish because he picked up the plates and went back inside the house. He looked so burdened and at a loss that Yusuf did not say the angry words that were on the tip of his tongue. What was all the fuss about?

He was already lying on his mat in the dark when Khalil came out to the terrace and lay at his usual place a few feet away. After a long silence, he said softly, 'The Mistress has gone crazy.'

'Because I was too long in the garden?' Yusuf asked, making the incredulity in his voice express some of the annoyance he felt.

Khalil suddenly laughed in the darkness. 'The garden! You think about nothing except this garden! You're going crazy too,' he said through laughter. 'You should find something else to use up your energy. Why don't you chase after women or become a holy man? Instead you want to turn out like that Mzee Hamdani. Why don't you chase after women? That's an enjoyable pastime. With your beautiful looks you can have the whole world. And if you don't succeed, there's Ma Ajuza waiting for you any-time . . .'

199

'Don't start that again,' Yusuf said sharply. 'Ma Ajuza is an old woman and deserves more respect . . .'

'Old! Who says that? I've used her and she's not old. I promise you, I've been with her,' Khalil said. In the silence Yusuf heard Khalil breathing softly, and then heard him snort suddenly with contempt. 'You find that disgusting, do you? But I'm not disgusted or ashamed. I went to her because I had a need, and I used her body for payment. She too had her needs. It may be cruel, but neither of us had any choice. What did you want me to do? Wait for a princess to fall in love with me when she comes to the shop to buy a bar of soap? Or for a beautiful jinneyeh to kidnap me on the night of my betrothal and keep me in a cellar as her sex slave?'

Yusuf did not reply, and after a brief silence Khalil sighed. 'Never mind, keep yourself pure for your princess. Listen, the Mistress wants to see you,' he said.

'Oh no!' Yusuf sighed wearily. 'This is going too far. What for? Just tell her I'll keep out of the garden if she doesn't want me there.'

'There you go with the garden again,' Khalil said irritably. He yawned twice before he continued. 'It's nothing to do with that! Not like you think.'

'I won't understand her,' Yusuf said after a moment.

Khalil laughed. 'No, you won't. She doesn't want to talk to you, though, she wants to see you. I told you she used to look at you in the garden. I told you that before. Now she wants to see you more closely. She wants you in front of her. To-morrow.'

'What for? Why?' Yusuf asked, confused by Khalil's words as well as by his manner of saying them. There was anxiety and defeat in them, a resignation to threatening and unavoidable difficulties. Tell me about it, Yusuf was tempted to shout. What's it all about? I am not a child. What are you setting up for me?

Khalil yawned and dragged himself nearer as if to speak gently to Yusuf. Then he yawned again, and again, and began to move away. 'It's a long story, truly it is, and I'm very tired now. Tomorrow, Friday. I'll tell you tomorrow when we go to town,' he said.

5

'Listen,' Khalil said. They had gone to Juma'a prayers, had strolled through the market without speaking, and were sitting on the sea-wall near the harbour. 'You have been very patient. I don't know whether you know anything about this, how much you've been told or how much you've understood, so I'll tell you from the beginning. You are not a child any more, and it is not right that you should not be told these things. It's just the way we are, all these secrets. Nearly twelve years ago the seyyid married the Mistress. He was a small trader who travelled between here and Zanzibar, bringing cloth and tools and tobacco and stock-fish, and taking livestock and logs over there. She was recently widowed and rich. Her husband had owned several dhows which sailed all along the coast shipping cargo of all kinds. Grain and rice from Pemba, slaves from the south, spices and sesame from Zanzibar. Even though she was no longer young, her wealth attracted men of family and ambition. For nearly a year she rejected them all, and began to get a reputation. You know how it is when women turn down proposals of marriage. There must be something wrong with the women. Some people said she was sick, or driven mad by her bereavement. There was other talk that she was barren, and preferred women to men. The women who brought the proposals to the Mistress, and took back her answers to the families of the men, said that for someone so ugly she gave herself too many airs.

'She came to hear about the seyyid, who was many years younger, through business gossip. Everyone spoke well of the seyyid in those days, so despite all the well-connected suitors she had, she chose him. Word was discreetly sent to encourage him, some gifts changed hands, and in a few weeks they were married. I don't know what agreements were made, but the seyyid took charge of the business and made it prosper. He got out of the dhow trade, sold all the boats. It was then that he became the seyyid that we know, travelling far into the interior to trade.

'My Ba had a small shop in a village on the Mrima coast south of Bagamoyo. I told you this before. My Ma was there and my two elder brothers and a sister. It was a poor life, and my brothers sometimes went away to find work on the boats. I don't remember the seyyid coming to see us before, but maybe I was too young. I know that one day I saw him. My Ba was speaking to him in a way I had never seen him speak to anyone before. Nothing was said to me, I was only a small boy, but I heard the way they spoke about the seyyid after he left. Ma said he was the son of a Devil and was now possessed by the daughter of iblis, or afreet or worse. That he was a dog and a son of a dog ... that he did magic and other things. Crazy talk like that. When the seyyid came again, several months later, he spent two days with us. He brought me a present, a lace cap embroidered with a design of jasmine bushes and crescent moons. I still have it. But I knew now from everything I had overheard that my Ba owed the seyyid money, which he had borrowed for my eldest brother to buy a share of a small business which failed. My brother and his friends bought a fishing boat in Mikokoni, and the boat struck a reef. Anyway, our shop was too poor to pay the money back. After the two days the seyyid left. I saw my father kiss his hand several times as they said goodbye, and then the seyyid came to me and gave me a coin. I suppose my Ba's gratitude meant that the seyyid had agreed to give him more time, but I don't think I understood that then. I was not told anything at the time. It was impossible not to see how Ba became miserable and bad-tempered. He shouted at all of us and spent hours on his prayer-mat. Once he beat my eldest brother with a piece of firewood, and no one could stop him because he screamed with anguish and tears when my mother and my other brother came near. He beat his son while he wept with shame.

'Then one day that devil Mohammed Abdalla came and took me and my sister away, and brought us here. We were to be rehani until our Ba could repay his debt. He died very soon after that, my poor Ba, and Ma and my brothers went back to Arabia and left us here. They just went and left us here.'

Khalil sat silently looking out to sea, and Yusuf felt the salt breeze over the water sting his eyes. Then Khalil nodded several times and continued.

'Nine years I have been with the seyyid. When we first came there was another man in the shop. He was about my age now, and he taught me how to do the work. His name was Mohammed. In the evening, after he had shut the shop, he had several sticks of hashish and then he went off to look for sex. My sister was to serve the Mistress. She was seven years old and the Mistress frightened her.' Khalil laughed suddenly, slapping his thigh. 'Mashaallah, she used to cry so much that they had to call me to talk to her and keep her quiet. So I slept in the house, in the yard. When it rained I slept in the food store. After we had shut up shop and Mohammed had gone off to do his dirty business, I went inside to sleep. The Mistress was crazy, even in those days. She has a sickness, a big mark on her face, from her left cheek down to her neck. She covered her face with a shawl when I was near, but she told me. My sister . . . she said the Mistress often looked at herself in the mirror and cried. When I was lying in the yard she used to come and watch me, and I pretended I was asleep. She walked around me saying prayers, begging that God relieve her from her pain. When the seyyid was home she was quiet, and turned her misery against Amina and me. She blamed us for everything and abused us with filthy words. When the seyyid went away, she became crazy again and wandered in the dark.

'Then you came.' Khalil took hold of Yusuf's chin and twisted his head from side to side, grinning at him.

'What happened to Mohammed?' Yusuf asked.

'He went off one day when the seyyid raised a hand to hit him because the figures were wrong. He just stood up and left. I don't know if he was related . . . He never spoke to me about anything except the shop. The seyyid went away for a few days and came back with you, poor little Mswahili boy from the wilderness, whose Ba was as big a fool as mine was. I think he wanted someone to learn about the shop for the day when I would no longer want to work for him. So you arrived and became my little brother,' Khalil said and reached out for Yusuf's chin again, but Yusuf hit him off.

'Get on with it,' Yusuf said.

'The Mistress hides from people. She never goes out. The few women who visit are relatives or people she cannot turn away. She made me put those mirrors on the trees so that she could see the garden without going out. That was how she saw you. Every day you went to work in the garden she watched you in her mirrors. You made her even more crazy than she already was. She said God had sent you to her. To cure her.'

Yusuf thought about this for a long moment, torn between awe and abandoned laughter. 'How?' he asked after a time.

'At first she said that if you prayed over her she would be healed. Then she insisted that you would have to spit on her. The spit of those God favours has powerful qualities, she said. One day she saw you holding a rose in the cup of your hand, and she became certain that your touch would heal her. She said that if you held her face as you held that rose then her sickness would go away. I tried to stop you going in there, but you were obsessed with that garden. When the seyyid came back she could no longer keep her craziness to herself, and she told him. One touch from that beautiful boy will cure this wound in my heart. That was when the seyyid took you away with him and left you in the mountains. Didn't you suspect any of this? Amina told me that the Mistress used to stand under the wall when you were in the garden and call to you to take pity on her. Didn't you hear her say anything?'

Yusuf nodded. 'I used to hear a voice. I thought she was grumbling at me, telling me to leave. Sometimes she used to sing.'

'She never sings,' Khalil said and then frowned. 'I don't think I've ever heard her sing.'

'I must've imagined it. There are times at night when I think I hear music coming from the garden, and that cannot be. One of the travellers who visited Hamid told a story of a garden in the Herat which was so beautiful that all who visited it heard music which ravished reason. That was how a poet described it. Perhaps that's what put the idea in my head.'

'That mountain air must've driven you crazy too,' Khalil said in exasperation. 'As if your noisy dreams are not enough, you now hear music as well. I have two crazies on my hands, lucky me. The seyyid was worried about leaving you here with her, but he did not want you along on the journey. Maybe he was visiting your Ba and he did not want any messy scenes. Or perhaps he doesn't want you to know what a champion cut-throat he really is. Not yet anyway. And now the Mistress wants you, you lucky devil. She hasn't been able to watch you because the seyyid ordered I take down all the mirrors after he took you away, but she hears you.'

'She was watching from the door yesterday,' Yusuf said.

Khalil frowned. 'I don't think so. She didn't say. But she saw you at the meal we had with the seyyid. Now she has a new madness and it's very dangerous. Dangerous for you. Listen, she says you are now a man and the way to cure her wound is to take her whole heart in your hands. Do you understand? I can't utter what is in her mind, but I hope you understand the direction she is heading. Do you understand? Or are you too young and pure-thinking?'

Yusuf nodded. Khalil was not completely satisfied with his response, but after a moment he nodded too. 'She has asked to see you. Commanded and begged and ranted to have you brought to her. If I did not bring you in to her, she said, she would come out and get you herself. We must do what we can to keep her calm until the seyyid returns. He'll know how to deal with her. I promised that I would take you to see her today. Keep as far as you can from her. Don't touch her whatever she says or does. Stay close to me, and if she approaches make sure that I am between you. I don't know what the seyyid will do when he returns, but I know that your life will be difficult if he discovers that you touched or dishonoured the Mistress. He would have no choice.'

'Why can't I just refuse to see . . . ?' Yusuf began.

'Because I don't know what she'll do then,' Khalil said, his voice rising a little with a hint of pleading. 'She could do something worse. My sister is in there with her. I'll be with you all the time.'

'Why didn't you tell me all this before?'

'It was better for you not to know,' Khalil said. 'Then it was clear that you were innocent of any wrong.'

After a moment Yusuf said, 'It was your sister who was watching at the door yesterday. I thought there was something odd. It must have been the voice coming from a different place. When you said about your sister I thought of a young girl, but I realize now that it must be her that I saw . . .'

'She's a married woman,' Khalil said briefly.

Yusuf felt his heart leap with disbelief. 'Uncle Aziz?' he asked after a moment.

Khalil chuckled. 'You'll never give up with this uncle business, will you? Yes, your Uncle Aziz married her last year. So now he's also my brother as well as your uncle, and we're one happy family in a garden of Paradise. She is the repayment of my Ba's debt. When he took her he forgave the debt.'

'So you're free to go,' Yusuf said.

'Go where? I have nowhere to go,' Khalil said calmly. 'And my sister is still here.'

6

He expected to be met by a ranting, dishevelled woman who would fly at him with incomprehensible demands. The Mistress received them in a large room whose windows looked out into an enclosed yard inside the house. The floor was covered with thick decorated rugs, and large embroidered cushions were arranged at intervals along the walls. Framed tablets of texts of the Koran and a print of the Kaaba hung on the whitewashed walls. She sat upright against the longest wall, facing the door. Beside her was a lacquered tray on which stood an incense burner and a rose-water fountain. The air was perfumed with aromatic gum. Khalil greeted her and sat down several feet from her. Yusuf sat down beside him.

Her face was partly covered with a black shawl, but he saw that her skin was the colour of dull copper and that her eyes shone steadily at them. Khalil spoke first, and after a moment she replied. Her voice sounded fuller in the room, with a quiet modulation which gave it authority and assurance. As she spoke she adjusted her shawl slightly and he saw that the lines of her face were finely etched, giving it an appearance of alertness and determination which he had not expected. When Khalil started to speak again she interrupted him gently and glanced towards Yusuf, who looked away before his eyes engaged with hers.

'She asks if you are well, and she welcomes you back to the house,' Khalil said, half turning to him.

The Mistress spoke again. 'She hopes that your parents are well, and that God will continue to keep them well,' Khalil said. 'And that you will kindly think to remember her to them next time you see them. And that all your plans will be blessed and all your wishes come true and more words like that. May God, she says, give you many children.'

Yusuf nodded, and this time he was not quick enough to evade locking into her gaze. Her eyes were watchful and intense, taking his measure, and he saw them brighten a little when he did not turn away. Yusuf dropped his eyes as soon as she began to speak again, which she did for some moments, her voice rising and falling with an attempt at charm.

'Now we begin, little brother,' Khalil said, readying himself with a small sigh. 'She says she has seen you working in the garden, and she has seen that you have . . . a blessing, a gift from God. All that you touch flourishes. She says God has given you the look of an angel, and sent you to this place to do good work. This is not blasphemy, she says. It would be worse if you failed to do the work you have been sent here to do. This is the kind of way she goes on although she says more than I've told you.'

Yusuf did not look up and heard the Mistress begin again. A note of pleading was beginning to appear in her voice, and he heard the name of God mentioned several times. As she spoke she gradually found her level again and finished with the same modulated calm with which she had greeted them.

'She tells you she has been burdened with a cruel illness. She says this several times, but also she says she does not want to complain. This she also says several times. She has been burdened with an illness, but she does not want to complain and so on. All kinds of medicine and prayers have not cured this illness, because the people she saw were not blessed. Now she asks if you will cure her. For which she will reward you in this world and will pray that you receive the noblest rewards in the next. Don't say a word!'

Suddenly the Mistress removed her shawl. Her hair was pulled away from her face, which was sharp featured and handsome. A purple patch stained the left side of her face, giving it an angry lopsided look. She looked calmly at Yusuf, waiting to see the horror in his eyes. He felt no horror, and was filled with sadness that the Mistress should expect so much from him. After a moment she covered her face, and softly spoke a few words.

'She says this is her . . .' Khalil paused to think of the word, making an irritable noise of impatience at himself.

'Affliction,' said another voice behind them. Out of the corner of his eye Yusuf saw a figure behind him in the room. He had sensed this other presence but had not looked. Now as he turned that way he saw that it was a young woman wearing a long brown dress embroidered with silver thread. She too was wearing a shawl, but it was pushed back to reveal her face and part of her hair. Amina, he thought, and could not help smiling. Before he turned away it struck him how unlike Khalil she looked, more round featured and darker

209

than him. In the light of the lamps in the room, her skin seemed luminous. The smile was still on his face as he turned to the Mistress, but he was not aware of it. The Mistress retreated further into her shawl so that all he could see of her was the shape of her face and her watchful eyes. Khalil spoke to her and then translated for Yusuf. 'I've told her that you've heard what she had to say, and seen what she wanted to show you. That you are sorry for the pain she feels. That you know nothing about diseases, and there is no possibility that you can do anything to help her. Do you want to add anything? Make it harsh.'

Yusuf shook his head.

The Mistress spoke heatedly after Khalil stopped, and for a few minutes they exchanged angry remarks which Khalil did not bother to translate. 'She says it is not your knowledge but your gift which will cure her. She wants you to say a prayer and . . . and . . . touch her there. Don't do it! Whatever she says don't do it! Say a prayer if you know one but don't go near. She says she wants you to touch her heart and heal the wound in it. Just say a prayer and then we go. Pretend if you don't know one.'

Yusuf dropped his head for a moment and then began to mutter what he could remember of the prayers the imam of the mosque had taught him. He felt foolish. When he said *Amin*, Khalil echoed the benediction loudly, as did the Mistress and Amina. Khalil stood up and pulled Yusuf up with him. Before they left, the Mistress asked Amina to sprinkle their hands with the rose-water and pass the incense burner before them. Yusuf forgot to drop his eyes as Amina approached and he saw the curiosity which lurked in hers before he looked down.

'Don't tell anyone,' Khalil warned. The next day they were summoned again, but Khalil went in on his own. *Oh no, we're not having this*, he said. The debate went on for a while, at least an hour. He came out sullen and defeated. 'I promised you'll go to say a prayer tomorrow. The seyyid will kill me.'

'It's all right, I'll just say a quick prayer and then we'll go,' Yusuf said. 'You can't leave the poor sick woman unattended to when a cure is within reach. I'll put a lot of power in tomorrow's prayer. In any case, it was one of the imam's most powerful . . .'

'Don't fool around,' Khalil said angrily. 'Where's the joke? If you don't take care, you'll be laughing out of your arse soon.'

'What's the matter with you? If she wants a prayer we'll give her one,' Yusuf said happily. 'Would you deny her the gift which God has sent her?'

'I don't like the way you're acting the fool about this,' Khalil said. 'This is serious, or it could be. Especially for you. It frightens me what's in her mind.'

'What is that?' Yusuf asked, still smiling but troubled by Khalil's anxiety.

'Who knows exactly what's in her crazy mind, but I'm assuming the worst. It's the way she doesn't seem to care, or to be afraid of what she's doing. And all this wild praise . . . an angel of God. This is more than crazy talk. You're not an angel. You have no gift. And it will be a good idea if you remember to be scared about this whole business.'

The Mistress smiled when they went in the next day. It was late afternoon and the inner courtyard was gently throbbing with heat. In the room where she received them, the sun filtered in through thin drawn curtains, and in the incense burner tiny fragments of udi smouldered and fumed. She seemed less anxious than on their first visit, leaning back a little against the cushions, though her eyes still glowed watchfully. Amina sat in the same place as before, and she too smiled when Yusuf looked in her direction. Yusuf dropped his eyes over his cupped hands to begin his prayer and felt a deep silence fall on the room. He heard the muted birdsong from the garden and a faint gurgle of running water. Suppressing a smile, he stretched the silence for as long as he could and then began to mutter as if drawing to a close. His *Amin* was loudly echoed, and when he looked at the Mistress, who began to speak soon after, he saw that her eyes were sparkling with pleasure.

'She says she felt the benefit after your first prayer,' Khalil said, frowning. The Mistress had spoken for longer than that. So obvious was Khalil's curt translation that the Mistress turned towards Amina with an inquiring look. 'She wants you to come again to say prayers,' Khalil continued reluctantly. 'And to eat in the house ... both of us. She says we eat outside like dogs or homeless vagabonds. She wants you to eat here every day. I think this is trouble. You must say this is impossible for you ... otherwise ... otherwise your gift will turn bad.'

'You tell her,' Yusuf said.

'I have, but she wants to hear you speak for yourself, then I'll translate. Say anything, but shake your head a few times as if you are saying no. One or two firm shakes of the head will do.'

'Please tell her that I feel foolish having this impossible conversation about eating in her house,' Yusuf said, and thought he felt Amina smiling behind him. Or he hoped she was. Khalil glared at him.

They went back the next day, and the day after that. While

they worked in the shop they hardly spoke about the Mistress, but after they had been to say their prayers over her wound, Khalil could speak about little else. Yusuf teased him, and tried to placate his anxiety, but Khalil could not bring his worries and his ranting to an end. He accused Yusuf of enjoying the flattery of the crazy woman and not realizing the danger he was in. The seyyid will say I did mischief, he said. He'll blame me. Don't you understand what the seyyid might do?

It took Yusuf a few days to begin working in the garden again. Khalil had asked him not to go back in there, but after a few days Yusuf shrugged and went in, bringing deep frowns on Khalil's face. Why do you have to go back there? he asked. Can't you grow your own garden out here? At first, after the discovery of all the whispered secrets and his part in them, he had felt embarrassed. The idea of the Mistress staring at him while he worked and making up fantasies made him squeamish. Mzee Hamdani took no notice of his absence, or made no sign that he had noticed, except that his songs of devotion rose more plaintively from the shade of the date-palm tree. One afternoon, there was so little to do in the shop and Khalil was so restless that Yusuf shrugged and went into the garden. Mzee Hamdani welcomed him silently, and stayed longer than he usually did. Yusuf cleaned the pool and weeded the grasses, softly humming one of the songs he had learned on the journey. He tried to resist looking at the courtyard door to see if anyone stood there, but he could not, and it was with a feeling of some anticipation that he awaited the approach of their visit into the house.

'She says she heard you working in the garden today,' Khalil said. 'You should work there more often. She says go in there any time.'

The Mistress spoke at some length. 'You have a gift, she

says, again and again. This is what she says all the time. You have a gift, you have a gift,' Khalil said and hesitated, as if looking for the right words. 'If the garden pleases you then . . . er . . . this is . . .'

'Joy for her,' Amina said. Although she spoke so little, only when Khalil struggled with a word, Yusuf was always aware of her over his right shoulder.

'And she likes you to sing,' Khalil said, shaking his head in disbelief. 'I can't believe I am sitting here doing this business. Don't smile. Do you think this is a joke? She says your voice is so soothing to her heart, that God must have taught you to sing and sent you as an angel of healing.'

Yusuf grinned at Khalil's discomfort. When he glanced at the Mistress he found that she was grinning too, her face transformed by pleasure. Suddenly she beckoned, so precisely and so simply that Yusuf had no way of refusing. He stood up and approached. As he came nearer, she lowered her shawl down to her elbows, and he saw that she wore a shiny blue blouse cut square round the neck and that its edges were embroidered with tiny silver caps. She touched the mark on her cheek and then pointed to it, inviting Yusuf to put his hand on it. Her grin was turning into a gentler smile, and Yusuf felt a recklessness come over him. He knew that his hand was heavy with movement. Khalil spoke gently, saying no, no. The Mistress slowly put the shawl over her face and muttered alhamdulillah. Yusuf stepped back from her, and heard Khalil sighing softly behind him.

'Don't go near her again,' Khalil said later. 'Aren't you afraid? Don't you understand what could happen? And keep away from that garden. And don't sing.'

But he did not keep away. Khalil watched him with increasing suspicion and argued furiously with him to stay away. But Yusuf spent more time than ever in the garden, and kept his eyes and ears sharp for any noise or movement from the house. Mzee Hamdani began to leave work for him to do, and spent more time in the shade singing his joyful qasidas in praise of God. Sometimes Yusuf heard Amina singing and his body stirred with a passion that he neither summoned nor resisted. And sometimes a shadow fell across the slightly open door, and he thought he understood the joy of secret love. When evening came he was eager for the summons to the house, despite Khalil's increasing reluctance and discomfort. One day Khalil became so exasperated that he refused to answer the call when it came.

'She can get lost. We're not going. Enough is enough,' he cried. 'If anyone found out about all this carrying on we would become a joke or worse. They would think we were mad. As crazy as that demented vegetable in there. Think of the shame on the seyyid!'

'Then I'll go on my own,' Yusuf said.

'Why? Don't you know what's going on?' Khalil asked, his voice rising to a pained shout as he got to his feet. He looked ready to beat Yusuf to persuade him to see reason. 'She will do vile things and then blame you. I don't like the way you think this is a kind of joke. You have lived through wolf-men and through the wilderness. Why do you want to mark yourself with everlasting shame?'

'There is no shame,' Yusuf said calmly. 'She can do me no harm.'

Khalil dropped his head into the palm of his left hand and they sat in silence for several minutes. Then Khalil raised his face and looked strangely at Yusuf, his look growing more aghast as he suddenly understood. His eyes were hot with rage and pain, and the corners of his lips quivered. He sat back on the mat without a word, staring ahead. When Yusuf rose to go inside he turned to look.

215

'Sit down, my little brother. Don't go,' he said gently, just as Yusuf stepped off the terrace towards the garden. 'Sit down here and let's talk about all this. Don't bring shame on yourself. I don't know what you're thinking of, but it will end badly. This is not a fairy tale. There are still many things here you don't understand.'

'Tell me, then,' Yusuf said, speaking quietly but standing his ground.

Khalil shook his head, exasperated. 'Some things you can't just tell like that. Sit down and we'll begin. If you go you'll bring shame on youself and on all of us.'

Yusuf turned towards the garden without a word, ignoring Khalil's frantic shout for him to return.

8

'Her name is Zulekha. She wants to be sure that you know her name,' Amina said. She sat to his right, in front of him but away from the Mistress. Under cover of listening he studied her face. Her face was even rounder than his hurried glances had led him to believe, and in her eyes he saw a careless amusement which was like gaiety. He nodded and saw her smile, but he felt the Mistress's eyes keenly on him and forced himself not to smile back.

'Khalil did not always tell you everything she said,' Amina continued. 'She knew that. He just said what he wanted. And perhaps sometimes he did not always have the words ... when she used difficult language.'

'You speak better than him. I'll tell him. How is that? What was it he did not tell me?' Yusuf asked.

Amina ignored the questions and turned to the Mistress, awaiting her words. The latter spoke briefly, in a tone as soft as caresses, then turned away from Amina to look at him.

'Khalil did not explain to you that her heart is wounded with shame as well as pain. She says the pain brings her happiness even as it twists her sinews. Your prayers have benefited her, I think. She says they have.'

Yusuf wanted to protest. *Don't take any notice of that stuff.* He looked at the Mistress and saw that her eyes glistened with moisture. He quickly bowed his head to say the prayers, suddenly certain that he was wading out of his depth.

'She wants you to come and eat inside in the evening. Or even sleep in the courtyard if you wish,' Amina said, now smiling openly. 'Khalil won't let you sleep in the house, though. He'll make a fuss and stop her. But she wants you to come whenever you wish, and not to wait for an invitation.'

'Please thank her,' Yusuf said.

'There's no need for thanks,' Amina said calmly, speaking for the Mistress. 'Your presence brings her happiness, and therefore it is she who should feel gratitude. She wants you to speak, to tell her more about where you come from and where you have been, so she can know you. In return, if there is anything she can do to make your life here more comfortable, you must tell her.'

'Did she say all that with those few words?' Yusuf asked.

'She said that and more which Khalil did not tell you,' Amina said. 'Her words frightened him.'

'Don't they frighten you?'

Amina grinned but did not reply. The Mistress asked something, and Amina turned to her with the grin still on her face. What she said also made the Mistress smile, and as Yusuf watched them he shuddered involuntarily and felt strangely vulnerable. He rose to his feet, making ready to go. The Mistress beckoned him as before and lowered the shawl to reveal her face. He reached out and touched the livid mark which felt hot under his palm. He had known he would if she

217

asked him again. She groaned softly and thanked God. He heard Amina sigh and rise to her feet. She accompanied him to the door into the garden, and because she did not shut it at once behind him, he turned and spoke to her. He could not see her face, but the shadowy light of the rising moon outlined her form clearly.

'For a brother and sister, you and Khalil look very different from each other,' he said. He was not bothered by their unalikeness, but was eager to detain her for as long as he could.

She made no reply, and because she was so still, he did not think she intended to. After a moment he turned and began to walk away through the gloomy garden, to see if she too would try to detain him.

'Sometimes I watch you from here,' she said.

He stopped and turned, then began to move slowly back towards her.

'You make it seem joyful . . . this work,' she said casually, deliberately removing any emphasis or intensity from her words. 'And I envy you as I watch. When I saw you digging the water channels I thought how inviting that looked. I walk in the garden at night sometimes when he's away. Once you found an amulet . . .'

'Yes,' he said, touching it through his shirt, where it hung on a string round his neck. 'I've discovered that I can summon a good jinn by rubbing it, and he will do whatever I command.'

She laughed softly, keeping her voice down, and then sighed again. 'What has he given you, your good jinn?' she asked.

'I haven't asked him for anything yet. I'm still drawing up my plans. There's no point summoning the jinn from his busy life just to ask for a trinket,' he said. 'And if I ask for something silly he might take offence and not come again.'

'When I came here I had an amulet, but one day I threw it away over the wall,' she said.

'Perhaps it's this one.'

'Not if a good jinn comes with it,' she said.

'Why did you throw it away?' he asked.

'I had been told it would protect me from evil and it did not. I hope your amulet has more virtue in it than the one I threw away, and that it will protect you better than it did me.'

'Nothing can protect us from evil,' he said, and began to walk towards the shadow in the door. Amina stepped back and shut the door while he was still several feet away.

The shop was shut and Khalil was nowhere in sight when Yusuf got back. Their mats were already spread for sleep and Yusuf stretched himself out, thinking of the questions that he had ready for Khalil's return. He waited patiently for him, glad to have more time to himself than he had expected. As the waiting lengthened, he began to feel anxiety about him. Where could he have gone? The huge moon was quarter risen in the sky, seeming so near and heavy that he found looking at it oppressive. Dark-fringed clouds raced in the vicinity of its halo, contorting into tortured piles and shapes. Dark clouds filled the sky behind him, blotting out the stars.

He woke up suddenly, lashed by warm flails of the storm-burst. Heavy rain was pouring around him, whipped on to the terrace by the rising wind. The moon had disappeared, but the falling water gave out a grey luminous glow which lit the shadowy knots of bushes and trees as if they were huge boulders on the sea-floor.

A CLOT OF BLOOD

I

'Let her speak for herself,' Khalil said when Yusuf asked him about Amina. He had come back at dawn on the night of the storm, looking tired and dishevelled, his hair in little knots that were tangled with tiny splinters of twigs and dry grass. He opened the shop carefully, avoiding drama, but giving no explanation for his absence. Without any obvious hostility he distanced himself from Yusuf, and throughout the day he lightly refused all attempts at intimacy, returning to a muted form of the jocular amiability of their early years. When Yusuf asked him how he had avoided getting wet in the storm, Khalil made no sign that he had heard. Yusuf made other attempts to pacify Khalil, but in the end wearily left him to his hurt.

Khalil fetched their plates of food in the evening and came out with a tight dissembling smile on his face which failed to disguise his misery and anger. *Why won't you talk?* Yusuf asked, but Khalil pointed to the plates of food and began to eat. They ate in silence, and afterwards Yusuf rose to return the plates and call on the Mistress and Amina. He thought Khalil would have said something while he was inside, forced the issue with them and uttered prohibitions and threats. He thought Khalil would try to stop him, perhaps even with violence, but he did not even look when Yusuf rose to go inside.

The Mistress was full of smiles and welcome, her high-pitched voice rising and falling in sharp melodies which filled the room. She was eager to talk, and told them of her arrival in the house, when she came to live with her first husband, may God have mercy on him. Her husband was a man mature in years, perhaps fifty or so, and she was very nearly fifteen. He had lost his wife and infant son only a few months before, through illness and other people's envy. This infant son was the only one of his children who had survived more than a few weeks. All the others had lived long enough to be named, and her husband remembered every one. Even to the end of his days he could not speak of his wife and children without tears, may God have mercy on all of them. The Mistress had grown up in the town, and knew about her husband's grief, which everyone considered did him credit. Despite his burdens he was kind to her. Until in his last year or two anyway, when his illness made him so irritable and difficult. That was how she came to live in this house and brought Mzee Hamdani with her, although he was not old then.

It was he who built the garden, Mzee Hamdani. Not from nothing, of course. Some of the older trees were already here, but he cleared the ground and built the pools, and played out there all hours of the day like a child. His singing used to drive her husband crazy, so she had to forbid it. Her father gave him to her as a wedding gift. She had known him since she was a child, him and another older slave called Shebe who died several years ago, may God have mercy on him. At her marriage to the seyyid, more than ten years ago, she offered Mzee Hamdani his freedom, as a gift. For although the law at that time forbade buying and selling of people, it did not require that those held as slaves should be released from their obligations. But when she offered Mzee Hamdani his freedom he refused, and there he is, still in the garden singing his qasidas, the poor old man.

'She says do you know why he was called Hamdani?' Amina said, her eyes dull with distance. 'Because his mother, who was a slave-woman, had him late in her life. She called him Hamdani in gratitude for his birth. When the mother died, her father bought Hamdani from the family which owned him. It was a poor family, deep in debt.'

In the silence, the Mistress stared at Yusuf for a long moment, smiling cheerfully. The smile remained on her face as she continued, but this time she did not speak for long.

'She asks that you should come and sit nearer,' Amina said. He tried to look into her eyes, to seek guidance, but she busied herself and avoided looking at him. The Mistress patted the rug a foot or so from her, smiling at him as if he were a shy child. After he had seated himself, she took his hand and placed it on her wound, keeping her hand on his. She shut her eyes and made a long hissing noise, between relief and pleasure. Sitting so close to her, he saw that the flesh on her face and neck was firm and moist. In a moment she released his hand and he rose quickly and retreated.

'She says you have not said a prayer,' Amina said, her voice small and distant. He mumbled his usual pretence and hurried away, his hand still warm from the face of the Mistress.

It was after that he asked Khalil about Amina. Khalil looked at him with hate, his thin face twisted with such scorn that Yusuf thought he would spit at him. 'Let her speak for herself,' he said, and returned to the packets of sugar he was arranging on the counter. A hard silence lay between them all evening. Yusuf was not anxious to broach it, although there were moments when he thought Khalil would speak, to vent his anger and anxiety at him. He felt a calm obstinacy about what he was doing, even if he felt anxious and unsure about how far he would allow matters to take him. At least he would know about the intrigues and the whisperings if he could, and he found an irresistible pleasure in seeing and listening to Amina. He did not know where he had found the strength to act in this way. Despite what Khalil said, and what he himself knew and said to himself, he would not refuse to go when he was called inside.

The next day he sought out Mzee Hamdani as he sat in the shade of the date-palm with his book of qasidas. The old man was irritated and looked around him, as if selecting another tree to move to, under which he could sit in peace.

'Please don't go away,' Yusuf said, and something intimate in his voice made the old man hesitate. Mzee Hamdani waited a moment and then allowed the taut muscles of his face to slacken. He nodded impatiently, reluctant as always to suffer anyone's words. *Get on with it.*

'Why did you refuse your freedom when she offered it to you? The Mistress?' Yusuf asked, frowning at the old man as he leaned forward, annoyed with him.

The old man waited a long time, looking at the ground. He smiled, his few teeth long and yellow with age. 'This is how life found me,' he said.

Yusuf refused to be palmed off with what he thought was an evasion and he shook his head urgently at the old gardener. 'But you were her slave . . . are her slave. Is that how you want to be? Why did you not accept your freedom when she offered it?'

Mzee Hamdani sighed. 'Don't you know anything?' he asked sharply, and then paused as if he would say no more. After a while he began again. 'They offered me freedom as a gift. She did. Who told her she had it to offer? I know the freedom you are talking about. I had that freedom the moment I was born. When these people say you belong to me, I own you, it is like the passing of the rain, or the setting of the sun at the end of the day. The following morning the sun will rise

223

again whether they like it or not. The same with freedom. They can lock you up, put you in chains, abuse all your small longings, but freedom is not something they can take away. When they have finished with you, they are still as far away from owning you as they were on the day you were born. Do you understand me? This is the work I have been given to do, what can that one in there offer me that is freer than that?'

Yusuf thought it was the talk of an old man. No doubt there was wisdom in it, but it was a wisdom of endurance and impotence, admirable in its way perhaps, but not while the bullies are still sitting on you and releasing their foul gases on you. He kept silent, but he saw that he had saddened the old man, who had never spoken so many words to him before, and now probably wished he had not.

'Where are you from?' Yusuf asked the old man, to flatter and placate him, and because he wanted to ask him about his mother. He wanted to tell Mzee Hamdani about what had happened to him, about how he too had lost his mother. Mzee Hamdani picked up his book of qasidas without replying, and after a moment he waved Yusuf away.

2

For three days he went inside every evening, braving Khalil's silent disdain. All his attempts to persuade Khalil into conversation had failed. Even the customers were asking solicitously after him. On the third night, as Yusuf approached the darkness that led to the garden, Khalil called out to him. Yusuf paused for a moment and then ignored him and walked down the invisible path which led to the courtyard door which was now kept ajar for him. He answered the questions the Mistress put to him, about his mother, about the journey to the interior and about his time in the mountain town. She leaned back against the wall, smiling as she listened to him. Even when Amina translated, she kept her eyes on him. Her shawl sometimes slid down her shoulders, revealing her bruised neck and her chest, and she seemed unconcerned to retrieve it. As he watched her reclining, he felt a cold hard core of loneliness in him. He asked questions too, intended for Amina, who deflected them with long replies that elaborated on the Mistress. He was content to listen. 'The wound came on her when she was young, soon after she was married to her first husband,' Amina said. 'To begin with it was only a mark, but as time passed it bit deeper and deeper until it reached her heart. The pain was so great that she could not bear to be with people, who would only mock her disfigurement and laugh at her cries of anguish. But now you are healing her with your prayers and your touch, and she can feel the relief.'

'How was it when you first came here? What did you think . . . about what you had come to?' he asked Amina.

'I was too young to think,' she said calmly. 'And as I was among civilized people, there was nothing to fear. My Aunt Zulekha was renowned for her kindness and piety, and the garden and this house were like paradise, especially to a poor country girl as I was. When people came to visit, they cut themselves with envy for the beauty of the garden. Ask anyone in the town if you don't believe what I say. And every year during the time of alms, Aunt Zulekha gave more and more to the poor. No one was ever turned away without something from this house. The seyyid's affairs were blessed, while the Mistress suffered from this strange disease. It's the way of God, whose wisdom we have no way of judging.'

He could not help smiling. 'Why do you talk in this queer way when I asked you such a simple question?' he asked.

The Mistress spoke suddenly, her voice edged with restraint. After a moment it softened, and Yusuf saw Amina pause uncertainly before she began to translate. 'She says she does not want to hear me speak so much, but to listen to you. How beautifully you speak, she says, even though the words you say are unknown to her. Even when you sit still, light glows in your eyes and from your flesh. And how beautiful is your hair.'

Yusuf glanced at the Mistress in astonishment. He saw that her eyes were watering and that her face was bright with daring. When he looked back at Amina, he found that she had lowered her face. 'She asks that you put your breath upon her face and so restore her,' she said.

'Perhaps I had better go now,' Yusuf said after a long, frightening silence.

'She says that the sight of you gives her so much pleasure it causes her pain,' Amina said, her face still lowered, but the laughter in her voice now unmistakable.

The Mistress spoke angrily, and even though Yusuf could not understand the words, he knew that she was telling Amina to leave. He too rose a moment after Amina left the room, uncertain how to make his exit. The Mistress was sitting upright with anger, her face pinched with misery. The bubble of her rage slowly subsided, then she beckoned him nearer. Before he left the room he touched her glowing purple wound and felt it throbbing under his hand.

Amina was waiting for him in the shadows by the courtyard door. He stopped in front of her, wanting to put out a hand towards her but afraid she would have no more to do with him if he did. 'I have to go back,' she said in a whisper. 'Wait for me in the garden. Wait.'

He waited in the garden, his mind racing with possibilities. A light breeze blew through the trees and bushes, and the deep, contented throbbing of night insects filled the scented air. She would reprimand him about the Mistress, echoing

Khalil's warnings and prohibitions. Or she would tell him that she knew that he returned to the house every evening to sit with her, Amina, because he nurtured naïve dreams. As time passed and the waiting seemed interminable, his anxieties grew. He would be discovered lurking in the garden at the dead of night, plotting a shameful robbery. A sudden, surreptitious crack made him think Khalil had come looking for him and would make a scene. Several times he had to restrain himself from leaving. When at last he heard a noise at the door, he hurried towards it with relief.

Amina hushed at him as he approached. 'I can't stay long,' she whispered. 'You see what she means to do now. I shouldn't have told you what she said, but at least you see what she means to do now. She is obsessed with this . . . You have to be careful . . . and keep away from her.'

'If I keep away I won't see you,' he said. After a long silence he continued, 'And I want to keep seeing you, even though you won't answer any of my questions.'

'What questions?' she asked, and he thought he saw her smile in the dark. 'There's no time for questions. She'll hear.'

'Later,' he said, his body singing. 'After she's gone to sleep. You can walk in the garden.'

'She's angry. We sleep in the same room. She'll hear . . .'

'I'll wait for you here,' Yusuf said.

'No. I don't know,' Amina said, moving away and shutting the courtyard door. She returned after a few minutes. 'She's dozing, or pretending to. What questions?'

He could not have cared less about any questions, but he was afraid that if he reached out to touch her she would never let him near her again. 'Why do you and Khalil look so unalike? And you speak so differently . . . for a brother and sister. Almost as if you're speaking different languages.'

'We're not brother and sister. Hasn't he told you? Why

227

hasn't he told you? His father saw some men struggling to load two little girls into a boat. They were wading out in the shallows, and the little girls were crying. His father called out and ran into the water. The kidnappers abandoned one of the girls but managed to run off with the other one. He took me home and later I was adopted into the family. So we grew up like brother and sister, but there is no blood between us.'

'No, he didn't tell me,' Yusuf said quietly. 'And the other one? The other girl?'

'My sister? I don't know what happened to her. Or to my mother. I don't remember anything about my father. Nothing. I remember we were taken away in our sleep and we walked for a few days. Do you have any other questions?' she asked with a bitter mockery which he heard clearly in the dark and which made him wince.

'Do you remember your home . . . where it is, I mean?' he asked.

'I think I remember what it was called . . . Vumba or Fumba, and I think it was near the sea. I was only three or four years old. I don't even think I can remember how my mother looked. Listen, I have to go now.'

'Wait,' he said, and reached out a hand to delay her. He held her by the arm, and she made no effort to release herself. 'Are you married to him? Is he your husband?'

'Yes,' she said calmly.

'No,' he said, his voice filled with pain.

'Yes,' she said. 'But did you not know that either? It was always understood . . . She explained it all to me when I first came here. Her! That amulet which you found, it was given to me when Khalil's father adopted me. They had a man come and prepare the adoption papers, and he also made an amulet for me. He said it would protect me always, but it didn't. I've got my life, at least. But I only know I have it because of its emptiness, because of what I'm denied. He, the seyyid, he likes to say that most of the occupants of Heaven are the poor and most of the occupants of Hell are women. If there is Hell on earth, then it is here.'

He could think of nothing to say, and after a moment he let go of her arm, overwhelmed by the intense calm with which she spoke of her bitterness and defeat. He would never have guessed from her quiet smiles and self-assured silences that she had to keep such miseries in check.

'I used to watch you working in the garden,' she said. 'Khalil spoke about you and how you were brought here. And I used to imagine that the shade and the water and the earth helped you ease the pain of what had been stolen from you. I envied you, and thought that one day you would catch sight of me at the door and force me to come out too. Come out and play, I imagined you saying. But then they sent you away because she began to get crazy about you. Anyway, enough of all that . . . Did you want to ask any other questions? Then I must go.'

'Yes,' he said. 'Will you leave him?'

She laughed softly and touched him on the cheek. 'I could tell you were a dreamer,' she said. 'When I watched you in the garden I imagined you were a dreamer. I'd better return before she begins again. Keep away from her. Do you hear?'

'Wait! How will I see you? Unless I come.'

'No,' she said. 'What is there to see? I don't know.'

After she had gone he felt the touch of her hand like a mark on his cheek, and touched it to feel it glow.

3

'Why did you make such a mystery of it and go into such terrible sulks? You could've told me all this simply,' Yusuf

229

said, sitting by Khalil, who was already stretched out on his mat.

'I could've,' Khalil said reluctantly.

'Why didn't you?' Yusuf asked.

Khalil sat up, drawing the sheet round his shoulders to protect himself from the mosquitoes which were howling round them. 'Because it isn't simple. Nothing is, and this wasn't something I could just say to you, hey, how about this one?' Khalil said. 'And as for what you call terrible sulking, it is because you make me feel ashamed of you.'

'All right, I'm sorry you were ashamed and not really sulking, but perhaps you can now tell me a little more about what is not simple.'

'Has she said anything to you? About herself . . .' Khalil asked.

'She said your father rescued her from kidnappers, and then adopted her as his daughter.'

'Is that all? Oh well, that's nothing much,' Khalil said, hunching his shoulders sulkily. 'I don't know where that skinny old shopkeeper found the courage. Those people had guns . . . perhaps. And he ran splashing into the waters screaming at them to let the children go. He couldn't even swim.

'We lived in a small town south of here, a poor place. I told you about it. The shop traded with fishermen and small farmers who came to sell their vegetables and eggs for a handful of nails or a piece of cloth or a pound of sugar. And any lucky little bit of smuggling that turned up was always welcome. That's what she was, magendo to be sold off somewhere, like her sister was sold off. I remember when she came, crying and dirty . . . terrified. Everybody in the town knew her story, but nobody came to ask for her, so she lived with us. My Ba called her kifa urongo,' Khalil said and then smiled. 'In the morning, my Ba called for her as soon as he was ready to eat his bread, and she brought it and sat with him while he fed little pieces to her. Like she was a little bird. Millet bread and melted ghee every morning, and she sat nearby chattering and opening her mouth wide for the small pieces he broke off for her. She followed my mother while she did her work, or came with me when I went out. Then one day my father said that we would give her our name, so she would become one of us. God made us all from a clot of blood, he used to say. She could speak better with the people there than any of us. She's a Mswahili, like you, although she spoke a little differently.

'Then the seyyid came. This part is very simple. When she was seven years old, my poor stupid Ba, may God have mercy on him, offered her to the seyyid as part of the payment. And I was to be rehani to him until she was of an age to be married, unless my Ba could redeem me before then. But he died, and my Ma and my brothers went back to Arabia and left me here with our shame. When that devil Mohammed Abdalla came to collect us, he made her undress and stroked her with his filthy hands.'

Khalil began to weep gently, tears sliding gently down his face.

'The seyyid told me after the marriage that if I wished to stay I could,' Khalil continued. 'So I stayed to serve that poor girl whom my Ba sold into bondage, may God have mercy on his soul.'

'But there is no need for either of you to stay here any more. She can leave if she wants. Who can stop her?' Yusuf cried.

'My brother, how brave you are,' Khalil said, laughing through his tears. 'We can all run away to live on the mountain. It is up to her to leave. If she goes without the seyyid's will I have to go back to being rehani, or pay the debt. This was the agreement, and this is what honour requires. So she won't leave, and while she stays, I stay.'

'How can you talk about honour . . . ?'

'What else do you think I should talk about?' Khalil asked. 'My poor Ba, may God have mercy on him, and the seyyid have taken everything else from me. If it was not they who made me into the useless coward you see here, then who did? Perhaps I just have the nature for it, or it is the way we live . . . our custom. But her, they broke her heart. What else is there to hold above that? If you don't want me to call it honour, then call it anything else you like.'

'I'm not at all concerned about your honour,' Yusuf said angrily. 'It's just another noble word to hide behind. I'm going to take her away from this place.'

Khalil lay down on the mat and stretched. 'The night the seyyid married her I was happy,' he said. 'Even though it was not such a sight as that Indian wedding we saw many years ago. There was no singing and no jewels . . . nor even any guests. I thought that now she would no longer be like a little bird in a cage, singing those broken songs of hers. Did you hear her singing at night sometimes? The marriage would wipe away her shame, I thought. She can leave if she wants! Who has stopped you leaving all these years? Where will you go with her? The seyyid will not even need to raise a hand against you. You'll be condemned in the eyes of all people, rightly so. A criminal. If you stay in this town, you'll not even be safe. Has she said anything to you? I mean has she committed herself?'

Yusuf did not reply, but he could feel his indignation subsiding and sensed the beginning of relief that his reckless resolve was being challenged. Perhaps there was nothing for him to do about it. And though the memory of Amina standing in the dark by the courtyard door was still warm in his hands, he could already feel it cooling into something more quiescent, a fond treasure to be unwrapped at a quiet moment. How could he talk about going away with her? She would laugh in his face and then call for help. Then he heard the bitterness in her voice as she spoke of Uncle Aziz and as she spoke of her life as Hell. He felt her hand on his cheek, her hand on his cheek. Her laughter at his question if she would leave Uncle Aziz . . .

'No, she has not said anything. She thinks I'm a dreamer,' Yusuf said after a long silence. He thought Khalil would ask more questions, but after a moment he heard him sigh and settle himself for sleep.

Yusuf woke up feeling tired and at fault. Throughout the night as he dozed and surfaced, he had debated whether he should leave matters alone or speak to Amina and force the issue with her. He thought she would not turn away from him with scorn, the way she had spoken of her life and of his, how she had watched him and run their lives together. There was something like that in the desire he felt for her too, and although he did not have all the words to hand to speak to her about his desire, he knew that it was not something slight which arose entirely at his own bidding. But all that was only gentle murmuring compared with what would follow if she were willing. Despite that, he was resolved to speak to her. He would say to her: *If this is Hell, then leave. And let me come with you. They've raised us to be timid and obedient, to honour them even as they misuse us. Leave and let me come with you. We're both in the middle of nowhere. Where else can be worse? There would be no walled garden there, wherever we go, with sturdy cypresses and restless bushes, and fruit trees and unexpectedly bright flowers. Nor the bitter scent of orange sap in the day and the deep embrace of jasmine fragrance at night, nor fragrance of pomegranate seeds or the sweet herbaceous grasses in the borders. Nor the music of the water in the pool and the channels. Nor the contentment of the date grove at the cruel height of the day. There would be no music to ravish the senses. It would be like banishment, but how could it be worse than this?* And she would smile and touch his cheek with her hand, making it glow. You're a dreamer, she would say to him, and then promise that they would build a garden of their own more complete than that.

He would feel no remorse about his parents, he said to himself. He would not. They had abandoned him years ago to win their own freedom, and now he would abandon them. If they had gained any relief from his captivity, it would now end while he went to make a life for himself. While he was freely roaming the plains he might even call in on them and thank them for giving him some tough lessons to set him up in life.

4

The shop was busy that day, and Khalil threw himself at the work with a gaiety and abandon which made even the most cast-down customers smile. He's recovered his spirits, they said. God be praised! His banter reached a new daring, at times on the verge of mockery, but delivered with such irresistible amiability that no one felt able to take offence. 'What's got into him?' the customers asked. Yusuf smiled and shrugged, then lightly touched his left temple. Several explanations were advanced. It was youthful enthusiasm, misplaced but healthy and pleasing. Might as well laugh now before life knots you up. Some sticks of hashish had done the trick, suggested someone else. He's probably not used to it and his mind has developed a fever. A woman who came to buy two ounces of coconut oil for her hair, and to whom Khalil delivered a rhapsodic allegory on the joys of a massage, wondered if someone had put pepper on the young man's penis. The old men on the terrace watched and cackled happily. Though Khalil avoided his eye, Yusuf could see the gleeful frenzy in his darting glances and stepped out of his way.

In the afternoon, when the pace slackened, Khalil ostentatiously wedged a box into a corner of the shop and sat on it for a doze. Yusuf could never remember him doing that before, and took this sudden slump to be a continuation of his sulks and craziness. He saw Mzee Hamdani struggling with buckets of water and guessed that he would be replenishing the pools. The water spilled and sloshed over the sides of the buckets before the old man had taken the few steps to the garden, splashing his feet and turning the ground muddy. Yusuf watched him with envy and irritation, not bothering to rush to his aid, but the old man was as preoccupied as ever and made no sign that he was aware of him. Later he saw him leave without a backward glance, shuffling across the clearing at the steady pace of a charging millipede. His voice rose intermittently in a chant that was impossible to hear clearly, and which sounded like words sung backwards.

At the usual time in the evening Yusuf went inside. He told himself it would be for the last time. He would say a quick prayer for the Mistress and see Amina and then . . . ask her to leave with him, if he dared. The courtyard door was ajar and he walked in, calling out gently to announce his arrival. The room was fragrant with incense and the Mistress was sitting alone waiting for him. He stopped at the door, afraid to enter. She smiled and beckoned him in. He saw that she was richly dressed, her long cream dress glittering with amber thread. She pulled her shawl away and leaned forward, waving him nearer with insistent urgency. He took two steps forward and stopped, his heart pounding, knowing he should leave. She began to talk quietly to him. Her voice was rich with feeling, and her smile grew softer as she spoke. Yusuf could not be sure what she wanted him to do, but he could not mistake the look of passion and longing on her face. She pressed the palms of her hand on her bosom and then rose to her feet. When she put her hand on his shoulder he shivered. He began to retreat and she followed. He turned to flee, but she clutched his shirt from behind and he felt it tear in her hands. As he ran out of the room, he heard her screams of agony but did not look back or hesitate.

'What have you done?' Khalil shouted as he ran past him in the darkening garden. Yusuf sat on the terrace feeling numb and disgusting, overcome with the unbearable squalor of his situation. He waited on the terrace for what seemed hours, veering between shame and anger. Perhaps he should leave at once, he thought, before all the messy consequences began. But he had done nothing shameful, it was the way they had forced him to live, forced all of them to live, which was shameful. Their intrigues and hatreds and vengeful acquisitiveness had forced even simple virtues into tokens of exchange and barter. He would go away, there was nothing simpler. Somewhere where he could escape the oppressive claims everything made on him. But he knew that a hard lump of loneliness had long ago formed in his displaced heart, that wherever he went it would be with him, to diminish and disperse any plot he could hatch for small fulfilment. He could go to the mountain town, where Hamid could torture him with self-righteous questions and Kalasinga could divert him with his fantasies. Or join Hussein in his mountain retreat. He could find small enough fulfilment there. Or go to Chatu, to become the court clown of his ramshackle fiefdom. Or to Witu, to find Mohammed the hashish smoker's mother and

the sweet land he had lost by his transgressions. And everywhere he would be asked about his father and his mother, and
his sister and his brother, and what he had brought and what
he hoped to take away. To none of the questions would he
have anything but evasive answers. The seyyid could travel
deep into strange lands in a cloud of perfume, armed only
with bags of trinkets and a sure knowledge of his superiority.
The white man in the forest feared nothing as he sat under his
flag, ringed by armed soldiers. But Yusuf had neither a flag
nor righteous knowledge with which to claim superior honour,
and he thought he understood that the small world he knew
was the only one available to him.

Khalil came striding at him out of the darkness, his arm
raised as if he would strike him. 'I told you this would only
bring trouble,' he said angrily. He pulled him to his feet and
started to drag him away. 'Let's get out of here. Let's go to
town. You stupid, stupid ... Shall I tell you what she is
saying? That you attacked her and tore her clothes like an
animal, after she had treated you with such kindness. She
wants me to fetch people from the town so she can make this
accusation to witnesses. They will beat you and spit on
you ... and who knows what else.'

'I didn't touch her,' Yusuf said.

Khalil let go of his arm and began to punch at him, falling
all over him in his rage. 'I know that, I know that! Why
didn't you listen?' he cried. 'I didn't touch her! Try telling
that to the crowd she'll gather here.'

'What will happen?' Yusuf asked, pushing Khalil angrily
away and rising to his feet.

'You must leave.'

'Like a criminal? Where will I go? I'll leave when I want.
And what will happen when I'm found?'

'Everyone will believe her,' Khalil said. 'I said I would

237

fetch the people she wants from the town. She'll scream for help otherwise. They will believe what she says. Maybe she'll stop by tomorrow morning if we ignore her, but I don't think so. You should go. Don't you know these people? They'll kill you.'

'She tore my shirt from behind. That proves I was running away from her,' Yusuf said.

'Don't be ridiculous!' Khalil cried, laughing with disbelief. 'Who'll have time to ask you that? Who cares? From behind?' He glanced at Yusuf's back and was then unable to restrain a demented grin. He fell into thought for a moment, trying to remember something.

They hurried to the waterfront and chose a dark spot where they sat talking for hours. Yusuf refused to leave in the middle of the night as if he really was a criminal, and despite Khalil's urging insisted that he would wait until the accusation had been made so he could make a defence before going. No, no, no, Khalil shouted at him, his voice cutting across the hissing of the unresting sea battering the wall at their feet.

It was almost midnight by the time they made their way back to the shop. The town was battened down and silent, patrolled by the lean dogs which haunted Yusuf's dreams. As soon as they arrived at the shop Yusuf sensed a disturbance in the air, as if something had happened while they had been away. After a moment he knew without any uncertainty what had happened. It was the perfume which announced Uncle Aziz's presence. He glanced at Khalil and saw that he knew too. The Pharaoh was back.

'The seyyid,' Khalil said in a strained whisper. 'He must've come during the evening. Now only God can help you.'

Despite everything, Yusuf felt a thrill of pleasure that Uncle Aziz was back. It surprised him that he felt no fear of the merchant, just excited curiosity to see how he would talk to

238

him about the accusations. Would he turn him into an ape and send him to the summit of a barren mountain as the jinn had treated the woodcutter? While Khalil talked about the dire fate awaiting him, Yusuf spread out his mat and lay down with such exasperating calm that Khalil was forced into silence.

5

Uncle Aziz came out at first light. When he appeared, Khalil threw himself at the merchant's hand with his habitual zeal, kissing it in between his excited greetings. Uncle Aziz was wearing a kanzu and sandals, but was without his cap, a small informality which made him seem comfortable and benign. The face he turned to Yusuf, though, was severe, and he did not offer his hand to be kissed as he usually did.

'What is this bizarre behaviour I hear about?' he asked, motioning for Yusuf to sit down again on the mat from which he had risen. 'You appear to have lost your senses. Do you have an explanation for me?'

'I did her no wrong. I sat with her because she invited me in. My shirt was torn from behind,' Yusuf said, his voice shaking in an unexpected and annoying way. 'That shows I was running away.'

Uncle Aziz smiled and then grinned, unable to restrain himself. 'Oh, Yusuf,' he said mockingly. 'Did I not tell you that our natures are base? Why did you have to live through it all again? Who could've thought such a thing of you? From behind? That proves it, then. No harm was intended or done because your shirt was torn from behind.'

Khalil launched into explanations in Arabic, which Uncle Aziz listened to for a few moments and then waved down. 'Let him speak for himself,' he said.

'I did nothing,' Yusuf said.

'You went inside often,' Uncle Aziz said, his face hardening again. 'Where did you learn such manners? I leave you my house and you turn it into a place of gossip and dishonour.'

'I went inside because she wanted me to, to say prayers . . . for her wound.'

Uncle Aziz looked silently at him, as if debating what he should say or do next. It was a look Yusuf was familiar with from the journey into the interior. After such reflection, the merchant almost always decided to let matters take their course rather than intervene. It was the silent moment before allowing havoc to have its head. 'I should have taken you with me,' he said at last. 'I should have anticipated . . . The Mistress is not well. If nothing dishonourable has happened, then we should leave matters there. Especially as your shirt was torn from behind. But this whole matter is not to be spoken of to outsiders. It was still wrong of you to go inside so often.'

Khalil again spoke quickly in Arabic. Uncle Aziz nodded sharply a few times, and then spoke back in Arabic. After a few exchanges, Uncle Aziz pointed to the shop by a curt movement of his chin.

'Why did you go inside so often?' Uncle Aziz asked after Khalil had gone to open the shop.

Yusuf looked at the merchant without replying. Uncle Aziz was now sitting on the mat which Khalil had been lying on. One leg was folded under him and he was leaning on an outstretched arm. Yusuf saw that as he waited for him to speak, the calm amused smile began to take shape on Uncle Aziz's face.

'To catch sight of Amina,' Yusuf said. The words took a long time to come out of his mouth, and he saw the smile broaden and then settle comfortably on Uncle Aziz's lips. The merchant glanced towards the shop and Yusuf followed his gaze. Khalil was by the counter, staring at them with a look of rage and hate. He turned away and continued opening the shutters.

'Is there more?' Uncle Aziz asked, returning again to Yusuf. 'You really have been brave, haven't you? How you've distinguished yourself in these last few weeks!'

Because Yusuf took so long to make a reply, debating how much he should say and what difference it would make, the merchant began to speak again. 'I visited your old town while I was on my journey and called on your father. I wanted to make an arrangement with him, to have you stay here and work for me for payment, and in return I would forgive all his obligations to me. But I found out that your father has passed on, may God have mercy on his soul. Your mother no longer lives there and no one could tell me where she has gone. Perhaps she has gone back to her home town. Where is that?'

'I don't know,' Yusuf said. He felt no sense of loss, but a sudden sadness that his mother too was now abandoned somewhere. His eyes watered at the thought, and he saw Uncle Aziz give a small nod of approval at this display of grief. The merchant waited, as if content to let Yusuf decide how far he wanted matters to go. In the long silence Yusuf could not make himself say the words that were burning in him. *I want to take her away. It was wrong of you to marry her. To abuse her as if she has nothing which belongs to her. To own people the way you own us.* In the end Uncle Aziz rose to his feet and offered Yusuf his hand to kiss. As Yusuf bent forward into the clouds of perfume, he felt Uncle Aziz's other hand rest on the back of his head for a second and then give him a sharp pat.

'We'll discuss the plans later, to see what work you can best do for me,' Uncle Aziz said pleasantly. 'I'm getting tired of all this travelling. You can do some of that for me. You might even get to meet your old friend Chatu again. By the way, take care, both of you. Khalil! You too. There's talk of war between the Germans and the English, up there on the northern border. I heard this from the merchants in town when I came in yesterday afternoon. Any day now the Germans are going to start kidnapping people to make them porters for their army. So keep your eyes open. If you see them coming shut up the shop at once and get out of sight. You've heard what the Germans can do, haven't you? All right, get on with your work.'

6

'He likes you,' Khalil said happily. 'I told you all this time. The seyyid is a champion, who can doubt that? He came back, took one look at the Mistress and thought to himself, *this crazy woman has been tormenting my pretty young man. These women are always trouble and mine is a top-class monkey, damn her.* Anybody can see she's crazy, with her whining voice and all that business about her wound. And your torn shirt! Oh your torn shirt! What a story! You have some fine angels looking after your affairs. Now the seyyid will find you a wife, to keep you out of trouble. One of these nice little girls living in a shop in the country. I think he already had someone in mind for you before he went away. Perhaps he'll buy me one too and we can have a double wedding. Perhaps they'll be sisters. It'll probably be cheaper to get two at the same time. Half the fee for the qadhi to perform the ceremony, and only one lot of washing after the wedding night as well. We can rent one of those houses on the other side of the road and live together. Our wives will have twins and help each other with all the troublesome chores, and we can sit on a mat on the house terrace and talk . . . about the condition of the world, maybe.

That would be a good one. Or the fulfilment God promises. Then in the morning we'll cross the road to look after our seyyid's business. What do you think?'

Khalil announced their forthcoming double wedding to the customers, inviting them to the feast their seyyid had promised them. You know the seyyid, he told them, everything will be halal and pure. He described the entertainment: dancers, singers, men on stilts, a procession of boys and girls with trays of incense who would be flanked by men spraying the air with rose-water, you name it. Feasts with all kinds of food. And rich music throughout the night. Yusuf smiled along with everyone else. It was impossible not to, as Khalil invented and embellished with frenzied abandon. When the customers asked Yusuf for corroboration, he told them that Khalil's mind had cracked. 'He's delirious from fever,' he said. 'Take no notice of him. Otherwise you'll make him nervous and then he'll get worse.'

When Mzee Hamdani arrived for his daily observances in the garden, Khalil called out to him, 'Walii, sainted one, we're getting married, both of us. Aren't you surprised? Our seyyid will be setting us up for life. Sing a qasida for us when you have a moment. Who could've predicted such luck for us? You won't be getting this one in the garden there any more, by the way. He'll have other beds to till soon, and bushes to prune.'

At first Yusuf took it that Khalil was clowning his relief that matters had not turned out worse. Uncle Aziz had lightly dismissed the affair with the Mistress and Yusuf had not dared make his challenge on Amina. When he was ready to do so, Uncle Aziz would deal with him in what ways he saw fit. Later he knew that Khalil was mocking him. After all the passionate and brave talk before, he could only keep a defeated silence to the merchant's chilling invitation. They were the same now, he thought, both freely in the service of the merchant. Kissers of hands. Khalil had fashioned an explanation for his abjectness, that he was there to atone for the wrong his father had done to Amina. Yusuf had no explanation for remaining in the merchant's service.

'The seyyid, you had better learn to say that now,' Khalil laughed.

7

The first they knew of the soldiers was when they saw men running on the road past the shop. It was late in the afternoon, a time when people strolled the cooling streets for air and conversation, and others made their way home from the town. Suddenly the small knots of people began to scatter, running off the road or towards the country, shouting about askaris. Khalil ran into the house, calling out a warning, while Yusuf boarded up the shop as quickly as he could. They sat in the gloomy cavern with hearts pounding, grinning at each other. At first the rising smells of the merchandise stifled them, but they breathed more easily as they adjusted to the stuffy atmosphere. Through the cracks between the boards they could see parts of the clearing and the road. Before long they saw a column of soldiers marching with unhurried precision behind their European officer, who was dressed in white. As the column came nearer, they could see that the German was a tall and thin young man, and that he was smiling. They exchanged smiles themselves, and Khalil moved back from his spyhole in the shop's boards and sat back with a sigh.

The askaris marched barefoot and in perfect order. The officer turned into the clearing in front of the shop, and the men turned sharply with him. Once in the clearing, the column fell apart like a necklace whose string had been pulled out. Silently, they found whatever shade they could, and threw their packs and themselves to the ground with wide smiles and sighs. The officer stood for a few moments, regarding the house and the closed shop. Then, still smiling, he started to stroll without any appearance of urgency towards them. As the officer moved away, the men began to talk and laugh among themselves, and one of them shouted a word of abuse.

Yusuf did not remove his eye from the spyhole, and watched the smiling German with a frightened grimace of his own. The officer stopped on the terrace and then moved out of Yusuf's sight. Amid shouted orders, a camp chair and folding table were brought to the terrace from among the resting askaris. The officer sat down, his face only inches on the other side of the shop boards. It was then that Yusuf realized that the officer was not as young as he had looked from a distance. The skin on his face was stretched tight and smooth, as if he had suffered burning or a disease. His smile was a fixed grimace of deformity. His teeth were exposed, as if the tightly stretched flesh on his face had already begun to rot and slough off round his mouth. It was the face of a cadaver, and Yusuf was shocked by its ugliness and its look of cruelty.

The askaris were soon forced to their feet by the sergeant, a strong-looking man who reminded Yusuf of Simba Mwene, and stood in discontented groups, waiting. They were all looking in the direction of the German officer, who was staring ahead of him, occasionally raising a glass to his lips. He did not sip the drink, but rested the lip of the glass on his sick mouth and poured. Eventually, he glanced at the soldiers and Yusuf saw him nod.

The askaris jumped into action before the words were out of the sergeant's mouth. With miraculous speed and precision they stood at attention in a file, and then peeled off in threes, running in different directions. Three of the soldiers remained behind to guard their leader. One askari stood on either side of the shop-front, while the third marched off round the side and eventually forced open the garden door. The officer raised the glass to his lips, tipping it up to pour the liquid into his open mouth. He sucked greedily, his face turning red with the effort. Some of the chalky-coloured liquid dribbled down his chin, and he wiped it away with the back of his hand.

The askari who had gone into the garden returned and made his report. It took Yusuf a moment to understand that he was talking in Kiswahili, saying that the garden had some fruit but that was all, and the door to the house was locked. The officer did not look at the soldier, but after he had finished and gone back to lounge under the tree, the officer turned and stared at the boarded-up shop behind him. To Yusuf it seemed that he was looking straight into his eyes.

It seemed a long time before the askaris started to return, singing and shouting as they drove their captives ahead of them. The clearing filled with a crowd of men. The German officer rose to his feet and walked to the edge of the terrace, his hands clasped together behind his back. *Gog and Magog*, Khalil whispered in Yusuf's ear. Most of the men brought in looked frightened as they were herded into the middle, silently looking around them as if they were in unfamiliar surroundings. Some others appeared happy enough, talking among themselves and shouting friendly abuse at the askaris, who did not seem very amused. They waited for a few minutes before walking among the clowning men, silencing them with sharp blows and wiping the grins off their faces.

When all the askaris had returned, and all the captives were gathered unsmiling in the middle, the sergeant marched up to the terrace to receive his order. The German officer nodded and the sergeant barked with satisfaction before turning back to the men. The captives were formed into two silent lines, and in the gathering darkness were marched off in the direction of the town. The German officer marched at the head of the shuffling column, his body upright and his movements precisely understated. His white uniform glowed in the fading light.

Before the column was out of sight, Khalil slipped out of the shop and ran round the side to see if all was safe inside the house. The garden lay in composed silence, its night music trembling imperceptibily in the gloom. Yusuf went to explore the debris of the askari encampment. He approached carefully, sniffing as if he expected the askaris to have left an acrid mark of their passage. The ground was churned by the feet of the men, and a disturbance lingered in the air. Just beyond the shade of the sufi tree, he found several piles of excrement, which the dogs were already eagerly nibbling at. The dogs glanced suspiciously at him, and watched him out of the corners of their eyes. Their bodies shifted slightly to shield their food from his covetous gaze. He looked for a moment in astonishment, surprised at this squalid recognition. The dogs had known a shit-eater when they saw one.

He saw again his cowardice glimmering in its afterbirth in the moonlight and remembered how he had seen it breathing. That was the birth of the first terror of his abandonment. Now, as he watched the obliviously degraded hunger of the dogs, he thought he knew what it would grow into. The marching column was still visible when he heard a noise like the bolting of doors behind him in the garden. He glanced round quickly and then ran after the column with smarting eyes.